CAPTAIN MARY, BUCCANEER

a novel

by

Jacqueline Church Simonds

Simsbury, Connecticut

Captain Mary, Buccaneer

Beagle Bay Books, Inc.
542 Hopmeadow Street #129
Simsbury, Connecticut, 06070, USA

Visit us at our Website: www.BeagleBay.com.

Library of Congress Catalog Card Number: 00-190379

ISBN 0-9679591-7-9

First Edition

Printed in the United States of America

This book is dedicated to:

My Husband, Robin Pinckney Simonds

*for believing in me even when I didn't, and applying
a loving boot to my backside to help
me achieve my dream.*

And to

My Mother, Virginia Jacques Church

a fellow artist and "the differentist" Mom on the block.

HISTORICAL NOTE

Captain Mary, Buccaneer is a work of fiction. However, it is loosely based on the lives of the eighteenth century female pirates Mary Read and Ann Bonny. Certain aspects of their lives are echoed in Captain Mary's tale. Neither Read nor Bonny served as captain of a pirate ship.

There is historical precedence for a female pirate captain. In 1807, Ching I Sao not only captained her own ship, but led one thousand pirate ships, called the Red Flag Fleet, and terrorized the Chinese mainland.

Acknowledgments

No first novel becomes published without considerable help. Special thanks go to my patient husband Robin for putting up with the vicissitudes of having a writer in the house: helping me stage many sea battles on our dining room table with salt cellars, forks and anything else that was in the way; reading innumerable drafts; and typesetting this book.

My gratitude to editor Vicki Hessel Werkley is unending for the many hours she spent poring over the manuscript and almost as much time spent on the phone coaxing me through the editing process.

Special thanks to Doug Andersen of Fly By Night Illustrations for so aptly visualizing Captain Mary and the *Fury*. I could not have wished for a more sympathetic and enthusiastic artist.

Last — but not least! — thanks to all my early readers for pointing out plot faults, sharing your ideas and giving me encouragement. You gave me the strength to finish this project. Without your loving support there would be no Captain Mary.

British Bahamas

Les Saintes

Cache Island

St. Barthelemy

Marie Galant

St. Martin

La Deserade

Netherlands Antilles

Dominica

Puerto Rico

Barbunda (BR)

St. Johns

Antigua (BR)

Guadalupe (FR)

Nevis (BR)

St. Kitts (FR)

Montserrat (BR)

Dominica (FR)

Les Saintes

Martinique (FR)

Netherlands Antilles

Barbados (BR)

New Granada Spanish

Trinidad (SP)

Tobago

British Giuana

*"She is Choice at odds with Necessity;
she is Love blindly butting its head against all the
obstacles set in its path by civilization."*

Preface, *Indiana*
George Sand (1804-1876)

CAPTAIN MARY, BUCCANEER

CHAPTER ONE

Off Guadeloupe Island, where the Atlantic Meets the Caribbean, 3 August 1721

Captain Mary leaned out over the *Fury's* bow. Her black eyes seemed to burn holes through the writhing gray tendrils of morning fog surrounding the ship. Furrows of concentration wrinkled her forehead, making her look older than her eight and twenty years. Drops of dew settled in the curly strands that had escaped her long braid of black hair. A rose-red silk scarf was tied around her head; the thick hoop earring in her left lobe gleamed dully.

As always, in the moments before battle, she felt taut as a mains'l in a gale. The only noises were the creaking of the hull and the faint slapping of oars as the men below decks rowed the *Fury* toward the lookout's mark. The briny tang of the calm blue-black sea smelled like blood spilled on a hot deck. Orange mats of Sargasso weed undulating on the still water stank like putrefying flesh — a haunting reminder of all the men she'd had to kill in the past. How many would she have to kill today? Mary shook her head, trying to rid herself of the fog-conjured images. She stared forward again until whirling green and purple spots spun before her eyes. She couldn't make out anything yet.

She glanced back to see if her crew was ready. Unlike some others in the Caribbean, the men of the *Fury* weren't privateers pirating in the service of one of the colonial powers. Her buccaneers, made up of men from many nations, owed their only allegiance to Captain Mary.

The men looked like specters as they stood at their posts, tensely peering into the shifting light. Their motley clothes seemed almost black in the half-light, but even so, she knew them by their individual costumes. Petronius, her tall first mate, was at the great wheel. He was the only one who dressed like a gentleman. The others were like magpies, drawn to all things bright, rather than such conventions as fit and color coordination. Ingram wore a black and gray tattersall vest over a red-striped shirt and yellow checked pants. Talinn, her quartermaster, sported an overlarge coat the color of a bruised eggplant, but had no shirt; his maroon velvet breeches fastened above the knee, making him look like a badly dressed boy. Jacoby — who, as the finest cook in the Caribbean, never fought — fancied a lady's orange dressing gown trimmed with cream marabou feathers, which he wore over more ordinary looking garb.

Captain Mary favored more sober attire. Her baggy dark green knee breeches were tucked inside thigh-high boot tops. Over an ordinary man's linen shirt, she wore a navy-blue wool hip-length coat with tarnished gold braid down the sleeves.

She turned back and searched the fog again. Perhaps because of her intense concentration, she smelled the everyday odors of her ship as if they were new. She detected the heavy mildew of the furled square sails. In the air was the soggy odor of rancid food in the holds. The scent of rotting wood from hidden places throughout the ship reached her, as did the everyday stench of the men themselves. Permeating everything was the salt reek of the sea. Only the tang of carbolic soap from the silvery-clean decks alleviated the general smell of decay.

There! A shadow was forming off the starboard bow. In a few heartbeats, the wraith coalesced into a two-masted brigantine, the same kind of ship as the *Fury*, but flying King Louis's flag of France. She pointed out where the ship lay. Petronius began steering to port so that they would slide in beside it. He whispered a command to Talinn, who dashed below decks. Immediately the sound of the oars slowed. The men stood poised, watching her. Affecting calm confidence, Captain Mary strode to her post amidships. At her signal, three men heaved bulky, cloth-filled fenders over the port side. A muted rumble beneath her feet informed her that the *Fury's* six cannons were being maneuvered to starboard.

There was a clatter as twelve oars being shipped echoed loudly throughout the *Fury*. "Poxy fools!" Mary hissed.

She turned her attention back to the French brigantine and gauged the distance. Not yet. From the corner of her eye, Mary saw Petronius raise his pistol and point to it. Immediately the ship resounded with the distinctive sounds of pistols, muskets and blunder-busses being cocked. The quiet metallic slither of steel sliding out of hard leather sheaths heralded the drawing of boarding axes, long knives, swords and cutlasses.

Nearer the *Fury* crept toward its prey.

Mary waited, trying to still her wildly beating heart. Although she'd led more than a hundred board-ings, her palms felt slick against the hilt of the inlaid sword in her right hand and the ivory grip of the pistol in her left. She drew a calming breath. Then she held up her hand, signaling the men that battle was near. They crouched at the rail, preparing to jump. A muted rum-ble sounded from the belly of the man nearest her.

The *Fury* slipped closer.

Catching a whiff of chicory coffee from the unsuspecting ship, Mary heard a Frenchman whistling a merry air, which trailed off as he went below. Soft groans came from their rigging. Unsecured chains tapped rhythmically on something wooden and hollow on their deck. The chinking slowed. It stopped. All was still as death.

"Fire!" Captain Mary's command shattered the silence.

Two of the *Fury's* cannons thundered. Iron pel-lets ripped through the fog, shredding the French ship's flaccid sails.

"Fire!"

Again the *Fury's* big guns barked. A cannonball shrieked over the French bow, another over the fo'c'sle. With a grinding crash, the two ships collided broadside. A great geyser of water leapt from between the vessels, drenching everyone on deck. The *Fury's* rowers ran up to join those topside just as the men at the gunnels threw grappling hooks onto the French ship's side.

Mary leapt atop the rail, sword raised. "For the *Fury*! For Gold! For Glory!"

With a roar, her crew scrambled over the sides. Men of the boarded vessel stumbled groggily up from below. Some were half-dressed and pulled on clothes as they came. Many struggled to buckle on their pistols or swords. Thirty-five terrified French crewmen tried to assemble themselves into a ragged military line to face the wild charge of eighty roaring pirates. An officer, wearing only his unbuttoned blue velvet jacket over yellow-stained long johns, dropped his pistol and disappeared below.

While she fought, Captain Mary kept an eye on her crew. She saw Webb, a gap-toothed Welchman, run at the stocky French helmsman. Holding his wavering rust-stained knife straight out, the buccaneer aimed for the Frenchman's stomach, but the pilot drew his pistol and fired point-blank into Webb's chest. The ball tore through his heart and exploded out his back. Gobbets of flesh, muscle and lung spewed into the faces of those fighting nearby. As if not satisfied with its work, the bullet sped on until it burst apart the blond head of the ten-year-old French powder monkey.

She watched as a panicking, bald French crewman fired both his pistols at the mass of pirates. Wild shots struck the mainmast. Waving a black-bladed scimitar above his head, Gerhardt, a pirate with a deep, wickedly twisting scar across his face, leapt at the man. The Frenchman shrieked in terror as Gerhardt swept his sword into the man's neck. The shouts ceased abruptly. Great gouts of blood erupted and then ebbed with the dying Frenchman's pulse. It showered friend and foe alike, momentarily blinding those nearby. As if an afterthought, the body slumped slowly to the boards. His head tipped at an extreme angle, exposing the gaping trachea and shattered vertebra. Surprised eyes stared up to Heaven for help that could not come.

Hurling pulleys and spars down on the pirates from his perch twenty feet above the deck, the French lookout laughed maniacally. He missed most of his targets, but the splintered wood served to make the footing on the blood-slick deck all the more difficult. One of the pulleys found its mark through the skull of Santero, an Arawak pirate, who fought at Petronius's side. The plummeting wooden tackle popped out the man's eyes, and brains spewed onto the deck before the body pitched forward. Petronius knifed the man he was fighting, then saw his fallen comrade. He scowled up at the lookout. The Frenchman snarled and pitched another pulley. He missed, almost hitting a crewmate. Methodically, Petronius took aim with his ivory and brass inlaid pistol and shot the lookout between the eyes. Blood jetted from the shattered forehead, raining down on those below. As he hurtled toward the deck, his right leg caught the mains'l footrope. It stopped the body with a terrible jerk, arms flapping uselessly at the fray.

Captain Mary watched a burly Frenchman holding off two of her pirates, Brepa and Snowby, with a dagger and an old sword. Snowby, a thin redhead with a sparse ginger beard, and Brepa, a bald man who looked to be made of ebony, used their long daggers to toy with their prey as cats will a mouse. Nicking the Frenchman on the shoulder, Brepa forced the Frenchman to turn and face him. Then Snowby slashed the Frenchman across his back, from kidney to kidney. Screaming in pain, he wheeled back to fight Snowby, but his movements were wilder and slower as his strength poured out with his blood. Still the Frenchman fought on, struggling to fend off the attacks of first Brepa, then Snowby. Finally, the pirates tired of their sport. At a nod from Brepa, the two lunged, running the Frenchman through on either side of his spine. The body twitched and flailed, muscles fighting even after life had fled.

Captain Mary took on the fiercest-looking Frenchman — the second officer with fancy gold braid on his red velvet coat. He had a jagged scar on his right cheek that parted the black beard. His sword, bright and beautifully etched with brass, clashed with Mary's less elegant — but razor-sharp — sword. He jabbed at her face. She dodged the blow at the last minute, then answered with a slice aimed at his ribs. The blade caught in a fold of his coat as he spun out of reach. For a moment Mary worried the tip was caught, allowing him a free blow. Just as he turned to strike at her jugular vein, the point shook loose, and she was able to parry with a ringing clang. He feinted at her left shoulder, then changed at the last moment to make a lunge at her belly. She blocked the blow just in time.

"Your swordplay is very crude, sir." Mary thrust to his right. Twisting her sword at the last minute, she cut a thin line on his cheek opposite the scar. "Now you've symmetry."

The words were hardly out of her mouth when he made a wild attack of fierce, hacking strokes aimed at her head, arms and chest. The blade seemed huge, hardly attached to the man but for the terrible rictus of hatred on his face. She countered each blow, teeth gritted.

Mary considered what ploy she might use to put

him away. As was the case with most men, she had at least half a hand's-span height advantage on her opponent. She was taller than most men, except for Petronius. This gave her leverage in battle. Her opponent's arms were longer, though, so he had the reach on her. Their skills were about equal, though certainly he'd been trained since a lad, and she'd only been holding a sword for ten years now.

He paused, mad eyes assessing for the next charge. His blade waved in front of him. His breath came in gasps as a horse's does when it is ridden too hard, too long. Blood seeped off his chin. In a flash, she saw it: *He's weary, not used to fighting. He'll make mistakes now.*

Mary made a sudden swipe at his groin. When he moved to block it, she kicked the sword from his hand. It went skittering across the gore-covered deck, then clattered overboard. Undeterred, he leapt at her with a feral snarl. Instantaneously, Mary's cutlass met his charge. Her blade rammed into his chest clear up to the hilt. Wordlessly, his arms wrapped around her, attack turned into a grim embrace. His angry eyes stayed riveted on hers. The force of his now-slack body sent the two staggering backward. With an abrupt bump, they slammed into the forward mast. Still, he said nothing. His stare grew cloudy. She could feel his heart's stammering beats through her buried sword. His sour breath became tainted with a fatal hint of iron. Red foam accumulated at the corners of his lips. "*Sorcière,*" he whispered, spraying pink spittle in her face. A terrible shudder seized his whole body. He gripped her shoulders in vicelike claws. Dark scarlet blood erupted out of his mouth onto her breast. His brown eyes rolled up, and — as life fled — paled to an ash-gray. He sagged in her arms, held up only by her sword.

Thou shalt not kill! She heard remembered shouting. Closing her eyes, she shut out the dead man on her blade. As if he were present, she saw the old priest in his dusty cassock standing horrified among the tall Carolina pines. Darius Manchester, son of the neighboring plantation owner, lay crumpled on the ground before her. Blood pooled beside him, welling up from where she'd shoved her knife in his belly just moments ago.

Darius had come upon her as she strolled through the newly plowed fields on her father's South Carolina rice plantation. She thought him an ugly little dandy, dressed in his green velvet suit and cream lace cuffs. He had thinning sandy hair, a sparse beard, and beady black eyes set too close to a misshapen nose.

His disgust at the muddy field he stepped through proclaimed him a city boy. He told her he'd come to take what was his soon by rights. "The priest is arranging our union right now. Of course, you'll have to convert. I can't have a Protestant for a wife." He seized her arm in a tight grip. "Come here, wench, and give me a sample of our wedding night." With a leer, he grabbed her breast.

When she struggled, he tore her shirtwaist, reached in and pinched her nipple as hard as he could. She clouted him in the ear.

Throwing her down in the mud, he hissed, "You like it rough, eh? I'll soon have you tamed!" With one hand he nearly throttled her, with the other he tore through her skirt and petticoats. Then he grabbed her crotch, squeezing so hard she yelped. "You've just begun to sing, my pretty," he said with a chuckle.

Several times the plantation had been attacked by Cherokee or gangs of escaped slaves, so Father had taught her how to defend herself. She always carried a hunting knife in its homemade sheath in the waistband of her skirt The deed was done almost of itself: Mary whipped out the knife and jammed it into Darius's stomach, all in one motion. Shoving his body off, she stood, shaking. She had no idea what to do next. What would her future be now? Surely no one would wed a girl who'd killed her intended!

The old priest who had seemed so nice despite his loathsome mission, appeared between the tall white pines. "Thou shalt not kill!" he gasped in horror. "Your soul is damned for all time, girl! The Lord said, 'Thou shalt not kill!'" She threw the knife down and ran to the stables to make her escape, never once looking back.

Though it had been a long time ago, it never failed to haunt her each time she killed — and she'd had to kill many to survive all these years.

Opening her eyes, she studied the dead Frenchman. Vomit gathered at the back of her throat. What was one more dead man? She swallowed hard, put her foot on his shoulder and shoved him off her blade. He lay at her feet, spent and lifeless. She used his coat to clean her blade. It also afforded her a moment to collect herself before her men saw how badly her hands were shaking.

Once she'd regained her composure, she checked to see how the others fared. The fighting had subsided. All the other French had either surrendered or perished; thirteen remained. She looked over the dead, noting she had lost three of her men. None of them were of great value, and she dismissed them from her mind. She nodded for Petronius to take a group of men below decks to search for Frenchmen who might be hiding.

"Hold them on the poop deck, Franz," Mary ordered.

"Aye, Cap'n." Franz shoved his man up the ladder. The other pirates pushed their captives to follow Franz to the upper deck at the stern.

In the quiet of the aftermath, all could hear bumps and thumps from below. Shortly, the rest of the captured crew emerged from the hold, followed by a number of pirates. Petronius held his knife to the throat of a man dressed in an expensive gold velvet coat with lace edging and blue leggings. His feet, though, were unshod, and his big toe peeked out of a hole in his stocking.

Petronius, limping a bit, dragged his prisoner over to Mary and said in his sing-song Bahamian accent, "Here's the master o' this ship, Cap'n. I had a hard time gettin' him t'come outta his hidin' place behind some crates." The pirates on the afterdeck laughed.

"*Prostituée!*" the captive commander shouted.

"Silence, fool," she snapped. "I'm Captain Mary. We've come to collect the tax my men and I impose on all the ships using the Guadaloupe Passage." She took a deep breath, trying not to lose her temper. "If you'll agree to behave in a civilized manner, I'm sure I can convince my first mate to remove that knife from your throat. What say you?"

The French captain struggled against the pirate's hold for a moment, then grumbled in accented English, "I will stand now, but I will take revenge on you later!"

Mary laughed hollowly. "Well said, Captain Braveheart!" She nodded to Petronius. He sheathed his knife and went back below.

"I am Captain Jean Lemeux of his Majesty's ship *Le Chat d'Soleil*." He straightened his rumpled coat.

"Is that so? And do the French —" A cut-off scream from below decks interrupted her. There was the sound of wood splintering, then shouts followed by a terrible groan. Finally, two men emerged, one holding up the other, whose arm was bleeding. "What's this, Snowby?" Mary demanded.

"Talinn got knifed in the arm, Cap'n! They was two men guardin' a brig down there. Petronius killed the guard what got Talinn after Talinn took out the first one." Snowby led Talinn to the starboard rail and helped him sit down.

"Murderers!" Lemeux shouted.

"That was unfortunate. Weren't you paying attention?" Mary demanded.

Talinn's face was almost gray with pain. "Took me by surprise. Didn't know anyone else was down there."

"Idiot," she said, "don't let that kind of thing happen again. You could have gotten yourselves killed."

"Sorry, Cap'n," he said, staring down at his feet.

Petronius came back up leading an emaciated man of medium height. His humble, brown-wool pants and linsey-woolsey shirt were torn and bloodstained. His face was a mass of bruises and swellings. Iron manacles bound his wrists and ankles.

"I hear we had an unfortunate mishap, Petronius."

"Aye, Cap'n. Things happened a little fast. This's the prisoner they was guardin'." Petronius let go of him. He staggered a moment, on the verge of collapse. With a visible effort, he kept his feet.

"Who is your rather ill-treated guest, Captain Lemeux?" Mary asked.

Lemeux spat at the prisoner. "He is the traitor, Doctor Alphonse Coulances, late of Guadaloupe. We are taking him back to France to face the King's justice."

"Rather a long way to drag a man just to execute him," Mary said with a sniff. "Why didn't the Governor just have him hanged and be done with it?"

"This I also would have done," agreed Lemeux. "I know his accomplice has already met the rope. The King wishes to set an example to people who would betray our colonies to the filthy English and Spanish swine."

"A doctor, hm?" she mused. "Coulances, my man is wounded. Help him over there, will you?"

"Why should I?" Coulances objected through split lips.

She leaned forward and said quietly, "Because I will throw you back in the brig and let you rot if you don't."

Bright green eyes took her measure. "Then I have little choice. Take me to him."

"Traitorous scum!" Lemeux snarled.

Mary turned to him. "May I have the key to his manacles, please?"

"Never. He is a prisoner of the King!"

She grasped Lemeux's shoulder tightly. His eyebrows shot up in surprise at her grip. "Captain, I will have the key even if I have to personally strip you in front of what's left of your crew. I will use my knife, and I promise you, I do more than tickle." He stared at her, hardly breathing, then swallowed hard. The key to the manacles appeared in his hand. "Thank you." She removed it from him.

Holding the key out to the *Fury's* carpenter, Mary said, "Karl, help the doctor with his chains. Assist him in caring for Talinn."

"Aye, Cap'n," he said, taking the key.

"Captain, if you will join the rest of your crew, please." Mary motioned for the man to be taken away.

"I will hang you myself," Lemeux growled as he was forced to join his crew.

Mary sighed. "I do tire of the constant threats."

Petronius winked. "You shoulda picked a more peaceable occupation."

She smiled as she studied her first mate in one of his rare humors. Tall and barrel-chested, he was an imposing man. But for the bloodstains on his lace cuffs, one would have thought him a man of means in his tailor-fit dove-gray velvet coat hanging just so over his pegged wine-red wool breeches. Like Mary, he wore a scarf around his head, though his was copper-colored. Down his back hung hundreds of long brown braids tied in an elaborate knot. There was a thick gold earring in his left ear. Many said that he was the spawn of the Devil because of his intense hazel eyes, unusual in an African.

He was a close man, revealing little about himself in the time she'd known him. Only last year he'd told her about his former life as a slave. His master had entrusted him with a trading ship, which he'd piloted among the Bahamian islands — until he'd gotten fed up and used the ship to escape. Usually, he was the most serious, directed man she'd ever met. Petronius in a teasing mood was a rare treat indeed.

"What would I have done?" She strolled beside him to the bow. "Taken care of a squalling brood? Tatted? Gardened? The mind reels at the limitless possibilities." He smiled thinly in response. Then she turned back to the business at hand. "What did you find in the hold besides the prisoner?"

"The usual," he said. Returning to his customary stern-faced demeanor, he ticked off the inventory on his long mahogany fingers. "There's molasses, cotton, hardwoods, spices, casks o' rum, fresh provisions and quite a few bottles o' good wine. The best news is that they have a goodly supply of powder, ammunition and a fine selection of firearms."

"All that and their captain cowers in his cabin," she said. "The French would do better hiring you or me to run their trade."

"Their loss is our gain." He shrugged. "Speakin' o' which, we have, as usual, left the captain's cabin for your personal inspection."

"I hope there'll be something of interest there. Have the crew load the goods and munitions you've found." Mary stopped Petronius and said quietly, "Count the guns. I think someone's been holding out lately."

"I noticed," he agreed. "Probably Ingram." He turned and began issuing orders to the *Fury's* crew.

Mary went below and entered the captain's cabin. It was dark, the portholes covered, telling her that just a short while ago, Captain Lemeux had been asleep. Perhaps he'd been dreaming of *La Belle France*. The sparsely furnished cabin reeked of a musky jasmine scent and sweat. She ran her hands along the wall until she reached the curtains and pulled them back. The cloth was a rich, yellow cambric print with blood-colored primroses. She smiled and slid them off the wooden rod. Lemeux's bunk was a tumble of bedclothes, hastily thrown aside. First she went through the simple but cluttered desk. She stoppered and took the ink as well as the pen with the good nib. Amidst the letters, journals, logs and poor-quality charts were some sheets of fine rag-bond writing paper, which she also took.

Next she opened the worn sea chest at the foot of the bed and rummaged through the contents. She took all the usable clothing, left the cheap glass-bead rosary, but took the cufflinks and silver shoe buckles. There was a beautifully bound volume of Moliere's comedies, which she took with delight, but left the ratty volume of *The Odyssey* in French, already having a superior copy. At last she discovered the strongbox which, by its weight, contained gold — though a rather disappointing sum. She dumped out the useless remainders and refilled the trunk with her finds and dragged it out onto the deck. Petronius awaited her expectantly.

"Rather less than one would've hoped. But we've managed a small profit this venture." She opened the chest and lifted out the strongbox, putting it into his hands.

"Common thieves!" Lemeux shouted. He struggled against his bonds.

Mary laughed. "Hardly common."

Petronius shook the box and grumbled, "Not much there. We'll never get rich at this rate."

"We can't all be Francis Drake and hit the Spanish gold fleet, Petronius."

"I don't see why not."

"Well, for one thing, he had to give all that gold to his god-rotting queen."

"Then this Drake-fella was an idiot," he argued.

"There's some say that," she agreed, slapping the cashbox. "I think it time we left Captain Lemeux's hospitality."

"What about the prisoner?" Petronius asked.

"Yes, what about him?" She ambled over to the men at the gunnels.

Coulances finished tying on the bandage. Mary inspected his work. It was professionally and economically done. Talinn looked much improved. The doctor patted Talinn on the back. "You should be able to use the arm within three or four days. Replace the bandage once a day. Let no sea water touch it."

"I thank you for your good work, Doctor. Would you be interested in forgoing a sea voyage to your homeland for a shorter trip with a band of pirates?" She offered her hand to help him up.

Unsteadily, he stood on his own to face her, which only emphasized the hand's-span difference in their heights. "And if I prefer not to?"

"I'm sure Lemeux would be delighted to take you back to . . . what was it?" She pretended to scratch her head through her scarf. "A hanging, did he say? Oh, you're right. That's a better choice than what I'm giving you."

He cleared his throat. "I think I could be persuaded to give up an audience with the King for such an interesting journey."

She bowed slightly. "Then you shall enjoy the hospitality of my ship, the *Fury*. I am Captain Mary. I'm sure we can find an island more hospitable to you." She turned and called to the cook, "Jacoby! Help this man aboard!"

Mary's crew struggled to load the last of the kegs from the hold.

Captain Lemeux shouted, "Take Coulances, you scabrous wench, and the entire French fleet will hunt you down!"

She watched as the captain's seachest was loaded onto her ship, then climbed on top of the railing. "*Au revoir*, Captain. Next time, have more gold on hand, will you?" She jumped to the deck of her ship, the last of the pirates to leave the pillaged *Chat*.

"Look lively, mates!" Petronius yelled. "Cast off the grapplin' hooks. Haul on those ropes, you laggards!"

In short order, the *Fury's* sails filled with the freshening west wind and pulled swiftly away. The heavy odors of the morning were replaced with the cleansing sea wind. The ominous-colored ocean of the morning was now cerulean blue with merry whitecaps. Fog thinned to a light haze. Once the *Chat* dwindled to a mere outline on the horizon, Mary commanded, "Jacoby, take the doctor to my cabin and clean him up." Shrugging off her bloody jacket, she handed it to him. "See what you can do to salvage that." She turned to the business at hand and put the doctor out of her mind.

"Mapana, go through the lockers of the men who were killed — Webb, Santero, and that other fellow. You'll know where to find them. We'll divvy their possessions with the rest of the goods." Mary joined Petronius at the mainmast as the crew assembled the small personal goods taken from the *Chat*. Guns, knives, swords, clothes, purses, jewelry and — of course, the strongbox of gold — were placed around the mast. Karl took care of the lock with a couple of stout blows from a hammer and iron chisel. Petronius counted the gold coins — twice and loudly — so that everyone was sure it was fairly done. Mary examined a piece of gold in the sun. The French must have seized it from the Spanish somewhere, since they were doubloons — eight-escudo coins with the king's head on one side and the Spanish coat of arms on the other. Stealing was a way of life in the Caribbean. "A hundred fifty!" Petronius called out.

After some figuring with a piece of charcoal on the deck, Mary announced, "Give one doubloon to every man. Petronius gets five, I get five, three go to Jacoby for being such a good cook — " A small cheer went up. "Three go to Talinn, our quartermaster, and three to carpenter Karl. The last three go toward a new set of sails for the *Fury*."

The men took their shares with little grumbling. All had agreed when they signed on how the spoils would be distributed. It was better pay than many of them had ever seen, and most were old navy or merchantmen.

She made sure everyone had gotten paid before she continued. "All right, then, you horrible pirates, you." The men laughed. "We'll start handing out the goods here, but before we get to that, I want to bring something to your attention." Mary glared about her. None of the men moved or dared speak. "One of you is holding out on us. Last ship we took, there were two guns missing by the time we divvied the loot." Men stared from face to face, trying to figure out the dog who'd done it. "Now, you know that taking something before it's given out is stealing from your fellow crewman. We may be pirates, but we don't steal from each other. Right?"

Many of the men nodded. A few still cast hostile glances at others in suspicion. Ingram glowered about him, looking as if he'd bite the thief. "Well, let's hope we've just been counting wrong," Mary said. Then she took her seat on a stool by a plank desk so she could record the transactions.

Petronius reached down and held aloft a pair of

black leather boots with thin brass chains around the ankles. "Who cares for this fine set o' boots! Good leather, nice polish, lots o' sole left on 'em." Brepa's and Franz's hands shot up,. "Both, eh?" Petronius took a gold coin out of his pouch. "Call it in the air, Brepa," he said, tossing it up.

"Heads!" Brepa boomed.

The coin clattered to the deck, spun, then lodged at an angle in a crack — head-side up. "Brepa gets 'em," Petronius announced, throwing the boots to him.

"Next we have a fine sword that used t'belong to a fella I met on the *Chat* . . . ." The distribution of the goods took quite some time as each piece had to be held up, examined, and then recorded by Mary.

When the division was finished, Mary said, "Now we need to discuss where we'll get more of these little goodies for you. Petronius and I fancy a trip north to St. Kitts. There's supposed to be a gold shipment going to the fort there, and — with any luck — we'll encounter it before the French. How say you?" A general rumble of agreement was heard. "All in favor, say *Aye*." Almost everyone responded in the affirmative, save one. "Cepa, if you think different, let's hear it."

Cepa shifted uneasily. "St. Kitts is *bueno*, Cap'n. But I hear a Spanish ship sank off the coast of Cuba. *Mi sobrino* tells me it was full to the decks with gold!"

The men started to talk among themselves, excited by the prospect of a share in a ship like that.

Petronius and Mary locked eyes. Not so long ago Petronius had insisted that they take just such voyage. It hadn't worked out so well. "Friends," she started, "let me tell you about a similar trip, some years ago. We heard a rumor just like Cepa's. Decided to go up north and find it. Our crew searched for almost three months. In the end, we had nothing to show for it but empty bellies and no gold at all." She didn't tell them about the mutiny she and Petronius had faced when some of the men wanted to continue their search using the *Fury*. They'd had to shoot the mutineers. Most of the remaining crew jumped ship at the first port they came to. "If that Spanish galleon sank, then only the fish know where it is, and fish don't talk. Give me a ship above water I can get at, any day!"

The men talked among themselves.

"I put the vote before you, again," she said. "All for St. Kitts, say *Aye*." After a pause, the men responded, *Aye!* Last, and reluctantly, Cepa echoed, "Aye."

"Fine. Petronius, will you set our course?" He went to take the wheel. Since Talinn was injured, Mary assisted in organizing the stowing of goods in the hold. First the crew had to drag everything out on deck so they could fit all the new goods in. This gave Talinn and Mary an opportunity to check everything over and throw out the rancid food she'd smelled earlier.

After that, she mediated an argument between Franz and Brepa. Franz felt that since the coin hadn't lain down completely, it shouldn't have counted. Mary settled the matter at once by tossing a coin up. It landed "heads" again. Franz shrugged, shook Brepa's hand and went back to work.

Then there was the sail-mending to oversee and the painting of the hull to direct and a hundred other things that filled her days.

CHAPTER TWO

It wasn't until the evening brought calm seas that she took the time to think of Coulances again. Tired and hungry, she asked Jacoby to have her dinner and the doctor's sent to her cabin. Selecting one of the wines captured that day, she took a bottle with her. She also took the new volume of Molière.

Coulances was sitting in the largest armchair by a lantern. Loosely held in his hands was a book, for it seemed he'd fallen asleep. At her entrance, he looked up, startled. He appeared a little better, if badly used. He'd brushed back his curly dark-brown hair, revealing a broad, albeit scratched, brow. His cheeks were still quite swollen. His nose was less puffy than earlier, and promised to appear strongly Roman when sufficient time had passed. He'd trimmed his beard and mustache to conform to his battered jawline. Overall, Mary thought he would be quite presentable once he healed. She was pleased to see that Jacoby had found him some clean clothes. "Good evening, Doctor."

He tried to stand, as a gentleman should when a lady enters a room. It'd been a long time since anyone had afforded her that courtesy.

Mary waved for him to sit back down. "Dinner will be served soon. In the meantime, I thought we might sample this fine wine." She took a seat in the chair opposite him.

"Such hospitality," he admitted, "one hardly expects from a pirate."

"One doesn't have to be a Philistine." She poured the wine into Venetian crystal goblets.

"Indeed." He took the glass and gestured at the room. "This is hardly the cabin of a barbarian."

Mary glanced around the room with its walls full of books, a beautiful mahogany bed covered by an azure bedcloth with intricate embroidery, the handsome desk with its fanciful marquetry depiction of the Lady and the Unicorn, emerald brocade curtains, rosewood chairs sumptuously upholstered in burgundy velvet in which they sat, and the table inlaid with mother-of-pearl between them. "I know quality when I see it."

"You are a most unusual pirate. You do not even fly the infamous skull and crossbones of your trade."

She held her glass up to let the light of the lamp play in the ruby depths of her goblet. "The skull and crossbones is a foolish invention used by braggarts and bullies. If I want to surprise an enemy, why would I scare them off miles away by flying that silly rag?"

"And the significance of your pennant? Why blue and green?"

"It's mostly blue to show my domain," she said,

pointing out the porthole, "the sea. The smaller triangle of green denotes a bit of land I call home."

"Which is where?"

She sipped her wine, then shook her head. "You don't need to know that, Doctor."

Dr. Coulances sat quietly, observing her. Mary shifted uncomfortably. She knew what he saw: a rather plain-looking woman, too tall and unfashionably thin. She'd been told she was comely, once. But she doubted that her sun-darkened skin could fetch the eye of any man now. She had wide black eyes, broad cheekbones and a sharp nose. Only her full red lips might be considered an attractive feature.

Mary tucked a loose strand of hair behind her ear. Most of her kinky black hair was held back in a braid. It, in turn, was wrapped in an eelskin sheath covering it from the nape of her neck to the small of her back. Her red scarf was stretched tightly across the top of her head and tied behind. The single gold hoop in her left ear denoted her initiation by "King Neptune" — alias Petronius — when she'd crossed the Equator.

She glanced down at her clothes — themselves a sight, since women weren't supposed to wear men's attire. In addition to her breeches and shirt, she wore old blond calfskin boots that were deeply stained with seawater and accumulated gore. Someone once observed that she could afford to dress very much better. She'd retorted that she dressed for battle, not for the salon. In truth, she didn't miss the fancy flummery of petticoats and laces one tiny bit.

Finally, Coulances held up the volume of Milton he'd been reading and indicated the leather-bound books on the shelves behind him. "You are very well-read, for a pirate. I've not seen such a collection of fine books and manuscripts since I left my patron in France."

"A particular weakness of mine. It helps to pass the time," she said. It reminded her that she still had the new book beside her. Mary got up and went over to the bookcase. Leaning over him, she shelved the volume beside a small edition of Shakespeare's sonnets. The *Fury* breasted a swell at that moment and Mary swayed into the doctor. As she straightened, their eyes met. Then they each looked away.

For a moment, he seemed fascinated by the proximity of her waist; or perhaps it was only the sight of her male attire that transfixed him. Then he turned to the shelves. "Literature, art, science." Tapping the brightly colored book spines, he said, "You have a wide-ranging mind, yes?"

A knock on the door interrupted them. At Mary's permission, Jacoby came in with their dinners and placed the gold-rimmed bone china plates on the table. "Pheasant, Cap'n!" he said, uncovering the dishes. "Them Frenchies dine good!"

"And now we do." She took her seat and bent over the food to inhale deeply. "Those birds have gone to Heaven twice, Jacoby."

He grinned hugely. "Always a pleasure to cook for the appreciative, Cap'n." Jacoby bowed and went out.

"Do the men eat as well, Captain?" Coulances asked, cutting into his bird.

"They do, Doctor. That's one of the reasons they're very loyal to me. I pay the best, I feed them well, and I treat them better than any other captain of military, merchantman, privateer or pirate ship in the Caribbean." He nodded and hungrily attacked his plate. She realized it must have been months since he'd last eaten a decent meal. They ate in silence for a while.

When they were finished, she refreshed their glasses. "What is it you did that so aroused the ire of your countrymen?"

He scratched at the healing scar barely covered by his beard. "I am a doctor. I heal the sick, the injured. I do not stop to ask them their politics or their nationalities when I work to staunch a wound."

"So you cared for injured who happened to be English or Spanish?"

"I treated patients in pain," he objected. "It had nothing to do with who they were."

"Surely you knew they were wanted by the authorities?" she prodded.

He shrugged. "That does not concern a doctor."

"It does if the doctor wishes to continue to live." She examined her nails. "Tell me what led to your capture."

He sat back and stared into his wine. "I'd been on Guadaloupe for three years. In that time, I treated most of the merchants and sailors of Pointe-a-Pitre. The rich see Dr. Roget, the Governor's personal physician. Additionally, I treated natives, slaves — owned or running away — whores, thieves, a pirate or two." He managed a smile. She raised her glass in salute. "And, yes, both Spanish and English. I was known among a certain class of people." He sipped his wine. "About a month ago, one of the locals brought me a patient. He was Welsh, I think. He'd received a bullet wound to the thigh and was bleeding quite heavily."

"What was his name, do you remember?"

"Yes, at the trial he was referred to as 'the spy, Timothy Wallen.'"

"Ah, I'd wondered where he'd got to."

"You knew him?"

"Yes." She finished her glass and refilled it. "It's amazing how unlike one view is from another. Wallen was a trader in information — no more a spy for Britain than you. Anything he knew was for sale to the highest bidder." She stared into her wineglass. "A useful little weasel. I shall miss him."

After a respectful pause, Coulances resumed, "Before I'd quite gotten the bleeding stopped, the Governor's guards ran in and arrested both Wallen and me."

"What happened to the person who brought Wallen to you?"

"That is a remarkable thing. She disappeared, moments before the guards came in." He sat forward a little.

Mary sighed. "She played you and Wallen very well and probably got paid by both sides for a short night's work."

"I treated her a year ago for a beating her procurer gave her," he argued. "How could she betray me?"

"Oh, people will do the damndest things for money, Doctor." She gestured at the cabin in which they sat.

"Do you do this only for money?"

"Sometimes." She smiled slightly. "Tell me, why you left France for Guadaloupe?"

Coulances refilled his glass. "For money." She laughed, then nodded for him to continue. "You noticed that I limp, Captain?"

"I had thought that was from the treatment the Governor's jailor gave you."

"I received beatings enough from those ruffians,

but they didn't give me that particular infirmity." He picked a crumb from his sleeve and appeared to examine it closely. "When I was a young lad, about ten or so, I lived in the village of Lisle. We were poor people. My *Père* was a carpenter of no discernible talent. We had little to eat. But then, no one in the village had much.

"One day, as I played in the road with my sister, a fancy carriage came 'round the bend at great speed. My sister leapt off the road; I didn't get out of the way fast enough. The wheels of the carriage knocked me down and ran over my leg. I heard a loud pop and felt excruciating pain. The driver stopped. The man inside the carriage emerged and picked me up. He took me with him in his carriage to his home. All the while, he held my hand and apologized. I remember the pain well, but I also remember noticing the plush plum seats, the blue velvet-covered ceiling and walls, the cut crystal vase with the single perfect white rose in it. Never had I seen anything so marvelous. I thought surely I was in Heaven."

Slowly, he twirled his glass in circles on the marquetry table. Mary didn't interrupt his thoughts. After a long while, he continued. "I was taken into a house unlike anything I ever imagined. It was filled with furniture and paintings and rugs and things I hadn't any word to put to. I was laid on the softest, warmest bed imaginable. Presently, a doctor came and set my leg. I screamed and passed out. When I awoke, I heard the doctor tell the man from the carriage that he doubted I would ever walk without a heavy limp — if, indeed, I walked at all." Coulances rubbed his leg in an absent fashion.

"There followed many days of pain, in which I was well-cared for. Slowly, I learned to walk again, though with a limp. Eventually, Monsieur Racine — for that was the name of the man in the carriage — told me that he'd spoken to my *Père*. He was going to keep me at his estate and educate me along with his own sons as a way of atoning for having lamed me. I could see my family whenever I wanted, if I would but return at night." He paused and stared into space.

Mary had been watching him. The way he spoke, the gestures he used, his very vocabulary intrigued her. Surrounded as she was by the uncouth, the criminal — her crew — it wasn't often that she had a chance to enjoy such company. Not that she hadn't held more than a few of the rich hostage. But they were all afraid of her or looked down on her. She liked Coulances's ease with her, after his initial distrust. It said much about his character. "That must have been very hard, being separated from your family."

He shook his head. "I had to be bribed to see them just once a month. I did not even miss them, sad to say."

"Why?" she asked. "How could you not wish to see your family?"

"My family had nothing. They were ignorant and content with their wretched lives. I reveled in the trappings of the rich: the food, the clothes, the learning. Monsieur Racine's sons were indolent scholars. They cared nothing for the knowledge that books possessed. They only wanted to hunt and ride. I had never opened a book before the accident. I was like a parched man in the desert who comes upon an unlimited spring." He rubbed his lower lip thoughtfully, clearly remembering with fondness his days as a student. "Soon, I not only took the same lessons as the older boys, but surpassed them in my studies."

"Monsieur Racine was pleased with my progress. He offered me the opportunity to be trained as a doctor if I would come back and serve as his physician. I readily agreed and went off to Paris with much delight. In a few years, I returned to the Racine estate and cared for my benefactor, whose health had begun to deteriorate. Foolishly, I thought that I was like family to all those at the manse. I ate with them, attended *soirees* with them, hunted with them — but in the end, it made no difference." He got up and refilled his glass, sat back down, then took several sips before he began again.

"Monsieur Racine was taken by consumption, and I mourned for the first time in my life. Yet, I expected that I would serve the new master of the manse, my former schoolmate, as I had his father. I was wrong. The new Monsieur Racine viewed me as a kind of usurper. He and his brother informed me that another physician would fulfill any duties I might have had. I was encouraged to see the world. They handed me a small sum of money and told me that my things were already packed and in a carriage awaiting me at the door."

Mary could almost feel his anguish. Strangely, she wished to comfort him: stroke his hair or hold him in her arms. This distinctly female compulsion surprised her. Long ago she'd put away the emotional softness expected of her sex. She'd watched men grovel on their knees for her compassion and felt nothing but contempt. How could he move her as they could not? Finally, to break the silence that tempted her into unwonted action, she said quietly, "That must have come as quite a shock."

Coulances laughed darkly. "I was devastated. For a month, I stayed in waterfront taverns and drank myself into a stuporous acceptance. Then, the lawyer for the Racines ran across me. He took great delight in informing me that I'd been hoodwinked. It seems the elder Racine left me a large inheritance if I had but stayed on the grounds of the estate. However, if I left for more than a fortnight, all the money would revert to the two younger Racines." He finished off his wine. "Do not tell me what people will do for money, Captain."

Mary went to the spirit cabinet tucked into the bookcase and poured two snifters of brandy from the crystal decanter. She handed Coulances one and sat back down. "What got you on the ship to Guadaloupe?"

"I couldn't stay in Paris." He took the glass and breathed deeply of its vapors. He smiled ruefully before he took a sip. "It seemed to me as if everyone knew of my life and was laughing at me. I heard a man in a dockside tavern talking about the need for doctors in the French colonial isles. My money was almost spent. I was inebriated enough to think it was a good idea. I signed on before I sobered up — which was somewhere around the Azores, I believe." He glowered at his brandy, took one last draft, and set the glass deliberately on the table. "So, there you have it. My life's story. Rather dull, really."

"That doesn't answer the question of how you went from a rich man's doctor to a healer of, shall we say, those less well-favored." Mary put her chin on her fist.

"I had no way of attracting Dr. Roget's patients away from him. The only people who needed my services were those with little or no money. As I treated them, I came to hear their stories. I realized that I was born of them, like them. Because of a stupid accident, I had been removed from my class temporarily, but now

I was returned to where I belonged. I found that they were no different from me. They merely lacked my good fortune. From that time on, it was pointless to deny anyone treatment. Do you see?"

"Yes, I do." She nodded. "Strange what games life plays with one, isn't it?"

"It must have been an interesting twist of Fate that turned an intelligent woman into a pirate," he observed.

She avoided his eyes. "There is no story to tell. I am simply a woman who is also a pirate."

"The words *simply* and *pirate* rarely go together, madam, even for a man. Nor do I believe that you have no tale to tell."

She found his gaze penetrating, as if he were searching her soul. Mary shrugged. "I like the sea air. This life agrees with me."

"A woman pirate. The concept is wholly contradictory. The idea . . . ." A great yawn overcame him. "Pardon me."

"It is I who must ask your pardon, Doctor. You're injured, and I have kept you up late talking." She picked up the plates and glasses. "We'll talk again, I'm sure. Sleep well." She headed for the door.

"Captain?" He stood unsteadily. "Surely I should sleep below decks with the men?"

"Rest, Doctor. I'll sleep in a hammock under the stars, as I do most nights."

"But —"

"No arguments." She pulled open the door. "Think of it as my apology for your ill-treatment by your countrymen here and at home. Now, goodnight," she said, stepping out onto the deck. As she let the door close behind her, she heard him yawn loudly and mutter goodnight.

Jacoby hurried forward and took the plates and glasses from her. She went to the quarterdeck and stood beside the wheel. The crewman at first seemed anxious about having her there, but when she took no notice of him and said nothing, he relaxed. She watched her ship sail on into the night, the bright stars of the Caribbean shining fiercely overhead. The wake beside the ship echoed the glow of the sky in the green luminescence that followed the hull. She felt suspended between sea and sky. The wind stroked her face, tugged gently at the stray strands of her hair. It was for this that she lived. Tonight, there was something especially sweet about the smell of the night, though she couldn't have said what. Mary strung up her hammock in the rigging and fell asleep feeling like a spirit of air and darkness.

A fortnight later, Coulances was still on board the *Fury*, despite ample opportunity to place him ashore. They sailed past British Montserrat when Captain Mary fancied she saw a French man-o'-war in the harbor, though the lookout swore it was a Flemish merchant ship unloading. They passed by Redonda Island because it was the hideout of an old rival of Mary's, Captain Dead-Eye. They'd had a recent skirmish with him, and she wanted to avoid him at all costs right now. At the embattled double islands of French St. Kitts and British Nevis, she believed they were being stalked by a French privateer, even though for two days the ship drew no closer than a blue-gray outline on the horizon.

Each evening Mary ate dinner with Coulances and then talked late into the night. There seemed no subject too obscure for their wide-ranging conversations.   Afterwards, when she climbed into her hammock, she felt strangely uplifted.

They were a day out of Saba Island with its dangerous turquoise reefs, when they spied a British merchant ship.   Normally, with such a large prize, the *Fury* would rely on stealth and ambush, shadowing its prey until an opportunity presented itself.   But the frigate's sails luffed while passing within the windshadow of a tiny archipelago's cliffs.   Just for a moment, it slowed and drifted slightly.

"Prepare to take that ship!" Mary ordered.

"Haul the mains'l, trim the top gallant!" Petronius sang out as he spun the wheel.   Her crew grasped the thick hemp rope of the *Fury's* main sheets. Teeth gritted, sweat popping off their foreheads, the men struggled down the deck, straining against the seemingly immobile sail.   It was like playing tug-of-war with the wind.   A giant made of air pulled against them. Slowly, the men won out.   Timbers groaning, the bow swung to port.   Spray exploded over the decks as they cut across the waves.   Bright diamonds of spume stabbed their faces.

The *Fury* flew at the other ship.   Wind screeched in the rigging; the sails roared.   Cannons rolling into place vibrated the quarterdeck.   Mary pointed at her cutlass, then to the port gunnels.   Flintlock and pistol, knives and axes appeared as the men ran to their stations. She knew that below, her men were loading short lengths of chain in three cannon, grapeshot in the other three.

The British ship took no countermeasures.   It continued on its course, sails still poorly trimmed to catch the Trade Winds. Petronius maneuvered the *Fury* across its bow. If they hadn't been seen before, they certainly would be known now.

"Fire!" Mary commanded.

Cannons spat whirling chains. They hurtled into the British sails and rigging. Sails, rope and splintered wood from the fore-mizzensail went careening onto the British deck.

"Fire!" she cried.

A shower of incendiaries shrieked over the English bow.

"Ahoy, the ship!" Petronius shouted in his booming bass voice. "Heave to, or we'll blow you outta the water!"

The *Fury* heeled around the British port side. Mary hung on to the rail against the starboard pitch of the ship. Uppermost in her mind was the vulnerability inherent in this move. Exposing the *Fury's* hull below the waterline was the most dangerous position in a sea battle. A well-aimed mortar would destroy them instantly. Her breath caught as she saw their gunports. She'd heard that some merchant ships were starting to arm themselves, but hadn't credited the stories. As they drew abreast, she watched for the glint of sun on metal. If their guns fired on the *Fury* — well, of course, she would fire back. Even though the *Fury* would shortly be headed for Davy Jones's Locker.

Squinting, she thought she could see the evil snouts of cannon in those ports. Just as she was about to order a full assault with their six guns, a man appeared at the gunnel and waved a bit of white cloth. "Surrender!" they heard faintly on the wind. "We surrender!"

"Prepare t'be boarded!" Petronius shouted. He maneuvered the *Fury* around their stern and headed in close to their starboard. "Drop the sails!" he ordered the

Fury's men. The cloth flapped and drooped at his command. Later, after the boarding, the crew would tie them down. But not with battle coming. Fenders dropped into position. Grapples were tossed onto the captured vessel. All hands pitched in hauling on the ropes, reeling in the British ship.

As the ships closed, Mary wryly noted that the gunports were painted on. It was a good job. Even this near, the cannon mouths looked real. But they'd almost led to this ship's destruction. She turned her attention to the British decks. Something was wrong. Besides the man with the handkerchief, she'd not seen anyone else. He behaved oddly, leaning on the rail, watching her men take his ship.

Mary leapt aboard. Again, she scanned the ship. Still, there was no one, save the man leaning on the rail. His face was terribly drawn and pale as parchment. Was this some kind of trick? A British trap? She drew breath to question him when the stench hit her, so foul she gagged. Hiding her nose and mouth in the crook of her arm, she waved her crew back to the *Fury.*

"What is it?" Petronius asked.

"Pestilence! Get the doctor over here. No one else." How well she knew that awful smell. When she'd lived in New Providence, the villagers suffered a terrible contagion. The fetid cottages of the sick reeked thus. Hundreds died. It was as if the odors of death and disease co-mingled, becoming a living presence that stalked the narrow lanes. It sought to suck the life from those not yet claimed. She'd been thankful to be spared, but counted it one more reason to leave that Hell-hole.

Cautiously, Mary approached the pale man. "Who are you?"

"David Agar. Captain of the merchantman

Goode Sheepherd . . . out of Dover two months." His breath came in ragged gasps. There were terrible sores around his mouth and lips. The sour smell of chronic diarrhea came off him. "It's the flux plague. We've lost fifty or more . . . in the last month. Men, women, children . . . babies."

"By Hades," Mary whispered.

The doctor, a handkerchief clapped firmly to his face, joined them. "Coulances," he said by way of introduction as he examined Agar. He peeled back the man's crusty eyelids, then gently probed his abdomen. Agar moaned in pain. Coulances stepped back in concern. "How long have you had this?"

"I felt the first effects . . . almost a fortnight ago." Agar was seized by a coughing fit that bent him over the rail. His brown-stained breeches turned damp. Coulances looked at Mary and shook his head.

"We should tow them into a port somewhere." She held Coulances's eyes to avoid watching Agar's suffering.

"Do, and you'll be delivering a death sentence to some innocent town." He helped Agar stand upright again. "I can't promise that we won't get it just from being here on deck."

"We can't leave them this way," Mary objected.

"They're beyond any help I can give them, Captain."

"No, please," gasped Agar. "Let us go on. We're missionaries . . . going to teach heathens . . . in the Amazon. Oh." The pain bent him double again.

Mary winced. What a horrid way to die. "You'll never get there, Captain."

"If it's God's Will . . . that we make it, we shall." Agar said straightening. "Have faith in the Lord Jesus."

Mary hadn't experienced much charity at the hands of God or his Son, but she admired the man's determination. "Is there anything we can do to help you?"

"We could use some water. And perhaps some food. For when we're better."

"I think we can spare you some."

"Bless you." Tears started down Agar's face. "Truly the Lord works in mysterious ways. That we should have such treatment . . . at the hands of pirates, and a wanton woman besides. It's a miracle."

Coulances's eyes crinkled in an ironic smile. Mary was glad that Agar couldn't see the scowl on her face, the sanctimonious old fool. "You wouldn't happen to have anything to trade for it, would you?"

"We have little . . . that would interest pirates, being missionaries." Weakly he waved toward the hold. "You're welcome to whatever you find. Not that I could stop you."

"Thank you, Agar." She started below.

"Captain," Coulances said, appearing at her side, "the flux vapors will be much worse in that closed space. You risk almost certain contagion."

"I've been around much worse, Doctor," she lied. In truth, sick people frightened her to her bones. But that wasn't going to stop her from seeing if she could make a profit from this little adventure. "Go back to the *Fury*. I'll see you when I'm done here."

Coulances opened his mouth, about to argue, but stopped at her determined face. "As you command, Captain," he snapped.

"Tell Petronius what we need. Ask him also for an ax."

"An ax? What would they need with that?"

She pointed out the broken mast that slumped over the starboard bow. "I'll have to cut that away if Agar's to keep sailing."

"You're both *toqué*." He rapped the side of his head with his fist. "Crazy, you know? Are possessions worth dying for?"

"Do you know anything better?" She slapped him on the shoulder and picked her way over the debris.

Below decks, the rank miasma stung her eyes and prickled her skin. Her throat refused the putrid air. Coughing hard, she forced the foul air past clenched muscles. She looked around, afraid to go on. Through narrow passageways, unholy dark shadows slithered. Cautiously, she edged slowly aft. Moans and sobs haunted her every step. Walls bowed in and out, as if gasping for air themselves. At any moment, Death's icy fingers would slither through the floor boards and wrap like iron around her ankles. *Stop it!* she admonished herself. *The men expect me to be their brave, daring Captain. Not a weak-livered fool!*

She straightened her shoulders, then strode into the first cabin. Clad only in their horribly stained undergarments, a gray-bearded man and a younger blond woman lay dead in their bunks. A living black blanket of flies crawled over the open-mouthed corpses. Still, someone had lit a lantern for the gruesome couple. Mary took it, having better uses for it than the dead. She removed the pot-metal pocket watch from the night stand and the plain silver buckles from their shoes. The cheap glass rosaries she left, still clutched in the couple's dead hands. Kicking through their soiled black dress and suit wadded up on the floor, she decided to leave the ugly brass buckle where it lay. She just couldn't force herself to touch those infested pants.

Methodically, she went through every cabin pretending not to see the rotting corpses. She ignored the heart-wrenching pleas of the rare survivors. Weak arms held out, they begged for mercy, for water, for their mothers. There was nothing Mary could do for them. She tried to imagine that the rooms were bare save for the few items that were of value. These she put in a fairly clean pillowcase she'd discovered. In the captain's cabin, where a dead little black-haired girl lay putrefying in the bed, she came upon a treasure she valued more highly than the gold in the strongbox. It almost made the horror worth it.

Satisfied that she'd discovered everything of worth in the cabins, she worked her way down to the holds. Oxen and donkeys, packed too tightly in their stalls, leaned against one another, dead or dying. There was no telling how long since they'd been fed. She inspected some of the crates in the next hold. Nothing of real interest. Cheap furniture that hadn't been worth the passage. Clothing that probably carried their disease and so was useless. She could think of no value to their farm implements. The only thing of amusement was a pipe organ. She wondered what the natives of Amazonia would have thought of that rare noise.

Like a swimmer whose lungs are starved, she clambered topside craving air. She collapsed onto the deck gasping in the cleansing salt breeze. It seemed to scour the foul stench out of her body. Once she'd stopped panting, the sound of chopping caught her attention. She couldn't imagine that Agar was managing such a thing. Turning toward the felled mast, she spotted Petronius cutting the timber into manageable sizes. Three of her men assisted him, kerchiefs tied around their mouths. She stood slowly and whistled up to him. "I thought I told you to stay aboard."

He wiped the sweat from his brow and frowned down at her. "Woman, if I let you do this, we'd be tied t'this scow till Judgment Day. This way it gets done and I can get the *Fury* the Hell away from here."

She grinned up at him — the old fake. He was just as afraid of the plague as she. Perhaps more. But he hated to see suffering. It was a trait that had always endeared him to her. "Need some help?"

"Yeah. Help toss those freed pieces over the side. Keep the spars. We'll use those for firewood." He went back to chopping.

In a little while, they had the debris cleared and were ready to leave. Mary found Agar propped up against the ship's wheel. "Well, Captain, my crew tied down barrels of food and water and you're clear of the mast. It's time for us to go."

"Thank you, again. I just can't get over . . . being taken care of by pirates . . . by a woman and a black-amoor. Amazing."

Petronius spat on the deck and headed back to the *Fury*. Mary turned to follow.

"Wait. Here. Take these rosaries." He held out two gold and pearl strands. Their crosses glinted in the sun. "Those who owned these . . . are with Jesus now. I'm sure you and that black . . . need to know the solace . . . of the Lord."

"Good luck, Agar," she said, slipping them into the pillowcase. As she jumped aboard the *Fury*, Petronius had the crew cast off from the *Goode Sheepherd*. Soon the *Fury's* restored sails filled with wind and the pestilence-stricken ship was behind them. She directed the men who'd been aboard the *Goode Sheepherd* to scrub down with carbolic soap, as a precaution. They grumbled about her superstition regarding soap, but she paid them no mind. Mary turned all her attention to washing her hands and face, deliberately not looking back. She didn't want to know the British ship's fate.

Later, she assembled the crew for the distribution of the booty. It was small pickings since there was little coin, and the rosaries were worth little, but still, it had to be given out fairly. She left the bag below the mainmast before going into her cabin for writing materials. Coulances elaborately ignored her, turning his back and holding his book closer. Returning to the deck, she set up her desk.

The business of distributing the booty proceeded smoothly, and soon the *Goode Sheepherd's* troubling fate was behind them. When it came time for the crew to vote on their next heading, Petronius hesitated, waiting for Mary's suggestion. She wished she had an answer for him. They didn't usually travel much farther north than they were at the moment. They didn't know the waters and had no charts. Running aground on one of the hidden reefs was a real concern here. Yet the Dutch West Indies were only a little farther north. She'd heard there were rich pickings in those seas. As an added incentive, it might just be a good haven for Coulances. The people there would probably delight in the addition of a doctor to their population. On the other hand, the *Fury's* holds were almost full. If they met another likely-looking ship, they'd have to start storing goods on the deck. She hated to do that. It left their cargo out to the mercy of the capricious Caribbean elements and could overbalance them in a storm — and it *was* Storm Season. No, it was time to see a certain banker. "Perhaps we should head south to Saint John's, friends."

"And then maybe home, Cap'n?" Petronius

asked.

She considered, briefly. "Yes, why not? It's been too long since we were in our home port."

The crew eagerly voted for heading south.

Mary strayed to the bow, considering the situation. Perhaps she was working too hard at the problem of where Coulances should go. What was wrong with putting him on Cache Island? The isle had suffered its own flux epidemic last year. They needed a doctor, but Mary hadn't gotten around to finding one yet. It was the perfect solution. The thought had been dancing at the edge of her mind for weeks now, yet it hadn't presented itself till now. And why was that? It seemed obvious now. She drew a deep breath. She knew why. Any real thoughts about putting Coulances ashore she'd delayed. The truth was, she liked having him aboard. It was an odd feeling, this attachment — and it made her uncomfortable.

That night she and Coulances dined on a sea turtle and turnip pie. Mary studied his face, now almost entirely healed from the beatings. He was not what was thought of as a pretty man. He had a strong, stubborn jawline, mostly covered by his beard. His hair had receded enough to show a broad, intelligent, slightly furrowed brow. His nose was a touch crooked and somewhat overlarge for the rest of his features, but Mary liked the way he looked all the same. She was glad to see that his time on the ship had darkened his too-pale skin. Though she knew if he stayed aboard, living her kind of life, his skin would go as dark as hers — and perhaps his nature as well. He couldn't continue on the *Fury*. But she hated to think of a time without these evening visits. He was one of the few people she'd met who shared her interests. It was possible he enjoyed her company as well.

Tonight, though, he was silent. Still brooding on their little adventure with the *Goode Sheepherd*, no doubt. "You are most quiet," she said gently.

"You are ordering me to speak?"

She smiled slightly. "It's customary to converse with one's hostess, is it not?"

"You are not a hostess. You are a pirate." He shoved his plate away. "You care for nothing but gold."

"True." She drank down the last of her wine. "I'm a pirate, and as one, I hunt for plunder." She folded her napkin in her lap and stared at Coulances

After an uncomfortable length of time, Coulances said, "I must admit, I thought well of your compassion. That is, your offer to tow those unfortunates to port was most thoughtful."

She said nothing. The only noise was the gurgle of water passing by the *Fury's* hull.

"And — you did leave food and water for them."

Still she was silent.

He threw his napkin on the table. "But then you stripped those poor missionaries of everything they had!"

"After obtaining permission from the captain," she reminded him.

Grumbling wordlessly, he acknowledged her point.

She got up and refilled her wineglass, then took her seat again. "Soon a storm will come and that will be the end of the *Goode Sheepherd*. Neptune will have his due."

He wouldn't look up from the table.

Mary folded her hands in her lap. "What do you think would become of me, a female pirate captain, if I failed to capture booty for my crew?"

He studied her for what seemed an eternity. "I suppose they would kill you."

"Probably not murder, but certainly I would be marooned." She knew that if the crew mutinied against her, they would try to make Petronius captain. What they didn't know was that she and Petronius were a pair — one couldn't be separated from the other. If he couldn't put down the mutineers, they'd very likely both be killed. "I must always behave as a pirate if I want these men to follow me."

"Perhaps."

Mary could tell it was an argument she wasn't going to win, as she hadn't with someone else she cared about. The only one who understood her need to be a pirate was Petronius, but he didn't seem to understand about her other needs. Changing the subject, she said, "I have an idea about what port would be suitable for you."

"Madam, you know I am more than grateful that you and your crew rescued me from my captors. I should be happy wherever you decide to land me." He got up, refilled his glass, and sat back down.

"Provided it isn't French land." She laughingly took a sip of her own wine.

"Even so." He attempted a smile and lifted his glass to her. "During this time I have been treated better — and had more stimulating conversation — than I've had in my whole Caribbean experience. And to think I should find such treatment at the hands of a pirate. I had almost forgotten what it meant to be civilized."

She folded her hands again on the table in front of her. "The wish for a richer life has returned to you then?"

"I admit I enjoy creature comforts." His brow furrowed. "However, I have learned that such things are fleeting. Indeed, they must be paid for. I am reconciled that this ease I find myself in will not continue."

She leaned her chin on her fist. "Quite bravely said. But what if you found yourself completely surrounded by thieves, whores, cutpurses, pirates and usurers, not one of whom had even heard of Homer or Milton? What then, my friend?"

"If they need a physician, then it would be my privilege to be among them." He steepled his hands. "I have told you my feelings on this matter. Why question me again?"

Mary bowed her head a moment. "Forgive my trying you so, Doctor. The port I've chosen is filled with such folk. There are few gentle people there. I know you'll do your best in such a milieu."

"Where is this port?" he asked, sitting far back in the chair.

"It's on what I am pleased to call my island." She sat back as well.

"Your island? How extraordinary!" He laughed. "How does one come by an island?"

She took a sip of her wine. "That's not so difficult in these waters. There're many tiny uninhabited isles, like the one that so foiled the *Goode Sheepherd* this afternoon. Cache Island's quite a bit larger than that one and has its own protected harbor."

"Cache Island? Dare one guess how it got the name?"

"It's not hard, is it?" she agreed. "We found the place almost four years ago. At first we only hid our booty there. Took on fresh water, scraped barnacles off our hull, that sort of thing."

"But there is a town there now?" He balanced his glass on his knee. "How did that come about?"

She stared into the golden lights in her glass. "A couple of crewmen asked if they might be left there. They had some idea of living free while guarding our treasure against other pirates. It seemed like romantic claptwaddle to me, but I couldn't see harm. I told them to build a hut, and we'd consider them the harbor masters. They're still there: Bellington and Omanshay.

"As you may imagine, a pirate crew isn't exactly the most dependable crowd. They come and go as their whim and Fortune take them. We added more crew. Then some of the old crew would ask to stay on land. Many asked to pick up sweethearts from islands we passed. A savvy mate wanted to go into business with me, supplying people there with food and other necessities. It seemed a good idea, so I made him a loan. Since then, I've gone into various businesses with quite a number of my former crew."

"It sounds like a thriving community," he observed.

She nodded in agreement, finishing her wine. "So thriving that the *Fury* wasn't enough to keep all my businesses going. I invited others — friendly pirates and privateers — to use the port. Provided they pay a small fee. Now we boast four bordellos, seven or eight taverns, innumerable stores of all sorts, and three banks. Every time I go back, it seems the town has doubled in size."

His green eyes twinkled. "And what is it called, this bustling metropolis of the Caribbean?"

She felt her face go hot as it hadn't in many years. "I'd nothing to do with naming the place."

"Are you blushing?" He laughed. "Now I have seen it all — a pirate who blushes. Tell me, what is the name of the place?"

"Mary's Town."

"But that's marvelous!" he exclaimed. "What an honor! Why are you embarrassed by it?"

"I don't know." She shrugged. "I'm just uncomfortable with it. I didn't make the place. Better to have called it Pirate's Town or Furysville. It couldn't have happened without the work of us all."

"Work." He scoffed, returning to his earlier attitude. "Thievery, you mean."

She smiled thinly. "As you say."

He cradled his chin in his hand and regarded her appraisingly. "I have been wanting to ask how a woman of your obvious intelligence and education justifies piracy. How did you come to be a pirate in the first place?"

"I became a pirate through an accident of Fate." She retired their empty wineglasses to the table beside them and poured brandy into the waiting snifters. The ship rolled abruptly to starboard, almost tipping the glasses and decanter onto the deck. With a well-practiced move of her arm, Mary saved the crystal and served Coulances as if nothing had occurred. "I stayed a pirate because that same Fate arranged that I couldn't live what you might call a normal woman's life. Besides," she said with a gleam in her eye, "it has its rewards."

"I should be scandalized by your attitudes . . . your behavior." He peered at her over the rim of his glass. "All my medical training says that yours is the weaker sex, incapable of decision, leadership or physical hardship."

She laughed. "You and all your experts never take into account the real life of women. Who is it runs households great and small? Who makes decisions every day — from how one can stretch scant rations to feed a family of ten, to disciplining the upstairs maid? And as for physical stamina, I advise you to try birthing a babe before you tell me how much hardship a woman may endure."

He held up his hand. "Peace, woman. I concede our society has it all wrong. But even you must admit you are an exception to all rules."

"I'm no different from any other woman you've ever met, Doctor." She gently swirled her brandy in the crystal glass. "I've simply had the opportunity in the last several years to do what I wanted, when I wanted. Very few women have that chance."

"Yet I notice there are no other women in your crew," he said.

"I've not met any that thought to join me in my vocation, though you'd be surprised what they would dare." Mary didn't mention the one woman she had begged to join her, once.

He shook his head. "I still say you are remarkable, and I will stand by that assessment."

"Then I suppose I shall have to take it with good grace as a compliment and let it go at that."

"Please do," he said in a low voice.

For a moment she gazed into his green eyes. It was as if they were drawing her into them. She blinked and focused on his lips instead, only to be fascinated by their warm fullness. He licked them slowly and she felt as if his tongue had lightly strummed the strings of her soul. She caught herself leaning forward and forced herself back. What was it about him?

An unrelated thought drifted through her mind. "Ah!" she exclaimed, seizing on the idea, "I'd forgotten!" She slipped out of the cabin for a moment. Very soon she returned with a parcel from the *Goode Sheepherd* still wrapped in the remnants of a dead woman's lavender shawl. "Here," she said handing it to him. "A little token of our adventure this afternoon."

He put down his snifter and took off the cloth, clearly not noticing what it was. Revealed was a book bound in thick, intricately tooled carnelian leather. In letters of gold was written *The Faerie Queen*. "This is marvelous. I read this in Paris and thought it extraordinary. What a fine copy."

"I thought you might enjoy it," she said with a smile. "Perhaps we may read it together."

He opened the book and turned a few pages. Reading aloud in a strong voice with care to accent the rhyme scansion, he began at the Preface. She took a turn at the first Canto. Switching at each section, they read through to Canto IV before deciding to quit for the night.

Mary walked up to the bow. She loosened her hair and let the wind whip through it. The scent of a tropical bloom came to her from an island somewhere ahead in the dark. Before nightfall, the watch had told her there were heavy clouds on the horizon. They'd probably have a blow by midmorning. By then they'd be close to Montserrat and could make a run to the harbor if it got too bad. But tonight was like honey. She breathed deeply, in love with the night.

"Evenin', Cap'n," the first mate said close to her ear.

"Petronius," she said, startled, "do you have the duty this night?"

"No, Franz does. I was . . . wakeful." He leaned against the rail, but watched her, rather than the sea.

Mary still looked out along their course. "It's a beautiful night to be awake."

"Hmm." He lit his clay pipe with a straw from the lantern, considering her thoughtfully. The flame illuminated his dark face, so like oiled teak. Unlike the rest of the crew, he was close-shaven, revealing a chiseled jaw, a broad mouth and high, sharp cheekbones. "It's a night. Just like many another."

"Ah, my friend, have you no appreciation of nature?"

"I appreciate that other things concern me more, Cap'n." Smoke streamed behind him.

Catching his mood, she turned. "Meaning?"

He folded his arms. "Didja hear the crew mutterin' after we divvied the booty, Cap'n?"

"Aye." She braced her back against the rail. "I warned you someone's holding out lately. I think it's Ingram."

"No." She could just make out the shake of his head in the dark. "No t'isn't Ingram made 'em talk, Cap'n. Though I agree he's our sneakthief."

"Well?" she snapped.

"Notice you took those embossed shoe buckles for yourself today. And before, a fine linen shirt."

"What of it?"

He paused so long, she thought he wasn't going to continue. "Was that for the doctor?"

"His buckles were lost in prison. You know that. His shirt was badly torn as well." She couldn't see where he was leading. "He needs to be properly clothed."

His clay pipe glowed redly in the night, making

his face a glowering, uncanny mask. "Cap'n, if he's gonna get a share o' the booty, shouldn't he do more'n be kept by you?"

She slapped his face as hard as she could. His pipe popped out of his mouth and fell in a shower of sparks onto the deck. Without a word, he bent over and picked the pieces up. He bowed stiffly to her. "G'night, Cap'n," he said in the same calm tone he'd bidden her good evening and strode down the deck.

Mary pounded the rail with both fists in time with her angry thoughts. *Insufferable, irritating bastard! How dare he!* First thing in the morning, she'd have the son of a whore flogged and then keelhauled. Talk to *her* that way! Who did he think he was?

She took a deep shuddering breath. He was Petronius, that's who. Without him there was no Captain Mary, no *Fury,* no Cache Island. No books or anything else she loved in this life. Bastard! He always knew how to irritate her the most. But why did he have to make her strike him? She felt just as stupid as the last time she'd struck him . . . oh, so long ago. She'd always regretted that moment. Now it looked like she'd another regret to add to a lifetime of secret humiliations. A pox on him!

The wind began to feel cool against her skin, and she realized she'd left her coat in her cabin. Well, she couldn't go get it now, could she? It angered her all over again, that cut of Petronius's that she was *keeping* Coulances. She hadn't bedded him once. Hugging herself to keep warm, she began to pace. Not that Coulances wasn't man enough for her tastes. He was, most certainly. But she'd hosted dozens of men, albeit hostages, and not touched them. She'd met no man who could stir her since Edmund — and look where that'd led her. No, letting one's feelings run away with one was a most dangerous business.

Still, Coulances was different from any man she'd met. So intelligent and quick-witted. She liked the way he looked at her. He was good company the like of which she'd not had in some time. He'd a merry spark to him that she fancied only she could bring out. It impressed her early on that he'd stood up to her. How many, once they lost their initial fear of her, sought to patronize her as if she were some wharf whore. No, he treated her with respect at all times. She found it refreshing . . . attractive, even.

Mary pondered the past fortnight. What stood out weren't the days, but the nights with him. She could recall practically every single word he'd said to her since coming on board. Fool. It could be depended upon that he had no such remembrance. This time they had was but a trifle — meaning nothing to either of them more than a few pleasant conversations. Yet, she would miss him when he was gone. Would he miss her? Certainly not. He was a man of science and reason. Still . . . a man for all that.

She halted and discovered that she was in front of her cabin door. Why was she here? To get her coat, of course. One couldn't be expected to lie in the night air without it.

There was a small sliver of light under the door. He, too, was still awake. Her heart thumped loudly in her chest. She rapped on the door. "Yes?" came his muffled voice.

Opening the door, she stuck her head in the room. "Are you dressed?"

Coulances gaped at her, momentarily confused. He sat at the table, a snifter of brandy at hand. The whale oil lantern was turned up high for reading. He wore only his new linen shirt and his long underwear. Hurriedly, he moved the book to cover himself. "No, I'm . . . uh . . . not."

"So I see." She couldn't help but laugh as she slipped into the room. "I forgot my coat."

He looked around the room. "There, on the chair in front of the desk."

"Indeed." She went over and picked up the coat. "Having trouble sleeping?"

"A little."

"I, too, seem unable to settle down for the night," she replied. "Do you recommend anything?"

He smiled. "You could join me in another brandy."

Mary put the coat back down. "I think I shall." She poured herself a splash.

"I have been reading the further adventures of the Redcrosse Knight." Coulances tapped the book. "Perhaps we could continue."

"Fine."

"Would you mind handing me that blanket so I might cover myself?" he asked.

She put down her glass and pulled the blanket off the bed. As she handed it to him, their hands brushed. She felt a tingling in her fingertips and looked into his amazing green eyes. He looked back at her and slowly licked his lips. Mary felt a quiver in her inner core.

"Thank you," he whispered.

As if it had a mind of its own, her hand reached out and stroked his cheek. His beard was pleasantly coarse against her fingers, his cheek warmly inviting. Eyes half-closed, he leaned a little into her caress.

She felt his hand slide up her waist, then around to the small of her back. Slowly, he rubbed her hard muscles in a circular pattern that she found sensual.

Mary bent down and kissed him. His lips met hers and seemed to blend into her skin. At first, their kiss was gentle, a fragile, exploratory thing. But as it lengthened, their passions ignited in a honey-flavored fire.

She felt his hand stroking her neck, her nape. There was a thunk as the book hit the floor. His tongue slipped into her mouth and danced with hers. Slowly she sank down into his lap. She let go the blanket and ran her hand through his thick curly hair. His other hand slid up her side. Gently he began to fondle her breast. She could feel him harden under her thigh.

"Mary, I have longed for you," he whispered in her ear. Slowly, he ran his hands around her breasts, down her sides and caressed her flanks.

"Alphonse," she moaned as she rubbed her hands over his chest and shoulders.

Coulances kissed her throat while slowly unlacing her shirt. He nibbled the tops of her breasts and pinched her stiff nipples.

"Come to my bed." She slipped out of his grasp and stood, pulling him upright to her.

He kissed her deeply again, squeezing her buttocks. "I have never made love to someone in breeches before."

"Good." She chuckled, pulling him down with her on the bed. "I'm not all that fond of buggers."

"For you, I'd be willing to give anything a try." He licked her nipple and rubbed her dampening crotch.

"Mmm," she sighed. Quickly he unlaced her pants and slipped his hand inside. "Oh, Alphonse.

More."

"Aye, Captain," he whispered.

Three weeks found them no closer to Cache Island. It seemed as if the entire Caribbean was filled with French military ships and privateers. It was clear that Captain Lemeux's threat to hunt them down was real. He'd set the entire fleet after them. Long ago the French had perfected a system of communicating with their far-flung ships by using a series of fast little boats to convey messages. By now, every Frenchman in the Windward and Leeward Isles knew the *Fury* had a captive Lemeux wanted back.

Just as they sighted the island of Antigua, a French man-o'-war appeared and bore down on them. The *Fury* managed to outrun the bigger ship and hid in a cove of an uninhabited island. After two days there, Captain Mary ordered them back into the sea lanes. She tried a more oblique tack toward their goal of Antigua. Once again, they sighted a French military ship — though probably not the same one. As before, they were forced to outrun a larger ship and hide out in a cove.

"Cap'n Lemeux's a man o' his word," Petronius observed after yet a third such incident.

"I'm beginning to lose my sense of humor about the French and their little ways," Mary grumbled. She commanded Petronius to head for Barbuda.

For Mary, each day was filled with frustration with the French. Each night was filled with lovemaking with her Frenchman. She lay awake long after he fell asleep beside her and tried to reconcile what she wanted as a woman with what she knew to be best for her ship and crew. Sometimes she inspected his face for hours as he slept, observing each eyelash, each line, each pore, and wondered how he'd achieved such a hold on her heart. She knew the crew was growing restive at the inconvenience this man, her lover, was causing. She thought of all the money she was losing on the saleable goods in the *Fury's* holds. But she couldn't surrender Coulances and let him be hauled off to his death. She would fight to defend him against the French — or her own crew.

The sleepless nights began to tell on her. She became more abrupt with the crew. The more snappish she became, the more grumbling she heard behind her back. Finally, a day after a French privateer got close enough to blow a hole through their deck, Petronius took her aside. "Cap'n." He spoke close to her ear so they wouldn't be overheard. "You're close t'mutiny here."

She bit back a stinging retort. "I'm aware of the situation."

He grasped her arm. "I tell you only 'cause I think we gotta remedy the problem, and soon."

"I'll not give him to the French," she rasped.

He let go her arm. "I guessed that, Cap'n. You have any plan at all?"

"No," she whispered after a long pause, "no, I don't. I lie awake all night and worry the problem, but it does me no good." She bowed her head. "Have you come up with anything?"

"None that you'd wanna hear, Cap'n." He smiled faintly at her sharp look. "I'm a practical man. If somethin' causes me trouble, I get rid o' it."

Mary scowled at him. "If you think of something more constructive, let me know. Otherwise, keep the crew from becoming a mob on me. Up the rum ration tonight."

"That could work," he said with a shrug. "Or it could make things worse. Hard t'tell what drunk men'll do." He turned away and started back to the quarter-deck, limping noticeably.

"Is that toe bothering you again?"

He shrugged and continued forward.

"You should see Coulances," she called after his retreating back. "He could cure it, I'm sure."

He waved dismissively and headed for the wheel.

"Stubborn bastard," she muttered to herself.

That night Mary was gloomy as she ate with Alphonse. Jacoby served them a disappointing dinner of salt cod and dried biscuits. The rations were getting thin, he explained. There wasn't much one could do with such meager fare. Mary glared at the wall and refused to acknowledge him. She knew Jacoby was implying they'd have more food if she hadn't given sup-plies to the dying people of the *Goode Sheepherd*. Usually they acquired their fresh provisions from captive ships, but there'd been no boardings since the French began harassing them.

"Mary," Coulances said, breaking the tense silence of the meal, "we must speak about the necessity of surrendering me to the French authorities."

"No!" She swept her plate off the table. The fine porcelain shattered on the floor. Food spattered the var-nished wainscoting next to the door. "I won't have it!"

"*Cheri*, I am endangering your crew, and you." He shook his head. "I won't have that. I don't want you hurt on my account."

She balled up her fists. "Don't tell me what you will and won't have, Alphonse. I won't give you to them. There's a solution to this predicament! It just hasn't occurred to me yet."

He looked at her sadly. "You are exhausted. I know you aren't sleeping. Surely it would be less trouble to put me on one of these little islands while you make good your escape?"

"You'd not survive, my dear." She patted his hand. "Exposed to the weather, wild boars and whatever other creatures there are, you'd have little chance. Moreover, the uncertain amount of time you'd be left there, the sun and thirst would certainly take you. No, that's not a possibility either."

Gently, he took her hand and kissed her fingers. "I am causing you pain, something I never wished to do."

She closed her eyes. "It's been my experience that love exacts a fierce price." Opening her eyes, she stared into the green eyes she'd come to love. "A way will be found; depend on it." Mary squeezed his hand.

Coulances leaned over and kissed her. Soon they were making slow, passionate love. But afterwards, Mary lay awake, alone with the same dark thoughts.

CHAPTER THREE

On a moonless night, after many days of playing hide-and-seek with the French navy and privateers, the *Fury* sought shelter on the west side of Basse Terre, Guadaloupe. Petronius shined a lantern at the coast, flashing it three times, then dowsing it. He repeated the signal as the stars wheeled above them. Finally, toward morning, a fishing skiff approached the *Fury*. A short, stocky man with thin gray-white hair and wire-framed glasses scrambled up the thick cargo net that served as a ladder. He hauled himself over the gunnel and scurried across the deck like a rat running toward a slab of rotting meat. "It's good to see you again, *Capitan*." He bowed deeply.

Captain Mary stood aloof, hands on hips. "What have you for me, Henri?" This simpering creature had once been a trusted member of her crew. She'd set him up as their courier two years ago to carry messages and mail to the *Fury* when they couldn't go to port.

Disturbing rumors about him began to surface a few months ago. His manner told her they were true.

He pulled a packet of envelopes from inside his shirt. They were tied with an old string and soiled from close contact with his filthy body. He offered them to her with a brown-toothed smile. "One comes all the way from Hispaniola, *madame!*"

"And how would you know that unless you'd read it, you sniveling dog?" She snatched the missives from his hand.

Henri trembled under her gaze. "I speak to the man who gave it to me. That is all. Truly!"

She tapped the letters in her hand, considering. It'd be better to kill the little nuisance now. However, at the moment, they couldn't afford to do that. There was much he could do for them still. She hated relying on people like this to help her. "I'll take your word for it, today, Henri. But don't let me catch you selling us out to the colonial governments, hear?"

"Oh, *non, madame.*" He seemed ready to grovel on the deck. "I would never do such a thing."

Petronius arched his brow ironically. Mary knew he wouldn't hesitate to kill Henri, even though they would face a certain amount of inconvenience. But he didn't interfere with her decisions. Not in front of the crew. Later was another story.

Putting away the letters, she said, "Henri, bring us some provisions: beer, meat — any kind, flour. Jacoby can give you a complete list."

"Provisions?" A subtle change came over his face, though it could have been a moth across the lantern flame. "It will take two, three days."

"Try to make it one day, Henri." She took out her knife. It flashed menacingly in the lantern light.

"Try very hard."

He backed away. *"Oui, madame.* Henri will be very fast."

Mary took out the first letter and slit it open. "See that you are." The little man rushed off to speak to the cook. She sighed and shook her head at Petronius. "I know what you're thinking."

He shrugged. "We'll see if the chance you're takin' pays off."

"We need the food."

"Haven't you heard my belly talkin'?" He slapped his firm abdomen. "The men aren't happy when they're hungry. 'Sides," he took out his repaired pipe and looked at it ruefully, "we're outta tobacco, too."

"Go add your filthy weed to the list, then, and leave me to read my letters in peace," she said laughingly. He gave her a mock salute and stalked off after Henri.

Mary gave the first missive a cursory read-through by the lantern's fitful light. It was from Donwelyn Briarley, Cache Island's governor. For the most part, it contained nothing but gossip and complaints that she wasn't spending enough money to expand the harbor. There was nothing important enough to linger over just now.

She put the first letter inside her shirt and opened the second. This one she glanced through, then read more carefully. It started out innocently enough:

Darling,   *27 September*
Thank You soe very muche for the Exotic Plant.
It survived the Trip quite welle and now fills My
Rooms with its Extraordinary Chocolate-like Scent.

*Every Moment it reminds Me of You. I can hardly
bear that We have been Apart soe long. I think of You
Constantly. I even Dream of you.*

*Last Night, I had the moste Amazing Dream yet.
We were in a far Place. I have never seen Its Like
before. There was a Room, a Dungeon? You were
bound on a Table, for indede, You were My Prisoner!
You — and I know this will amuse You no end —
were in a very Formal Dress of Deep Blue Silk with
elaborate Flanders Lace Cuffs and Bodice. I was
dressed in the Tight-Fitting tan Breeches and Shirt
that You gave Me last year.*

*Very Slowly I used a Knife to cut Your Dress to
Shreds. Your Wonderful Blacke Eyes bore into Mine.
You looked Small and Threatened. It Thrilled Me that
You were helpless and in My Power.*

*Finally, You lay before Me Naked. Methodically,
I explored Your Body with My Tongue, Teeth, and
Fingers, leaving no Crevice unexplored!*

It went on for many more paragraphs describing
exactly what her lover would do in those circumstances.
Mary refolded the letter and put it into her bodice as she
stealthily looked around. Had any of the crew seen how
her cheeks suddenly flushed red? How rapid was her
breathing? How her pulse raced? Usually, she would
have read her letters in her cabin. But she didn't dare go
there now, with Coulances in her bed. She didn't want
to answer a lot of questions about the letter-writer.

She took a couple of deep breaths, trying to calm
herself. Slowly, her heart pounded less. The letter
against her breast felt hot and scratchy, as if trying to
work its way into her skin. Mary tried to ignore it by
turning her attention to the remaining envelope.

These missives were rare. The last time she'd gotten a letter from Hispaniola it was bad news. She broke the messy-looking wax seal and unfolded it. "*Madamme Marie*," it began, addressing a persona she used when pretending to be someone other than a pirate.

> *U doe not nowe us. Nanete took sick last month and she di. Me and my Gigi we takin care of ur Mellisa. She doein fine. Nanete she tol us u a riche woman. We figger u cann pay muche muche mor than u waz payin her. Maybe if u don Mellisa don stay fine. We figger Mellisas life worthe 2000 golde peeces a monthe. Send soon or she mite take sikk too.*
> *Juan Carlo*

Mary stomped to the bow, angrily balling up the letter. She'd long feared that one of her enemies or the damned colonial powers would take her daughter Melissa and use her as a way to capture the *Fury*. It'd never occurred to her that a common kidnapper would be a problem.

As soon as this foolishness with the French was straightened out, she would order the *Fury* to Les Cayes on Hispaniola to rescue Melissa. By Hades, she'd torture those miserable whores's whelps slowly, taking days to kill them. She'd savor repaying them for every bloody moment they'd endangered her baby. If, indeed, Melissa still lived. It could be that they'd done away with the child. It wasn't unheard of. No. Mary couldn't allow herself to even contemplate such a thing. Melissa must be alive. Anything else was unthinkable.

She let the gentle Caribbean wind cool her emotions and forced her reason to take control. Killing this

Juan Carlo and his Gigi might be satisfying, but what of Melissa? One couldn't simply sweep in and slaughter the people who'd been caring for the girl. That would be horrid for the child. She would see her mother as a brutal killer. Bad enough to have her brought up by others. Melissa didn't need to know that Mary was a pirate.

"Somethin' wrong?" Petronius put a hand on her shoulder. "Is the baby sick again? You know, little ones get sick all the time. My little —"

"Nanette's dead," she said, cutting him short. As she said it, Mary felt the first pang for Nanette's loss. She'd been a sweet woman with a calm and caring nature — as good a nanny as a midwife for her daughter. Mary shoved aside her feelings for later. "Melissa's being held for ransom. The kidnappers are demanding two thousand a month in gold."

He leaned on the rail, facing her. "So, soon as we can, we go t'Les Cayes and kill the swine."

Mary shoved back her wild curly hair, still loose from her earlier lovemaking with Coulances. "Aye, that'd make me happiest. But it won't work."

"Why not?" he demanded.

"Think, Petronius!" she snapped. "Where am I to put that child? Shall I give up pirating to rear her?"

"Well, what're you gonna do about it?"

She twined a hank of black hair around her fingers as she thought. "Two thousand's a lot of money. They're greedy. Maybe they'll settle for less. Perhaps five hundred a month?"

His face showed he was caught between amusement and incredulity. "You're gonna negotiate with kidnappers?"

"Why the Hell not? People negotiate with us." Petronius said something in reply, but Mary paid him no heed. She was casting about in her mind for a crew-man who could be trusted utterly. She'd be vulnerable to this man in two ways. Once she revealed the exis-tence of her daughter, he'd never again respect her — a woman — fully as an equal again. It wasn't his fault. It was just how society was. Therefore, she'd have to pen-sion him off somewhere, and preferably not Cache Island where he could talk.

Because that was the second problem. No mat-ter how loyal, sooner or later he'd have to tell someone about Captain Mary's little girl. It was human nature not to keep secrets. And when he did tell, surely that person would use Melissa to get whatever he wanted from Mary. It would take a dedicated crewman and a lot of money to make this work. A name popped into her mind. Yes, he might do. "Henri hasn't left yet, has he?" she asked.

"No. I think the little rat's below, samplin' our rum."

"Good. Do I remember correctly that Franz speaks French as well as the Frankish dialect?" Franz also was one of the few crewmen who could read and write.

He nodded. "Aye, he's from Alsace-Lorraine where they speak both, or so he's told me. Are you gonna use him t'make the deal?"

"He's been with us three years, now. He could retire well. Settle down in Hispaniola, don't you think?" How much would Franz demand to cash out of the *Fury*? How much would buy a man's silence? She cal-culated what she had on board. Only enough to whet both the kidnappers's and Franz's appetites. Well, it would have to do for a start until she could get to St. John's. "Tell Henri to wait for someone to join him.

Have Franz meet me here."

Petronius went to do as she'd asked. Mary hurried to her cabin, stopping first to grab a lantern. Closing its shutter so that it emitted only a sliver of light, she crept into the room and made her way over to the chest. It was nearly hidden by the coverlet and blankets Coulances and she had thrown off in their passion this evening. He lay curled in a ball in the middle of the bed, features relaxed in deep slumber. The pillow beside him was dented where her head had lain only a short while ago — although it seemed a fortnight. Setting down the lamp, she covered him with the bedclothes, but he didn't stir. Then she went through her trunk and took out a good sum of gold, wrapping it securely and noiselessly in an old velvet cape. She left quietly and hurried forward to meet Franz.

Quickly she explained the situation to him. His eyes widened when she mentioned a daughter. Then a shadow of a smile crept on his face. Mary guessed that he was picturing her as a mother — a woman who should be home tending her babe by the hearth. In that moment she also knew he'd lost all the respect for her as a fellow pirate, or a superior — his captain — that she'd built up with him and the others over these last few years. She couldn't restore his faith in her ability to command, but she knew well how to bind him to her.

She mentioned the large sum she proposed to pay him, if he did what she asked. With the possibility of becoming wealthy held out to him, he listened carefully. By his questions, she believed Franz was concerned with the welfare of Melissa and keeping Mary's anonymity — as well as making a lot of money for little work. She instructed him never to refer to her daughter as a person or by name, only "the package," even when speaking directly to Mary. When all had been arranged, she handed him the heavy bundle. "Do this favor for me, Franz, and I'll see you'll retire a very rich man. All right?"

"*Ja*, Cap'n, I'll get your ba — " She shot him a hard look. "Uh . . . package back to you, safe and sound. I swear it."

She slapped his shoulder. "Good. Go grab your things and shove off with Henri. Catch an island sloop out to Hispanola from Pointe-a-Pitre." He hurried down below. Presently he returned. She noted he carried a single bundle under his arm. It had to be the gold. He had hold of Henri's arm and rushed over to Mary.

Mary gave Henri a letter she'd written to her lover on Cache Island a few days before. She debated whether to send it, especially after the one she'd just received. But what she felt for Alphonse was so powerful. How could she lie or keep it a secret? Henri squinted at it, trying to read the recipient's name in the dim light, then slipped the letter into his grimy shirt. He tipped his hat as Franz led him over the side.

She watched the fishing skiff slip into the morning fog toward the coast. She could do no more than she had, either about their problems with provisions, or Melissa, or her lover. It didn't soothe her nerves, though. She paced the deck as the sun burned off the clouds. To keep everyone busy, she set part of the crew to fishing, the rest to cleaning the ship.

Mary kept up her nervous walking all that day, barely giving Coulances a few words when he came out on deck. There was a cold prickling on her back, as she'd felt many times before sudden danger. Petronius said she was better than a weather glass — except she predicted trouble instead of storms. This time, she'd knowingly created the possibility of disaster by trusting Henri. But she had to take the chance. It was either that or give in to the bloody French — and she would never do that while there was breath in her body.

The sun was well on its way to the westward horizon when Jorge, their lookout, cried out, "Sails ho!" Coming up from their stern quarter, around the rocks at the edge of the island, was a brigantine, tacking hard for them. The ship flew a black flag with a large grinning skull over crossed swords at her mainmast. Four blood-red pennants signaling no quarter fluttered at her mains'l spars. "The *Evil Eye!*" he shouted.

"Weigh anchor! Hoist the sails!" Mary commanded. "Ready the cannon! To arms, to arms!" The crew raced to their stations. Her heart hammered as the sails seemed unwilling to shake out of their shrouds. If the *Evil Eye* caught them in this cove, they'd be dead in the water. How humiliating to be caught like some witless merchantman!

Petronius took the wheel from Talinn. "Trim the mains'l! Haul the jib, there, you laggards!" he shouted. He swung the sluggish *Fury* out of the tranquil waters of the cove into the chop of the Caribbean.

Breasting the increasing swells, the *Evil Eye* bore down on them, trying to cut off their escape. The *Fury's* masts creaked and chuckled as the wind bellied out the sails. Surging forward, the ship gained speed. "Point three cannon to port, the others starboard," she ordered. Mary heard the rumble of the cannons' wheels in answer to her command. There was no way to know where to place all their firing power until the *Evil Eye* engaged them.

While she waited for the *Fury* to gain position, she thought back to two years before, after one of the

Caribbean's more vicious storms. The *Fury* had come across a Portuguese caravel. Its crew was struggling to fix the broken mainmast when Mary's men attacked the ship. The pirates quickly had the ship in their control. While they were pillaging their captive, another ship appeared on the horizon. Shortly they were joined by a brigantine flying a pirate flag. The bowsprit proclaimed it the *Evil Eye*. As soon as they were in range, they started firing on the frigate and the *Fury*. Mary had her men abandon the crippled Portuguese ship and go back to the *Fury*.

The *Evil Eye* had already damaged the *Fury* before Mary and her crew could get away from the Portuguese ship. Spars and rigging littered the deck as the *Fury*'s men raced to their posts. Petronius maneuvered them away from the caravel so that they could have a clear shot at the other pirates.

The two ships fired round after round of cannonballs, mortars, chains and grapeshot. Soon, the *Fury*'s sails were shredded. A cannonball came through their hull just at the waterline. Mary's men had to leave their posts to patch the gaping hole that could easily sink them. Reluctantly, Mary ordered Petronius to retreat from the battle.

As they'd turned into the wind, she heard a terrible cackling coming from the other ship. At the bow stood a figure from Hell. He was dressed all in black. Long, stiff burning rags jutted out of his sooty tri-corner hat. "That'll teach ya to get in Captain Dead Eye's way!" he hollered.

Mary took aim with her blunderbuss and fired. Dead Eye was waving his cutlass at the *Fury*, then suddenly disappeared. She smiled at the obvious hit. Later, she heard she'd shot two fingers off his right hand.

Mary had been disappointed. She'd been aiming at his black heart.

Someone grabbed her arm, shaking her out of her reverie. "What's going on, Mary?" Coulances asked.

Mary whirled to face him. "It's the *Evil Eye*. Get back to your cabin," she ordered.

"Perhaps I can help," he objected.

"If you know how to pray, do so — but do it in the cabin. Now!" She shoved him toward the hatch. He went slowly aft, his limp all too apparent. Stopping at the entrance, he turned. There was anger in the set of his jaw. Pain in his eyes. Mary ignored it and glared at him until he started down the gangway.

She spun around at the shriek of an incoming cannonball. Shredding a corner of their foresail, the black whistling blur missed the gunnel by a hand's breadth, then shot into the sea. Mary directed her men to tie down the damaged sail that was flapping in the wind. She could tell that the tattered cloth had affected their speed. Where moments before the *Fury* had been knifing through the swells, now each wave felt like a hammer against her hull. "Hurry!" she shouted up to her men. As soon as the sail was lashed into place, the *Fury's* bow seemed to leap out of the water. They slipped away from the approaching *Evil Eye*.

But the loss of speed allowed the *Evil Eye* to beat forward of the *Fury*, positioning itself at the best possible angle both to fire and steal their wind. It got off another salvo as the *Fury's* sails began to luff. Three flaming missiles arced toward Mary's ship. Two fell into the sea, exploding in geysers almost as tall as the mainmast. The third incendiary seemed to be coming right down their bowsprit, looming bigger and bigger. Petronius spun the wheel hard to port. Struggling with the insufficient wind, the *Fury* dragged her head reluctantly onto their heading. The burning missile hurtled into the water on their starboard side. Sizzling salt water erupted over the decks. Shaking off the corrupt brew, the drenched crew raced to secure rigging loosened by the explosion.

"Close haul those sails, mates!" Petronius called out. "Ready about." He swung the wheel hard to starboard. "Hard a' lee." Mary and most of the crew clung to the rising port rails as the starboard side dipped close to the swells. His maneuver slipped the *Fury* directly behind the *Evil Eye*, but out of their windshadow. Both ships tacked close to the wind. The *Evil Eye's* pilot feinted, pretending a premature tack. Petronius, wise to such tricks, had already anticipated the move and held his line. After a while, he wheeled the *Fury's* bow off starboard — briefly — then brought her back on their previous heading. The *Evil Eye* ignored the move. Again, the pilot pretended to turn off the *Evil Eye's* course, but Petronius wouldn't take the bait. And so for many leagues, neither gained an edge over the other. Both ships beat out toward the setting sun, each master goading the other into a mistake that could be fatal.

Mary wanted to break out of this game. Dodging about in rough seas seemed pointless to her. Hand-to-hand combat was something she could understand and control.

The wind shifted subtly from southeast to east-southeast. Petronius took advantage of it and bore to port. "Ready the starboard guns!" Mary commanded. The *Evil Eye's* pilot struggled to keep the gap closed, but overshot his mark in the lessened wind, widening the distance.

"Fire!" Mary shouted.

Immediately the first cannon spoke, then the next, then the next in deadly syncopation. Flaming mortars, lethal chains, deadly grapeshot hurtled into the sails and through the decks of the other pirate ship. Wood, cloth and water exploded around the *Evil Eye* as the *Fury's* arms hit home. "Reload the cannon! Prepare to fire!" Mary cried.

The *Evil Eye* answered with a salvo of flaming cannonballs. Mary saw one, just for a moment, suspended over the deck in front of her. Then, with a banshee shriek, the mortar crashed into the wood. There was a horrendous thunder clap followed by the noise of shattering timber. With a whoosh, flames and pieces of splintered deck rushed at her. The smell of scorched iron and burnt wood hit her with the shock of the explosion. She was hurtled aft, arms and legs flopping uselessly. The mainmast flashed past her. *So this is what it feels like to die.* Her body started to twist right. From the corner of her eye, she saw the heaving sea rushing to meet her. Suddenly, pain screamed from her back as she crashed into something solid. She tried to take a breath, but her lungs refused to cooperate. Still struggling to get air, her body slumped to the deck. The world went black.

Moments later, Mary awoke to hear someone screaming. When her eyes focused, she was relieved to discover it wasn't her voice. Lying in the scupper mere inches from her face, Albert moaned in agony. The left side of his face was horribly burnt, the eye gone. Blood pooled darkly around him, telling her he'd a hole in his belly. Then his noise stopped. He shivered like a mast in a hard gale. Turning to her, mouth agape as if trying to tell her one last thing, his remaining eye poured tears. Then his head sank back onto the deck. His shivers ceased.

She closed her eyes. But for a few feet, it could be her lying there. Perhaps he'd even broken some of the force of the explosion — somehow saving her life. Mary took a deep breath. He'd been a good man, though he'd only been with them three months. She wished she knew a prayer for him.

Mary struggled up on her elbows, trying to find out what had happened to the rest of the ship. Choking thick clouds of dark-gray smoke hung over their debris-ridden deck. Her men carried buckets of water, fighting the hidden fire. An orange dagger of flame shot up through the sooty fog. Then, there was an angry hiss as gray smoke turned white from the dowsing of the fire.

Painfully, she shoved herself up, coughing as the smoke reached her sore lungs. Her back was all one massive ache. Shooting pains darted down her legs as she stumbled through the chaos. From the port gunnel she could see the *Evil Eye* was coming about the *Fury's* stern. It was going broadside for a final, killing salvo. She grabbed Watu and Gerhardt as they hurried by. "Get the crossbows. Come on!" They snatched up their weapons, then raced after her as she hobbled aft.

Mary held Watu's arm and pointed out the tall man dressed all in black on the deck of the other ship. The smoldering tapers in his hat made him seem to glow in the gathering dusk. "Kill that bastard, Captain Dead-Eye, and I'll give you your weight in gold." She lit two bolts with the lantern and handed them to the men. "Fire at will." Both got off their shots just as a volley came from the *Evil Eye*. Two of the cannonballs shredded the topsail and ripped off the spars, which rained onto the deck.

She watched as Captain Dead-Eye dodged the

burning arrows just in time. But the flames ignited loose gunpowder on the deck. Sparks fired the fallen, shredded sails and the *Evil Eye* crew had to turn their attention from the *Fury*. Quickly, Mary lit two more bolts. She had Gerhardt and Watu aim for the mainsail. They fired, unleashing the burning arrows to arc gracefully into the *Evil Eye's* rigging. The mainsail burst into flames, touching off the sails above. Burning cloth tendrils drooped onto the frantic crew of the *Evil Eye*.

Petronius maneuvered the *Fury* around so they were broadside to the *Evil Eye*.

"Fire!" Mary shouted.

The *Fury's* guns spoke again. Mary watched as two of their mortars struck the *Evil Eye* amidships. The successive explosions thundered through the hull, then ripped a huge crater from the lowest holds to the upper deck scattering men, timber and guns high into the air. The crew of the *Fury* cheered as the opposing ship shuddered and wallowed. Yelping men dived into the black water as the *Evil Eye* broke apart, her timbers squealing. The water around her boiled as she started sinking below the waves. Dusk came on, turning everything to different shades of gray. It was impossible to see who had survived. The air hung heavy with the odors of gunpowder, burnt wood, corrosive seawater and scorched flesh. Mary wished she had some way to search the inky waters for her enemy.

"Petronius!" she called forward. "Set sail for Marie Galant Island."

"Aye Cap'n," he shouted over the din of the sinking ship.

Mary turned back to watch the *Evil Eye* collapse under the waves with a terrible roar. Debris littered the water but she couldn't see anyone. There was a possibility that some of the *Evil Eye's* crew might live. It disgusted her that Captain Dead-Eye might escape her once more.

She limped back to the main deck. By the light of two lanterns held by members of her crew, Coulances was binding Brepa's messy-looking leg wound. His ebony face was contorted in pain as the doctor tied the bandage tightly. He'd be no use in the coming days.

"You all right, Cap'n?" Talinn asked, apparently noticing the way she held her aching side.

She waved his concern away. "Just a bad fall. How much damage?"

"The sails're in sorry shape. We have those extra ones, but there ain't 'nough to replace all of 'em. We've a nasty hole in our deck. Goes clear through the upper hold. But the ball got stopped by all those bolts o' cloth ye had us store down b'low. Made a mess o' it."

"It's worth the loss if it saved our lives." Privately, she was upset at the expenditure of that fabric. It would've been worth quite a bit in St. John's.

"We don't have much wood to repair that. Or the spars and crossbars that need repairin'."

Mary took a deep, painful breath, trying to shed her frustration. There was no question about it. They'd have to end this harassment soon or lose the ship. She just didn't know how, yet. She pointed to Albert's burnt, broken body lying in the scupper. "Toss the body overboard and clean up his mess," she ordered.

"Aye, Cap'n." He called a few men over to assign the task.

Coulances appeared at her shoulder. "Captain, were you injured?"

"Merely bruised, Doctor," she lied. Actually she felt terrible. What she'd like was to lie down in her big

Cache Island bed with its starched linen and down pillows. A nice fantasy, but hardly useful at the moment. "How long before Brepa will be better?"

"A fortnight or so, I expect. If he's kept quiet." Coulances turned at the sound of the men heaving Albert's body over the side. The crewmen paused, watching the corpse slide along beside the hull, then bob in their wake and disappear. Coulances turned back to her. "That was rather . . . unceremonious."

"I usually have a service for fallen mates. We don't have time for that right now." She could tell he disapproved, but what did he understand about the expediencies of piracy? There was something else to his manner though. It occurred to her that she'd treated him roughly before the battle. "I apologize for speaking sharply to you earlier. I was worried about your safety and my ship."

"Of course." Holding her eyes, he bowed slightly. It was clear the apology was accepted only in the interest of civility. She'd pushed him away in battle, when men are expected to fight. Yes, she could see it in the set of his back as he walked away. She'd damaged his pride. An unforgivable offense she wasn't sure she could heal. Yet another reason to put him off the ship, though her heart begged her not to part with him.

A few days after raiding the small village of Petit Bourg on Marie Galant Island for much needed provisions, Jorge called out, "A ship!" and pointed to the northern horizon.

"French?" Marie shouted.

"Dunno yet."

"What size?"

"Sloop!" he hollered back.

It was too small to be any threat. Certainly it couldn't be a military vessel. Mary was about to tell the helm to avoid it, when a plan burst full-formed upon her. "Hard for that ship!" she ordered.

Talinn swung the wheel to the new heading. The crew swiftly moved to prepare for a boarding. She could feel their mood shift as they readied themselves. For the first time in days, they grinned as they went about their tasks. The insults they barked at each other were jests rather than serious jibes. This was what they were pirates for!

Petronius appeared at her side. "A little sport for the crew? Good. This might break their evil temper."

"Perhaps." She smiled.

He regarded her cautiously. "Somethin' else you have in mind?"

"There just might be a solution at hand." She folded her arms and watched the outline on the horizon begin to enlarge.

"You'll put the doctor off on the other ship. Very good." He also folded his arms.

"You have but the tip of it, Petronius." She continued to stare ahead.

"I don't understand," he said.

She took a deep breath of the salt air. "I've figured a way to have my prize and keep it near."

"You're gonna keep him still?" Petronius asked.

"Oh, aye." She nodded. "Just not aboard the *Fury*, my friend." She watched the wind fill the sails. "We'll take that ship," she said, pointing to the nearing sloop, "and we'll make her ours."

"Finally you'll listen t'me," Petronius nearly crowed. "We'll be the only pirates with our own fleet!"

She flipped her braid behind her. "Almost. We'll put part of our crew aboard as well as the doctor. Then we'll have her sail for Cache Island."

"And after that?"

"It will sit in the harbor, as a hospital ship."

"No." Petronius grabbed her by the arm, then when he noticed men watching them, dropped it. Lowering his voice, he continued, "We should use this new ship t'work the shallower waters. There's more money t'be had, woman. You've no ambition!"

Mary put her hands on her hips. "And you've too much! Can't you see the doctor is an asset to us? Remember the flux epidemic on our island? You lost a child in that, I know."

A rare, haunted look came into Petronius' eyes. "Yes. Louisa-Térèse."

"Perhaps you wouldn't have if we'd a doctor there, hm?" she pressed.

His brow furrowed. "I still don't understand. How'll this stop the French? They'll still come for us."

She began to pace. "We'll set loose the captain of this ship after letting him hear that I've given the ship to the doctor. I'll order her to sail to the American Colonies while he's still on board. He'll tell the authorities, who'll tell the French. Then Lemeux and his friends'll turn their attention North while the doctor sails South."

"But what if they don't believe this tale? They'll still harry us, yes? And even if they think we parted ways with the doctor, won't they raid Cache Island lookin' for him?"

She stomped her foot. "Dammit, Petronius! For every plan I think up, you come up with a reason why it won't work! I'm trying to solve our problem!"

He held up his hands. "No, no, it almost floats, this plan o' yours. We just need t'caulk the planks, that's all."

She went to the railing and glowered down at the water churning behind them. "I'll write to Lemeux and the Governor giving my word that I've released the doctor to his own devices. The captain of yon ship will carry these letters to the proper recipients."

"You're known for many things, but not for lying." He shrugged. "It might work. What makes you think the captain o' this ship will cooperate with you?"

Mary pointed to the flag on the ship ahead of them. "Because it's a French ship!" She laughed at her luck.

Petronius shook his head, "You are somethin'! I wouldn't be surprised if the captain was Lemeux's own brother."

She smiled. "I doubt we'll be that lucky."

"Who'll captain this new ship o' yours?"

She surveyed her crew, busy at their tasks. "Ingram."

"What!"

"It's the easiest way to get rid of him. Think on it. He wants more? Give it to him. Let him captain this new ship, but let the ship only stay in Cache Island's harbor. There he can do little mischief but fancy himself well-taken care of. Oh, this will cost me — no doubt! But it'll work."

He looked skeptical. "And when the French sail into the harbor?"

"When there's danger, Ingram'll sail 'round to one of the coves. The French will discover their prisoner isn't there, and they'll sail away." She slapped his back. "*Voila*! The island gets a much-needed doctor, and I . . . get what I need. What do you think?"

He rubbed his ear. "It might work."

The ship in front of them fired off a cannonball. "Well," she said, buttoning her coat, "shall we board her?"

"Aye, Cap'n." He hurried off to give orders to the crew.

It wasn't difficult to take the French ship. The sloop was facing into the wind and wasn't as maneuverable as the *Fury*. One shot was all they managed with their single ancient gun before the *Fury's* crew rushed on deck. The sloop, called the *Nacre*, was fitted out for inter-island trade and so had little of value beyond fresh provisions — for which the *Fury's* crew was very glad. The captain of the *Nacre* was an older man who seemed resigned to whatever indignity Fate had for him this time.

"Louis Dumond," he replied to Mary's question. "I suppose you will now kill us or maroon us for the pitiful goods we carry?"

"Neither, Captain Dumond." She felt an odd sort of compassion for him. "I don't make a habit of killing unnecessarily."

He looked at her for the first time. "And what do I owe you for the gift of my life?"

She patted his shoulder. "I'm afraid the price is quite high today, Captain."

"Ah, I might have guessed. You will ransom us, then."

"No, I'll be taking your ship from you altogether. You and any crew that chooses to join you will be put in your dinghy to row for shore." She prepared herself for a fight. Well she knew that this tiny boat was his livelihood. There were many who would kill her for the insulting deal she'd just offered. But Dumond had shown concern only for his life and his crew's. Perhaps he'd be sensible and live.

"That's all?" he asked, his surprise evident.

"I'll also charge you with delivering two letters to the garrison at the first French island you reach."

He searched her face. "You're jesting with an old man?"

"No, Captain." She hid a small grin of triumph. "I need your cooperation in a matter which doesn't concern you. Will you carry out my wishes?"

"Yes . . . yes!" He cackled. "I will see my daughter again!"

"As long as you assist me, sir." She went over to the captured crew. Fear was apparent on their faces as she approached. Mary said in the French she'd learned at her mother's knee, "Crew of the *Nacre*, no harm will come to you if you continue to cooperate. We'll be taking this ship as our own." Her own crew looked at her quizzically. "Those who don't wish to serve as pirates will be released with your captain. You have an hour to decide." Switching back to English, she said, "Crew of the *Fury*, let these men free. I'm sure they'll be on their best behavior. We'll meet by our ship."

Her men huddled about her. "What's it about, Cap'n?" "Are we scuttlin' the *Fury*?" "Do we really need new mates?"

She held up her hand. "Peace! We're taking this ship and putting the doctor aboard her. Meanwhile, we inform the French that their prisoner has left our hospitality." The men chuckled appreciatively at the plan. "We'll need a new crew for this ship. Know that the *Nacre* won't be a'pirating. Choose where you'll serve."

"Cap'n," Karl asked, "who'll skipper the *Nacre*?"

"I've decided to have Ingram captain this new ship." Mary offered her hand to the man who shook it in bewilderment. The other men patted his back or glared at him.

"I . . . I thank ye, Cap'n," Ingram stammered.

"In a little while I'll give you your sailing orders. Ready yourself for your commission, sir." She addressed the whole group, "I want your decisions as soon as possible. Tell Petronius which way you choose — but make up your minds before we finish cleaning out the *Nacre*."

Mary climbed over the railing to her own ship and strode to the cabin. Hand on the doorknob, she paused. It was easier to face her entire crew than what she had to deal with in the next few moments. She drew a deep breath and opened the door.

"Ah, Mary!" Coulances looked up from a fragile-looking creation he'd made from the painted French playing cards she kept in the desk.

She tried to smile and closed the door. "What game are you playing?"

"An amusement I learned at the Racine estate. One tries to build a castle of cards up as far as possible before it collapses."

She leaned over to inspect the delicate structure whose very existence would have been impossible if the sea had been rough that day. "I have never seen the like!"

He set up a few cards, so that she could see how it was done. "Now you try," he said, handing her the rest of the deck.

Mary tried to do just as he had, get the cards to balance just so against each other — but at her mere touch the entire creation fell in a heap. "I'm so sorry."

"Not at all. That is part of the game. It can be rebuilt." He sat in the nearest chair and started to collect the cards. "All is well, I trust?"

"Well, and not so well, my dear."

He looked up from his task. "What is it?"

"I've devised a plan to keep you safe from your countrymen." She sank into the opposite chair. "Unfortunately, it means we must part for a time."

Coulances reached out and took her hand. "I understand. It is necessary, *cheri*."

She looked into the intense green eyes of her lover. "I don't want to lose you. You've become very dear to me."

"As you are to me."

"We've taken a ship on which you'll sail." She took her hand back and made her voice harder. "I'll inform the French that you're sailing for the American Colonies when, in fact, you'll sail for Cache Island."

"So we will be seeing each other in the future, then," he said with obvious relief.

She nodded. "Yes, though not so much as I would like." Mary got up and stared out the porthole. "You won't be living on the island itself."

"Why?"

"It's too dangerous. You'll stay on the ship. At the first sign of mast or sail, the ship will leave the harbor and make for one of the safer coves."

He stood. "But how will I treat patients?"

"Your patients will be rowed out to you."

"Impossible!" He waved the notion away impatiently. "When a person is gravely ill, travel on water will make the condition worse."

She narrowed her eyes. "They'll be fortunate to have a physician at all, Doctor."

"Really, Mary, it is totally unacceptable!"

She gripped the arms of the chair. "Nevertheless, this is what must be done to keep you safe. I'll command that you not be let off the ship, no matter what you say."

"You would order me around?" he barked, slapping his chest. "I am not one of your crew!"

"I know, Alphonse," she said quietly. "But I shall have my way in this."

"I will not have it!" He stomped out, slamming the door behind him.

She rubbed her face with both hands and sat at the desk. For the first time in many years, she found herself trembling. Even his defiance moved her. She could never let him know how thoroughly he was able to affect her. She wanted to give in to his demands, if only to keep him from being angry with her. Irritated, she threw back her braid. She should have put him off the first chance she had! Now look at the mess she'd made of things. He was yet another person she must control and plot for.

Mary balled up her hands, angry at herself. She must not give in to this. She had much to do. Drawing out a sheet of paper, she quickly wrote a letter to the French authorities. Then she copied it but addressed it to Captain Lemeux. Next she wrote two very different letters to people on Cache Island. The last one was the most difficult.

She got up and opened her door. "Ingram!" Mary shouted. Going back to her desk, she started writing another letter. This one was for Alphonse. The words seemed to jam up in her mind. She doubted if the letter would end up making any sort of sense. There was a rap at the door. "Come."

Ingram swaggered in wearing a linen shirt and checked breeches in an eye-popping red and purple that Mary knew he didn't own. He put his hands to his hips and gave her a smile.

She glared at him. "Did you draw those from the stores, Ingram?"

"Aye, that I did, Cap'n." He tugged down one sleeve. "You wouldn't want the cap'n of yer new ship to look as shabby as the rest of the crew, would ya?"

"You presume much. Sit down."

Obeying, he said, "Not but what I figure I'm owed."

"Owed? We've known for some time of your thieving ways, Ingram. I don't want you on my ship any longer."

He stared at her slack-jawed. "I don't understand, Cap'n."

"If I keep you on the *Fury* and tell the crew you've been stealing from them, or one of them should discover it on their own . . . well, I'm sure you know what would occur." Mary hoped Ingram was remembering his friend Nelek. About five months ago, Mary had caught the man stealing from the general booty. There was only one remedy for his behavior, and she'd ordered him keelhauled.

The men, angry that one of their own had stolen from them, dragged Nelek up to the bow, screaming. Mapana, Brepa and Ramiro fetched a long chain from below decks. Petronius attached a stout rope to the links and sent Ableman to the stern. Then the crew rigged the chain and rope so that it formed a loop around the bottom of the ship to the deck.

Drega and Jorge punched and stabbed Nelek as they dragged him up from the hold where he'd been imprisoned in a large empty oak water barrel. Talinn and Paolo wrapped the chain around him.

"No! Please, God, no!" he shrieked, as they threw him off the bow. Ableman grabbed the rope that came up out of the water at the stern and ran toward the bow. Other crewmen raced to join him, hauling on the rope as fast as they could. Mary pictured Nelek being dragged along the keel as Ableman ran forward. The barnacles on the hull were sharp as saws and would cut Nelek to ribbons. There was a benefit to this punishment; the *Fury's* hull got a cleaning — at least as long as the body held out.

The chain followed the rope over the aft rail and Nelek came after. He flopped onto the deck like a soggy bag. They hauled Nelek over to Mary. Half his face was missing — the nose and most of the left cheek had disappeared. Gaps from missing teeth allowed bloody sea water to escape down his chin. Nelek's chest was a bloody mess. His right eye fluttered — life still held on. Mary sucked in a deep, sickened breath, but ordered, "Again."

Eagerly, the men carried Nelek to the bow and pitched him over the rail. Again, Ableman at the stern ran forward and was joined by willing helpers. Again, they hauled Nelek out of the sea and brought him to Mary. His right arm was missing and the left foot was torn off. The head with its shredded face bobbed, then twisted forward as Nelek struggled to breathe. Mary clenched her teeth against the vomit on the back of her tongue. She could only nod for the men to proceed.

Franz at the stern sang out, "Sharks!"

The men ran aft to scan the waters. Sharp fins knifed after the *Fury*. As Nelek was hauled up from beneath the ship, the deadly creatures attacked. The men screamed with delight while giant teeth ate away the last of Nelek. Only one crewman, Ingram, staggered away from the crowd. He'd slumped against the port rail and puked repeatedly.

Mary saw now that Ingram paled and swallowed hard. Yes, he recalled the incident. "I'm saving your scruffy neck." She laced her hands together on her knee. "In return, I want a favor, but I'm willing to pay handsomely for it."

"Thank ye, Cap'n," Ingram whispered. He wiped his sleeve across his perspiring forehead. It came away damp and gray.

"You'll sail the *Nacre* to Cache Island." She rose and paced in the small cabin. He watched her, sweat slipping down his face. "You'll keep her in the harbor, ready to sail at a moment's notice. If you sight another ship, or even think you see one, I want you to sail to one of the windward coves. Is that clear?"

He nodded, eyes wide. "Aye, Cap'n."

She clasped her hands behind her. "Further, I command you never . . . ." Mary stopped in front of him and bent down until their noses nearly touched. "Never let the doctor off the ship." She straightened and glared down at him.

He looked confused. "Never?"

"Not ever. He may receive visitors and patients, but he mustn't be allowed ashore. If I discover that my orders are in any way not followed — " She bent down again. "I will come for you. I will find you wherever you go to hide. I will kill you even more slowly than I disposed of your old pal Nelek." She stood. "Is that clear?"

He shuddered. "Aye, Cap'n."

She inspected him. "I'll pay you before you set

sail today — minus the price of your clothes. See if you can find a coat that fits you. Each time we're in port, I'll pay you again. Rest assured it'll be a sum more than you're likely to deserve."

"Thank ye, Cap'n." He went to the door. "I'll do everything just like ye told me. I promise."

"You'd better hope to," Mary snarled as she turned back to her desk. She heard the door shut behind her. Ingram was pathetically easy to bend to her will. All she had to do was appeal to his greed and fear. She had no doubt he would serve her well. She sighed and picked up her pen.

Once more she attempted to put her feelings on paper. What could she say to Alphonse? How could she make him understand? Either he'd comply or he wouldn't — and get himself killed. Mary struggled for a while. Finally she gave up and read through what she'd written:

Darling Alphonse   *18 October*
I wish that We were Two Different People in an entirely Different Situation. That is not to Be, however. We are Who We are and the Facts remain. You cannot Imagine how muche It pains Me to have to be separated from You. I have come to rely on Our Talks, Your Goode Sense, and Our Splendid Lovemaking. I shall long for Your Touch.

You must keep Yourself safe, My Deare. I will ache to be with You againe. I find that before, I had been lacking Some Thing for which to Live. Now I have found that Reeson. Stay Safe in My Harbor. Be there for Me when I come Home.

I know this Exile will be difficult for You, despite Your protestations to the Contrary. I am afraid that,

*for the moste Part, I cannot relieve That. I must write
to You (when I may) in Code, lest My Enemyes (and
Yours) suspect the Connection between We Two and
hold You for Hostage or Bounty. It is a Ruff Sort of
Business I am engaged in. The Rules demand that,
despite My Sex, the Play is Dedley. Hold tight. I will
see You as offen as I may.*

With a kind of relief, she signed and sealed it.
She'd done what she could. Gathering up the letters,
she went out on deck. The crews were busy, transfer-
ring supplies from one ship to another, depending on
what was needed in each. As usual, Petronius, with
Talinn as his deputy, had things well in hand. Mary
joined him at his post. "Everything sorting itself out?"

"Aye, Cap'n." He directed a cask of rum to their
hold. "It looks like we'll only lose three crew plus
Ingram. Eight of the *Nacre's* crew'll stay with her, five'll
join us and the rest'll go with her captain."

She nodded. "About what I expected. Any
problems?"

"No, everyone seems well pleased with the
arrangement. Except your doctor." He pointed to the
lone figure in the bow.

She watched Coulances for a moment. "Aye.
Well, he's going to have to choose for himself now. I've
done all I can."

"Here, you!" Petronius shouted at a man who'd
just dropped a cask of gunpowder. "Watch what you're
doin'. Clean up anythin' you spilled. Clumsy oaf!" He
turned back to her. "We should be ready t'cast off in a
few minutes, if these idiots don't blow up the whole
ship first."

"Keep them in line, Petronius." She made her

way up to the bow.

Coulances didn't turn around as she approached him, but she knew he'd heard her footfalls. "About ready to go aboard the *Nacre*, Alphonse?"

"I suppose so, Captain, since I've no possessions to take with me."

She leaned against the rail. "Don't make this any harder than it is already."

He turned. "I feel like a prisoner. Am I to have no rights, no say, in how I conduct my life?"

"Fine," she said, hanging her head. "Have the ship drop you off at any likely island. I don't care. I wanted to keep you safe and somehow keep you near. That's obviously an impossibility."

He stroked her cheek. "I want to be with you, *cheri*. Why must it be in such a restrictive fashion?"

She looked him in the eye. "If you don't do as I've planned, you'll be killed. That's all there is to it. I've had enough death and separation in my life!" She stopped, biting her lip to force the tears from her eyes. "I thought, just this once, I could stop the same thing happening again. I guess I was wrong."

This time, it was he who hung his head. "I'm sorry, *cheri*. I don't mean to add to your troubles. Perhaps in a few months the military will cease to look for me and I can go ashore, eh?"

"If I get word they think you dead or safely in another jurisdiction, I'll write Captain Ingram to allow you to go live on the island. This I promise." She put her hand over his.

He took her into his arms and held her for a long while. She laid her head on his, breathing in the strong, earthy smell of him. She felt the slender body she'd gotten to know so well. A lock of his hair brushed the tip of her nose, tickling her gently. The threat of tears stung her eyes. Blinking them back hurriedly, she straightened and held him at arm's length.

With a sad smile, he said, "I suppose I should go aboard now."

"Why don't you go into my cabin and pick out a few volumes to go with you?" she suggested as they walked aft. "I'm sure it will often be quite dull for you. You'll need something to divert you."

"Perhaps the *Faerie Queen*, to remind me of you."

"Of course," Mary whispered and took his hand. Coulances squeezed her fingers, then turned and went to the cabin. She wanted to call him back, tell him she'd changed her mind — that she'd never let him go! It was tempting to give up this pirate's life and settle down with Alphonse. They could live on some little isle where no one had ever heard of the pirate Captain Mary. Perhaps they would have children. Wouldn't a green-eyed babe of his be beautiful?

The sea heaved, forcing a swell between the two ships. Water leapt up and splashed the deck just in front of Mary, drenching her up to her thighs. "Fool," she whispered. The same thing would happen with Alphonse as had happened with all the men she'd ever loved. Betrayal and humiliation — that was how love ended. Better to put Alphonse on a ship far from her where he couldn't cause her pain.

She climbed over the rail and onto the *Nacre*. Captain Dumond was watching the activity aboard his ship with a bemused smile. "Ready to depart, Captain?" she asked.

"Oh, yes," he nodded, "little to take. I was just admiring the efficiency of your crew. I wish I'd been able to get my crew to work this well. Maybe we could have escaped you!"

"Perhaps, my friend." She handed him the letters. "You'll deliver these for me?"

He glanced down at their covers, then shook her hand. "Aye, I shall. I suppose the next time I see you, you'll be hanging at the end of a rope. But for what it's worth, I appreciate the courtesy you've shown."

She bowed. "I trust I'll avoid the noose, Captain, but you're welcome. Now, why don't you and what's left of your crew launch your dinghy." He called to his crew, made his way over the side and down to the waiting craft.

She went down to the captain's cabin in which she intended Alphonse to live. It was small and somewhat airless. The bunk looked hard and uninviting. Mary made a mental note to get some decent furnishings to replace these meager offerings, or Alphonse would truly think he was in a cell. Straightening out the blanket, she left her letter on the pillow. She hoped it made some kind of sense.

Returning topside, she saw Ingram strutting around the deck, resplendent in a long, gold wool and silk coat a trifle too large on him. Mary walked up behind him and tapped him on the shoulder. "Pleased with your command, Ingram?"

He whirled to face her. "Oh! Oh, yes, Cap'n. I was just havin' a look about."

"Here are two letters I want you to deliver on Cache Island." A thought occurred to her. "You can read, can't you?"

"Aye, Cap'n, and right well, too!"

"Good. See that you give these to the addressees personally."

He looked at the names and nodded, then put

them inside his coat. "I'll do that, Cap'n."

She folded her arms. He was still too full of himself. Time to take the wind out of his sails. "You'll be sleeping in the hold or on deck with the rest of your crew."

"But . . . but . . . ." he sputtered.

She was enjoying torturing him. "If you want, you may put a tent up by the mast. The doctor must have the cabin as his quarters and a place to see patients."

Ingram's face turned a mottled purple; his mouth opened and shut twice. He scratched the back of his head furiously. Finally he blew out a long, frustrated breath. "Aye, Cap'n," he said faintly.

"Oh," she glanced up, "don't forget to strike those colors just before you get to Cache Island. You wouldn't want the folks there to get panicked and start firing on you."

"Er, ah . . . no!" He looked shaken. "Shouldn't I take down the flag now, Cap'n?"

She tried not to laugh at his nervousness. "No. Let the French think you're one of them. You'll disappear all the better."

"Aye, Cap'n. Just as you say." He sounded doubtful.

She looked over at the *Fury*. "Ah, here comes the doctor now." The crew was helping him over the rail. She went to speak to him.

Ingram called after her, "Ah, Cap'n, don't ya think the Frenchies'll know us by the name of the ship?"

Ingram wasn't as stupid as she'd thought. "Then change the name, Captain."

He scurried over to her. "Ya know if ye change the name of a ship, it's very bad luck, Cap'n," he whispered.

She clapped him on the shoulder. "I'm aware of the superstition, Ingram. There are ways around that, though. Get a bottle of wine and we'll christen her directly."

Ingram ordered one of his crew to fetch a bottle.

Mary turned and discovered the doctor at her elbow. "Well, it looks as though the time has come."

He avoided her eyes. "Indeed. I . . . I am at a loss for words."

She nodded, not trusting herself to speak further.

Ingram interrupted them by practically sticking a bottle of red wine in her face. "Here, Cap'n!"

She snatched it out of his hand. "Thank you, Captain Ingram. See you have the new name on her bow and stern by this evening."

"Aye, Cap'n." He hurried off to talk to his crew.

"What will you change the name to, Captain?" Coulances asked.

"Oh, I'll not actually change the name, my love, merely translate it a bit. In a way, I'll name it after you." Mary strode up to the bow. Lifting the bottle, she shouted, "I christen thee . . . the *Pearl*!" She smashed the bottle on the gunnel.

"Three cheers for the *Pearl*!" Captain Ingram ordered. The crews of both ships cheered.

Mary returned to Coulances. "Like the fairy tale, I name it for a pearl of great price." She drew him toward her, took his face in both hands, tilted it up and kissed him long and slowly. The crew cheered again. When they quieted, she whispered in his ear, "Take care, my darling. I will see you as soon as I'm able."

"Come soon," he whispered back.

She turned to Ingram. "Make sure to keep him

safe, Ingram!"

"We'll do that, Cap'n!"

Mary climbed over the railings of the two ships. "Cast off!" she ordered.

"Aye, Cap'n! Cast off!" Petronius called.

Orders were given on both ships to haul up the sails, and the two began to part. Mary stood at the stern, watching the *Pearl* turn her head south. She could see Coulances in the stern, waving. She waved back. He got smaller and smaller as the two ships went their separate headings. Finally, she could hardly tell if Coulances was waving or not. It didn't really matter, she supposed.

"They're well away, now," observed Petronius, who stood behind her.

She sighed. "There he goes."

He leaned on the rail next to her and lit his pipe. "I know you're sad t'see him off. Are you as relieved as you are sad?"

She straightened abruptly and swung to glare at him. Finally she blew out a breath. "I hate it when you see me that clear."

He chuckled. "We're the same, we two. Lovers are fine, but they're best when they leave."

"Aye. I start to feel strangled when they make their demands. This one more than most. I don't know what it is."

"Sure you do," he said, slowly tamping at the coal in his pipe. "Coulances is the first one in a long time you actually cared about. And he's as smart as you."

"Yes. He's not easily fooled. I wish I'd the heart to send him off somewhere else."

"Mmm," he said with a nod. "What's gonna

happen when the other one meets him? Did you give a thought to that?"

She gazed out to sea. "They won't meet. He'll be stuck on the *Pearl*."

Petronius guffawed. "You old sly boots, you! You'll get t'see both when we're in port. Now if only I could work this trick for my little morsels."

She laughed. "Ah, no you don't! Captain's privilege! Besides, can you imagine if you and I kept all our lovers on separate ships? That harbor'd get awful crowded."

"Not t'mention how tired we'd get on shore leave," he agreed. "No, I admire the plot. I just don't see how it's all gonna work out."

She tried to make out the *Pearl's* outline on the horizon. She could just see the blue-gray shadow of a ship. Or was it only her imagination? "I don't either," she whispered.

CHAPTER FOUR

Once again, Captain Mary used the cover of early morning fog to creep up on her prey. The dual crosses of St. George and St. Andrew on the opposing ship's flag showed the ship to be from Great Britain. On the stern, in lettering of gold, was the name *Mars Thunderbolt*. It was a frigate, bigger than the *Fury*. But Mary was counting on surprise, speed and the ferocity of their attack. She waited, pulse secretly pounding, on the starboard side with her armed boarding crew. No warning cry was heard as her men rowed the *Fury* nearer.

Incrementally, the *Mars Thunderbolt's* hull appeared. Its three tall masts disappeared in the close-hanging mist. Gray-white sails drooped with dew. Mary could hear water trickling down the rigging. At the frigate's prow, the painted wooden figurehead of a dark-haired woman wound in thick draperies stared sightlessly into the gloom, a grim expression on her face.

Mary heard someone on the aft deck cough in a way that told of the advanced stages of consumption. She caught the faint smell of English bangers cooking. There were quiet bumps as the *Fury's* oars were shipped below. They glided on the still water. Mary chafed with impatience at their sluggish approach. The two ships seemed suspended at the moment of coming together, as if they were caught in an amber bubble just as they were and kept on some portly gentleman's desk as a curiosity.

"Fire!" Mary cried, breaking the spell.

Two cannons roared. Grapeshot hurtled into the *Mars Thunderbolt's* sails. The hot iron balls shredded through the cloth, leaving gaping rents.

"Fire!" Two more cannons spat out their deadly loads. Lethal chains shrieked across the frigate's deck. Just as a red-haired Englishman emerged from below, the sharp, whirling metal caught him. Links whipped through his chest, nearly slicing him in half. Blood sluiced down the ladder onto the deck below. He collapsed soundlessly, a surprised expression on his face.

Another set of spinning links arced toward the bow. Cutlass raised, a big-bellied officer stood by the foremast, shouting orders. His commands became howls of anguish as the chains sawed off his right leg just above the knee. Skittering over the deck, the bloody severed limb and irons went tumbling off the port bow.

Tossing grappling hooks over the *Mars Thunderbolt's* gunnels, the *Fury's* crew hauled the two ships together. Water jetted up from the meeting of the hulls, drenching everyone. Mary shook herself off, then noticed a squad of British marines, armed and ready, scrambling up from below decks. They looked to be battle-hardened men spoiling for a fight. She realized it wasn't going to be an easy taking.

"For the *Fury*! For Gold! For Glory!" Mary cried as she and her crew swarmed over the rails and charged the massed defenders on the main deck. They were met by the grim resolve of the English. As one, the Redcoats advanced, firing their pistols. Mary threw herself to the deck and heard the whine of a bullet fly over her. There was a scream as Ableman took one in his leg. Watu shouted in surprise as a shot ripped through his shoulder.

Throwing down their emptied guns, the Brits drew their swords and advanced. Mary leapt up and engaged the grim-looking fellow who charged her. With a determined roar, the rest of her men charged the *Mars Thunderbolt's* crew. There was little room to move in the crush that followed. For a moment, Mary could make no clear sense of the battle. It seemed as if knives and swords, fists and feet were coming from every angle as the opposing crews fought.

The air was filled with the thick, acrid smoke from the *Fury's* cannons and the small arms of both crews. Choking on the fumes, Mary jabbed her sword between the ribs of the old man she'd been fighting. As he collapsed to the deck writhing in pain, a younger, black-bearded man challenged her immediately. From the corner of her eye, as she parried hacking blows, she saw Talinn fighting a bald sailor over by the hatch. A crewman raced up from below. He stopped, aimed at Talinn's back, and shot at him, just missing his head. Talinn ran the bald man through, then whirled to decapitate the gunman.

Mary's opponent momentarily exposed his left side to her. She took the opportunity, aiming a blow under his arm and into his chest. He grabbed at her sword, then slid down it to the deck. She turned to see Mapana and a Brit locked in a deadly knife fight on the starboard side. Neither could gain the advantage, and so they struggled, arms wrapped around each other in a deadly dance. Slipping on the gore-covered deck, they caromed off other fighters. Suddenly, the sailor's foot caught in the blood-filled scupper. He was wrenched out of Mapana's grip and thrown into the pooled blood. Mapana slit his throat, then hurried to Jorge's side as he struggled with two opponents.

The shriek of a war whoop behind her made Mary spin around. Leaping from the yardarm, the look-out held his sword high, ready to cleave her in two. Quickly, she switched her sword to her left hand, drew her pistol and emptied it, killing him in midair. The dead body hurtled to the deck. Mary threw herself out of the way, knocking one of the British overboard. The corpse slammed into one of his own crewman, shoving the man into Petronius' knife. Immediately another crewman came at her, brandishing a bright steel sword. Mary dropped her emptied pistol and used her sword double-handed. With one slice, she neatly chopped off both his hand and weapon. Before he realized what had happened, she rammed her sword guard into his chest and sent him into the drink.

Despite the fact that they were outnumbered two-to-one, the *Mars Thunderbolt's* crew fought on. Just when Mary thought the Brits routed, those they'd thought wounded got up from the deck and re-formed into a new skirmish line. As soon as one Redcoat fell, another leapt to take his place in the British assault. They pressed the fight from the quarterdeck, the bow, the stern. Their tenacity was starting to tell. Mary watched as three more of her men succumbed to the

Mars Thunderbolt's crew.

She knifed the sailor in the back who'd been manning the forward cannon, then swung the gun around to face the main deck where the fight raged on. Grabbing the flaming firing wick and holding it over the cannon's fuse, she roared, "Hold! Hold I say or I'll blow every mother's son of you straight to Hell!"

Slowly, the fighting ended as the crew of the *Mars Thunderbolt* dropped their weapons. "Men of the *Fury*, assemble the captives on the poop!" Mary commanded. With secret relief, she extinguished the flame.

When the pirates had the *Mars Thunderbolt's* crew and the men and women passengers from below herded to the stern, she was able to assess the battle. Twenty British lay dead on the deck, five of the *Fury's* crew. The *Mars Thunderbolt's* many injured were gathered just below the poop deck. Twelve of Mary's injured men were taken back aboard the *Fury* so that Jacoby could treat what wounds he was able.

Brepa and Mapana held the struggling British captain. He was a short, bald man, his cheeks purple with rage. "Cowards!" he shouted at his pinioned crew. "Fight this rabble! You are British naval men!"

Mary sheathed her sword with an angry snap. "Calmly, Captain. Your crew fought bravely and well. I can assure you that once we've taken what we want, we shall leave with no further bloodshed."

The British captain ignored her and taunted his crew. "Bested by a woman! A tart! They're probably all women and you sit tamely by!"

The English crew became restive. Mary's men tightened their hold on them.

"Captain," Mary said tensely, "my crew is as manly as any of yours. I warn you that I, and I alone, have control over your fate this morning. Gentler words should be used."

"What kind of men are you that you would let criminals and trollops overrun you?" The British captain struggled free of his captors, ran over and beat one of the crew about the head and neck with both fists. "Boothby, you'll face court martial for this!"

Cepa and Petronius recaptured the captain. Boothby breathed hard but refused to look up from the deck. His face flamed red. The British crew stood in shocked silence.

"What is your name, sir?" Mary demanded.

"Captain Bailey Sayers Effington of His Majesty's Navy," he declared. "If it were not for the cowardice of this crew, and especially the first mate, you would not have the honor of being aboard."

"Captain Effington, it's always been my understanding that the captain of the ship is directly responsible for the behavior of the crew." She paced in front of him. "If there was any cowardice during our skirmish, which I did not see, then it would have to be in your treatment of your first mate."

The British crew grumbled, Mary thought, in agreement.

"What would a woman and a criminal know of British tradition? I run my ship as I see fit. I certainly don't take orders from a whore!"

Mary backhanded Effington so hard he staggered against Petronius. Blood welled up on his upper lip, spilling down his chin. One of the female passengers screamed. Mary turned and stalked down the length of the ship. It wasn't the name-calling that bothered her. She'd been insulted in four different languages — and much more inventively — before. It was the manner in which the fool treated his own crew that irked her. They'd fought well enough. But to blame one's first mate for failing to win a battle — then to strike him in front of the rest of the crew — was unconscionable. It was a wonder Effington's crew hadn't mutinied before this.

She came to the foremast and stopped abruptly at a sight she hadn't taken in during the heat of battle. Two men had been stripped and tied on either side of the timber. Obviously they'd been flogged. Their backs were striped with bloody streaks. Flies fed on the torn flesh. Pus welled up at the edges of the weals. What took Mary's breath away were the other injuries. Beneath the evil-looking whip weals were deep burns the size of an ember from the cookstove, all over both men's buttocks. Evidently, Captain Effington, like many another sailing master, enjoyed torturing those he considered a bad element on his ship.

Ah, but it was the manly way to run a ship. Fear, humiliation, threats and torture were what most captains used in place of genuine command and authority. This idiot more than most. Behavior like Effington's was condoned by most navies — the fools! Not that Mary thought she had the only answers to captaining. There was no "right and wrong" to commanding a ship. Rather, she'd studied captains who had uncoerced command of their ships and tried to emulate them.

Mary took out her knife and slashed apart the ropes. She eased the men to the deck, being careful to lay them on their stomachs. Walking slowly back to the waiting crews, she had time to think. Being outside the law had certain . . . advantages. There were remedies that one could take on one's own initiative.

As she neared the group, she could hear

Effington shouting: ". . . an embarrassment to the throne! Is this how you fight for King and Country? Oh, woe that I have lived to see such lily-livered churls inherit our great Isle!"

None of his crew would meet Effington's eye. One of the younger men sniffled, on the verge of tears.

"That," Mary interrupted, "is entirely enough, Captain."

"Look at this strumpet!" Effington crowed. "A woman dressed like a man!"

Mary looked down at her clothes, then shrugged. "Better a woman dressed as a man, than a man who acts like a scolding fishwife."

Her men guffawed. She saw some of the *Mars Thunderbolt's* crew and passengers stifling chuckles.

"A more depraved sight I never saw," Effington continued to rave, ignoring the jibe. "And you poor excuses for men let the likes of her best you!"

"Petronius," Mary said. "I think we've all had about as much of this irritating little carbuncle as any of us can stand, don't you?"

He released Effington and stepped forward. "Aye, Cap'n. What're your orders?"

"It's time we hoisted this blowhard up where he'll do the most good." She whispered her idea to Petronius. He grinned, then took the *Mars Thunderbolt's* captain by the arm.

"You . . . you wouldn't hang an officer of His Majesty's Navy!" Effington sputtered.

"Not hang precisely, Captain." Her smile was wicked. "Petronius, carry out your orders."

"Aye, Cap'n." He nodded toward the captives. "And the crew?"

"Oh, they may join in, if they've a mind to." She

stood, arms folded, considering the captive crew and passengers.

"You can't do this to a man in British uniform!" Effington shouted.

She nodded. "Quite right. Have him stripped before he joins the birds."

"Aye, Cap'n." Petronius and the others dragged away the squirming officer.

Mary began to pace in front of her captives. "I'll repeat what I said before. We are here to take some items from your stores. A sort of passage tax, if you will. We have no further interest in battle. If you cooperate, you will live to see another day. Further, I would offer any of you work aboard my ship. You've all shown bravery and the ability to tolerate . . . adverse conditions."

The men shuffled their feet, but none replied.

"You wish to stay and serve under that petty despot?"

One of the men, an older fellow lacking many of his front teeth, said, "Naw, it ain't 'im, is it? It's this 'un," he tilted his head at Boothby, "we stays fer, mu'm."

"And what does Boothby stay for?" Mary asked.

"I am a member of His Majesty's Navy. The honor is to serve . . ." Boothby paused, "with these fine men."

Some of his crew muttered their appreciation.

She crossed her hands behind her back. "Will you guarantee the behavior of your men while my men finish their work?"

He glared at her. "Under protest. For all your manners, you're still a pirate. Still a rogue."

She grinned. "Oh, aye. All of that!" Mary

stepped closer to Boothby. "I will permit two of your men to go forward and attend to the unfortunates I found there."

Boothby's eyes widened in gratitude. "Thank you, ma'am."

At that moment, Effington, clad only in his stained-yellow long underwear, was hoisted into the air. He yelled wordlessly as the rope tied around his chest pulled him higher toward the crow's nest. Both crews and the passengers roared with laughter.

"Cepa, Paolo, guard the crew. Mr. Boothby will need some excuse for not coming to his captain's aid. Allow a detail to go to the bow." Mary saluted Boothby. "The rest of you swabs, get to work!"

Mary went below to the cabins. Effington's quarters were well-appointed. She availed herself of the rich bedding, luscious curtains and a silver dresser set. These she took out to the mainmast and left in a heap. She returned to the cabin and opened Effington's trunk. Underneath the fine clothing — which she placed on the bed for removal — was a carved mahogany cask. It was too heavy to lift. She'd have to get to a couple of her men to come in for it. Petronius would be delighted at its weight. It must be filled with gold coin.

On the table there were some maps held down by a chipped crystal decanter. It was half-full of a what proved to be — after a small taste — a very dull claret. A heavily engraved silver candlestick held down the other side. She threw it on the bed, to be taken outside later. A handsome astrolabe of fine brass, ivory and ebony squatted in the middle of the papers. She carefully set that on the bed as well. Spreading the charts out, Mary studied them. These had to be the latest maps the English had for the Caribbean. Without question, they were the finest she'd ever seen. Petronius was always on the lookout for new maps. With the few pitiful charts they'd been able to acquire in the last two years, he was constantly forced to draw and redraw the shores and reefs of the islands around which they'd navigated on their travels. She rolled the charts back up and put them, along with the astrolabe, in the trunk with the gold.

After taking the latest load out to the deck, she returned below decks to go through the passengers' cabins. These were sparsely furnished, but the luggage contained more of what she sought. In one cabin she discovered three books. One was a volume of Machiavelli's *The Prince* in quite good condition. She had heard of this book. It was said that anyone who aspired to power must know it thoroughly. She kept that and rifled through the other two volumes; one a dog-eared — not even complete — copy of *The Canterbury Tales*, the other a very poor edition of Apuleius's *The Golden Ass*. She left those. There were also items of interest in a monetary sense: pouches of gold coin and jewelry, which she took, dumping them into a rumpled pillowcase. In the next cabin, she was delighted to find a handsomely bound report titled in gold on thick hide: *The Royal Botanical Society of Britain: Report on the Islande of Jamaica*. It was a complete survey of that island's flora and fauna done some three years prior. There were many detailed — and inaccurate, to Mary's amusement — drawings. The inscription, done in such intricate script that it was almost unreadable, was from the president of the Society to "His Honoure, the Governour of Jamaica." That, Mary felt, was worth all the trouble Effington put her to.

She went back out on deck and added her finds

to the pile Then she instructed Talinn and Cepa to remove the trunk from Effington's cabin. Glancing around, she noted that her crew had boxes, crates and barrels lined up to be loaded onto the *Fury*. Effington still hung in the air, cursing fluently.

"Cap'n!" Petronius called to her from the hold. "We found a load o' furniture. Care t'come down'n choose what we'll take?"

"Aye! Be right there!" Mary slid down the ladder into the deepest hold. An inky darkness closed in on her, illuminated only fitfully by the lantern Petronius had brought down. Shadows clawed and slithered among the furniture as he shone the light around the tightly packed, narrow room. Only a slim alley allowed the two to slip between tables, dressers and chairs. Petronius held the light up high as Mary peered at each piece. "It looks to be very fine mahogany, don't you think?"

"Aye. Worth a bit on Saint John, I'll warrant," he agreed.

"Nicely made." She rubbed the edge of a bow-front chest, but the stain didn't come off on her hand. "And there's a desk, chair, bed and armoire I can send to the *Pearl*."

"Mmm," Petronius grumbled, "you'll be takin' those as your share, then, will you?"

Mary glared at him. "I haven't given much thought to how we should deal with the accounting of the *Pearl*. We'll work it out tonight, all right?"

He shrugged. "I wasn't arguin', Cap'n."

She snorted. "Like Hell!" Mary started up the ladder, then paused. "Do we have room for all this below decks?"

"Some. Not all." He swept the lantern around

the hold. Mary could tell he was checking his mental inventory of the *Fury*. "We'll have t'put the largest pieces on deck. Cover 'em with the spare sail."

"Damn," Mary sighed. "We'll have to chance it doesn't storm. As soon as we're loaded, set sail for Antigua." She scrambled up the ladder to the deck. "You men!" She stopped Jorge and Drega as they carried rum casks to the *Fury*. "Man the winch there and help Petronius down in the hold. We've a load of furniture we're taking on." The men handed their casks to other crewmates and went to work.

"No! Not my furniture!" cried a bewhiskered prisoner in a blue nightshirt. "Please! I'll pay you double what it's worth!"

Mary laughed. "With what, sir? I've got all your gold as well!"

The man moaned. "You're a heartless, thieving trollop!"

"How original," she said wryly.

"I will see you die, filthy harlot!" Effington boomed from the rigging. "I will track you down, wherever you go, and send you to Hell!"

"To do that, sir, you'll have to get down first!" She saluted her adversary, then clambered over the railings to her own ship.

"To Hell, wench!" Effington hollered.

She shivered slightly. The man sounded like the voice of doom. For a moment, she considered shooting him, but decided there'd been enough death that day.

CHAPTER FIVE

Several days later, the *Fury* reached a cove east of Codrington, Barbuda in the early morning hours. Mary had Gerhardt and Watu row her and an impressive array of baggage into the port. She swept into the harbor master's office and booked passage on the morning packet ship for the short trip to the nearby island of Antigua. All eyes turned to her. She made quite an impression in her dress of pale-pink silk with balloon sleeves. The bodice was tight fitting, showing off her unfashionably thin waist to its best advantage. Her firm breasts were pushed up by a tight corset, creating a décolletage that revealed a tantalizing — though chaste — view of their supposed creamy fecundity. Supposed because Mary had applied a heavy layer of powder from hairline to the tops of her breasts to conceal her sun-darkened skin. Light rouge and lip paint gave her the unreal-look of a porcelain doll so sought after by high-class women. At her wrists was elegant Flanders lace;

her slender, work-roughened hands with their chipped and broken nails were sheathed in pink lace gloves. Peeking out from beneath the yards of silk skirts and linen of her snowy petticoats, pink leather high-top shoes showed off her dainty feet. A glimpse of her glossy black ringlets was afforded by a pink lace bonnet with long satin ribbons tied into a perfect bow beneath her chin. She carried a pink lace parasol with a long ivory handle — where a long thin blade was hidden, just in case — as an additional shield against the harsh Caribbean sun. A matching pink silk and lace reticule dangled from her wrist by pink silk ribbons. Gold bracelets, jewel-encrusted rings and necklaces further heralded her membership in the moneyed class.

The sun was almost directly overhead when the ship arrived in the port of Saint John's. There she checked into "The King's Slipper," the finest tavern in town. The owner, Mr. Deal — whose sharp, narrow features reminded Mary of a weasel — knew her immediately. "Madam de Tocqueville!" he cried, unwittingly calling her by her mother's maiden name. "What a pleasure it is to see you again! Are things well in Barbuda?"

"Oh, well enough, well enough, Mr. Deal." Mary arranged her silver and pearl necklaces so they framed the expensive enameled watch she wore on a heavy gold chain. "But plantation life becomes so dull after a time. I crave more genteel company."

He beamed at the compliment. "May we hope that you'll be here for an extended stay?"

"I'm afraid not." She pouted prettily. "I believe I'll only be here a week or so."

"Well," Mr. Deal sighed, "we shall enjoy the honor of your presence, no matter how long you are here. Will you be going to your room now?"

"No." She tucked a stray hair back under her bonnet. "I'll be visiting my uncle directly. Have my luggage delivered to my room immediately."

"I shall, Madam. And I can assure you that Naomi is available to be your personal maid again." He beckoned to the bellboy to take her things.

"Excellent." She chuckled to herself. If Mr. Deal only knew that most of the baggage contained not dresses for her, but presents for Petronius's beloved Naomi and their children. Behind the door of room number sixteen, Mary and Naomi would lie in the big bed and giggle half the night over some of Petronius's less-wise choices — once a sea turtle painted purple with a pink and orange starfish stuck on it. Mary always enjoyed these visits. It was a delight to have a female friend who demanded little more of her than admiring the willowy black woman in the latest dress from France.

"My regards to Mr. Trimmer!" Mr. Deal called as she swept out into the street.

Saint John's wasn't large. There were a few streets parallel to the harbor and two cross streets. Mary tried to remember to use a proper woman's mincing steps and not her usual ground-covering stride down the main avenue. After so long at sea, it felt as if the land was rolling underneath her. The heavy skirts wrapped uncomfortably around her legs as she turned right at the first intersection.

It would have been more fashionable to hire a coach, even for this short distance, but Mary wanted the town to see her. It wasn't mere vanity — although it was fun to be looked at — she wanted people to know there was a wealthy woman in town. It tended to stir up opportunities.

She headed toward an imposing two-story brick building with a very discreet sign. It announced in gold letters that the edifice belonged to the "Antigua Security Bank & Trust." Mary approached the large oak door fitted with highly polished brass filigree hardware.

A bewigged black boy dressed in fancy livery pulled the door open for her and bowed deeply. "Good morning, Madam." He waved her in grandly.

Mary nodded with just the right trace of hauteur as she folded her parasol. Her arrival caused a stir among the clerks at their high desks. An elderly man came hurrying out of a side office. "Madam de Tocqueville! What a delight to see you again! If we'd known of your arrival, we would have had some tea and cakes prepared. As it is, we've only the meager tea we allow our clerks."

"Never mind, Mr. Padgett," she said disdainfully. "Is my uncle about?"

"Oh, yes, Madam. He's in his office upstairs as usual this time of day. Let me send the clerk to fetch him down." He snapped his fingers. "Dickson!"

She headed for the stairs. "That won't be necessary, Mr. Padgett. I'm quite able to make the climb to his office."

"But Mr. Trimmer doesn't like to be distur — er, interrupted by visitors." Padgett stammered. "If you'd just let me have you announced."

Mary almost laughed at the man's upset. Things had certainly changed since her last visit. "All right, Mr. Padgett, have it your own way," she said with a sigh. Dickson scrambled up the stairs. "Have you a chair a lady might sit upon? I find the day's travels have caught up with me."

"Of course! Of course!" He motioned at the

other clerk to fetch one.

The man rushed into Padgett's office, then hurried back out bearing the head clerk's chair. He placed it in the middle of the room and made a show of dusting it off.

"That's fine, Skunge," Padgett said, shooing the clerk away. "I'm sure it's clean enough! I've just been sitting on it!"

"Thank you, Mr. Padgett, Mr. Skunge," Mary said, sinking into the chair. "Do you think my uncle will be long?"

"Oh, no, I'm sure not, Madam." Mr. Padgett became more nervous when Dickson failed to reappear immediately. "I'm sure he's just finishing up some business."

"I don't like being kept waiting." Mary pouted. Inwardly, she was fuming. How dare Trimmer keep her down here while he did . . . what? No. Surely not that. Hadn't she told him she wouldn't tolerate that in the bank?

"No, no," Padgett agreed hastily. "It's most disagreeable to wait. I don't know what's keeping — Ah," he exclaimed as Dickson came down the stairs.

The clerk appeared quite flushed. "Mr. Trimmer will see you now, Ma'am."

"Oh, he will, will he?" she said archly. "Isn't that kind of him!"

"I'm sure he meant no offense." Mr. Padgett said. Anxiously he trailed Mary as she made her way up the stairs. "He's a very busy man."

Upstairs, Mary came to a door with frosted glass. On it was etched "Ethan B. Trimmer, Bank President" in beautifully flowing script. She rapped her brass parasol handle sharply on the "B".

"Come in!" called a voice full of false heartiness.

Mary threw open the door. It hit the wall hard enough to threaten the destruction of the glass. "Uncle!" she cried in a voice full of poisoned honey.

"My dear n-niece," Trimmer exclaimed as he came across the room to plant a chaste kiss on her cheek. He was a man of spheres: his head was round with no hair on top, just at the sides. Large mutton chop side whiskers emphasized his plump cheeks. His torso was like a fat autumn apple. His handsomely tailored coat, vest and shirt strained to cover his expansive middle and the thick gold watch chain that arced from his vest button to his left pocket was stretched tight, as if there to prevent an imminent explosion of flesh. In contrast, his legs looked too thin to support such weight. He was perspiring heavily. Mopping his brow with a lacy handkerchief, he showed sausage-thick fingers that were strangled by gaudy rings. On the whole, he appeared every inch the prosperous banker. "Would that you had let me know in advance of your c-coming. I would have met you at the d-dock."

Mary glared at him, though she kept her voice full of false cheerfulness. "Oh, I wouldn't want to disturb your schedule, dear Uncle. I know how extremely busy you are."

Trimmer paled under her gaze. "You must join me for d-dinner at my home tonight, my d-dear."

"How lovely." She took a seat in front of the banker's desk.

"Padgett!" he yelled down the stairs. "Inform my housekeeper that my n-niece will be joining me for dinner."

"I'll send Skunge right away, sir!" came the reply.

"And make sure no one disturbs us. We have much b-business to discuss." He closed the ornate door, much more carefully than Mary had.

"Sit, Trimmer."

"You've been away so l-long!" Hurriedly, he took his seat, "I had become concerned!"

Mary barked a laugh. "I'm willing to wager half this month's consignment that you've been on your knees every day, praying the *Fury* was at the bottom of the sea!"

"Oh, no." Trimmer clasped his hands together. "Quite the opposite! I pray daily for your safe return and —" He allowed a smile to creep onto his face, " — with holds full of r-riches."

She chuckled. "That's why you continue to live, Trimmer. You still manage to amuse me."

"May I pour you a sherry?" He shoved his bulk out of the chair and opened a cabinet. It contained crystal decanters of every size and description, filled with rare spirits.

She shifted with annoyance in her chair. "Fine." The whalebone stays of her corset were constricting and the petticoats were wadded up between her thighs. "Bloody hell! How can women put up with these poxy skirts?"

He placed her delicate crystal sherry glass in front of her. "But you look so ch-charming in them, my dear." He watched her for a moment. "Except when you fidget."

Mary couldn't stand the irritation any longer. She flipped up her top skirt and yanked the offending cloth from between her legs. Grunting in satisfaction, she pushed the skirt back down and sat back in her chair. "I hate these fashions."

"When was the last time you wore w-women's clothes? Regularly, I mean," he asked with an unsteady laugh.

"Apparently many petticoats ago." She took a sip of her sherry.

"You must tell me about those times. I'm sure I would find the tale most—" He rubbed his pudgy lower lip. " — stimulating."

She ignored the comment. "Since when did you need such an elaborate ritual for a visitor to be announced?"

"Ah." He suddenly found the papers on his desk fascinating. "I w-was occupied with some accounts. Our b-business has been expanding lately and it causes me a great deal of w-work to keep up with."

"Liar." Mary held her wineglass in front of her chin. She looked through the sherry and pondered his yellow, wavering image. "Don't dare lie to me. You were with one of your little friends, weren't you?"

"I-I . . . it's just that . . . well . . . it . . . ."

She wagged her finger. "I told you, not in the bank, Ethan. I didn't build you those rooms so you could have your little trysts here. What would people say if that became known?"

Trimmer took out his handkerchief and held it tightly to his lips. Sweat beads dotted his brow. His jowls quivered. "You said you'd never t-t-tell," he whispered.

"And I won't, if you stop having your playmates in the office." She placed the glass on the edge of the desk. Mary felt the usual queasiness she had when dealing with him. If he weren't so damned valuable she'd love to skewer the fat bastard. When she thought about those poor boys, it made her blood boil. But he was the key to her entire financial empire. If she wanted the *Fury* to turn a profit, Trimmer had to live — much as it disgusted her. "Keep it at home or I'll make sure the whole island witnesses your humiliation. Is that understood?"

He wouldn't look at her, folding and refolding his handkerchief. "Y-yes, I'm s-s-sorry. W-Won't happen again. I p-promise."

"See that it doesn't." She steepled her hands together and studied him. His diamond stickpin jumped with his quick heartbeats. The rings on his trembling fingers held emeralds and rubies of enormous size. "I note other changes, as well. A doorman, a new junior clerk, your fancy door, some new jewelry — you've been skimming the profits, haven't you, Trimmer?"

"Oh, n-no," he exclaimed, hands raised. "No, I swear. Every p-penny is accounted for! It's St. John's! More people have been arriving. R-rich people! They want to invest somewhere and I — that is, the bank! — gives them the opportunity. We're doing remarkably w-well. Truly!"

"How wonderful for us all," she said flatly. "I'll enjoy looking at the books."

"Which b-books? The regular books or the one's concerning our consignments?" Even the top of his head shone damply.

"Both." She examined the seams of her lace gloves. "Now."

"You know I promised years ago not to take f-funds that weren't mine. Besides, you pay me exceedingly well. We can go over the b-books tonight. It would look strange to my clerks, me showing my n-niece the bank's records. Don't you think?"

She took up her glass again. Trimmer was always nervous during these visits, so it was difficult to tell if he was trying to hide something. Petronius was convinced Trimmer was up to no good. Mary had argued that he was firmly under control because of his . . . proclivities. Now she wasn't so sure. "All right. Bring me the consignment accounts now. I'll examine the bank's records after dinner tonight."

"Fine." He wiped his face. "I'll have Padgett bring them right up."

"No. I want you to get them yourself." She rested the glass on the elaborately carved arm of the chair. "You've been getting grand ideas about your place here. Sitting behind a desk all day will do that to a man, I expect."

He stood blinking at her. "B-but a bank president doesn't fetch account ledgers personally. That's why one has clerks!"

"Oh, but you do, my dear," Mary said with a sneer. "And while you're about, why not order in some sort of meal for us. I'm famished."

Trimmer's mouth flapped open and shut. Finally, he turned and walked mechanically out of the room.

Mary rested her head in her hand and chuckled. "Oh, what fools these mortals be." And Trimmer was worse than most. She thought back to when they'd first met.

It had been in the second year of her captaincy. The *Fury* was doing very well and her holds were filled to bursting with booty. In February, Mary and the crew discovered an archipelago they'd named Cache Island. They buried their gold there, but neither she nor Petronius was happy with the arrangement. Mary stopped at each port town and tried to deal with the low-lifes who would handle stolen goods, for a price. But she found no one whom she could trust on a long-term basis. Only a tenth of the *Fury's* goods could be converted to gold. Then there was the problem of where to put the gold itself. Mary opened several small accounts in various island banks, but it was difficult. Bankers were a suspicious lot, and they mistrusted her story. She told them she was a widow having to run an outlying plantation. This was the only way she, or any woman, could conduct business given the European strictures against allowing women to dirty themselves with financial matters. Those bankers with whom she was able to open accounts wanted to manage her money, her fictional plantation, and her life in every sense. The unmarried ones were the worst. She despaired of ever working out a way for the *Fury* to profit beyond mere piracy.

Exploring the waters off Saint Lucia, the *Fury* came across the *Albermerle*, an inbound British ship. It wasn't a particularly fruitful boarding. The passengers weren't very wealthy, and the holds contained nothing that was easily traded for gold. The only thing of interest was the miserable-looking man in the brig. Lip curled in disgust, the British captain told Mary that the prisoner had been caught doing something unspeakable when they were just a week out of England. Information from a passenger stayed the captain from executing the man right away. He said the prisoner was wanted for embezzling a large sum of money from one of Liverpool's largest banks. The prisoner was being held for justice at His Majesty's colony on Saint Vincent.

Mary ordered the prisoner be kept in cell, then went to talk to him. He was terribly thin from his diet of gruel and ghostly pale from his long confinement. She called to him in a deep gruff voice through the grille in the door. "Hello, prisoner! What say you?"

"S-s-say?" he asked in a trembling voice. "What's there to s-say? I am being taken to my death and the ship's been captured by p-pirates, or so the guard yelled as he ran away."

"It has indeed been taken by pirates," she confirmed.

"Ah, then perhaps they will do me the service of k-killing me now instead of dragging me thousands of miles to face a judge," he whimpered.

"Who are you?"

"I'm Ethan B-Berril Trimmer, late of Liverpool," he said with a shadow of pride. "I was head clerk at the largest b-bank there for ten years."

"Why did you leave such a fine position?"

"The love of m-money," he sobbed. "The love of fine things to eat and to drink, to t-touch and hold. All that lovely m-money, just lying around. What was the harm if I took small amounts out and had a little fun with it?" After a pause, he muttered, "If only I hadn't g-gotten greedy."

Mary's deep laugh echoed through the hold. "I believe they call that embezzling, Mr. Trimmer."

"I know what it's c-called!" Trimmer snapped. "I know that it's wrong, what I did. I left just before the magistrate called for me. Figured that there'd be no trouble if I took myself off."

"So the captain of this ship jailed you for embezzling? That seems rather extreme. Couldn't he have waited to arrest you before you got off the ship? You hadn't hurt anyone, had you?"

There were sniffling sounds from the cell. Then,

in a hollow voice, Trimmer said, "I did s-something else."

"Yes? What did you do?"

"I . . . it . . . he . . . . Oh!" he moaned.

"You did something very bad, didn't you?"

"Oh! M-mercy!" he wailed.

"Tell me, Trimmer, or you'll never see the light of day again!"

"There was a ch-child. A little b-boy. The sailor found me — Oh, God, I'm a wicked m-man!"

"You're a filthy bugger, aren't you, Trimmer?" Mary grated. "Steal from your employer, bugger little boys, what else? Kill your Mummy?"

"You leave her right out of it!" he shouted.

Mary smiled. "What would you do if you could get out of that cell? How would you feel if you were free?"

"F-free?" Trimmer whispered. "No magistrates. No rope. Just f-free?"

"Yes. Would you be grateful? Loyal to the one who freed you?"

"My G-God, yes!" he sobbed.

Mary swung open the brig's door and let him see her by the light of the lantern at the guard's station. "You must swear total loyalty," she said in her normal voice.

Trimmer blinked at her from where he squatted in the filthy corner. "You're a w-woman! Wearing a m-man's clothes!"

"I'm a pirate. By name, Captain Mary." She bowed slightly.

"You? A p-pirate!" He laughed shrilly.

She shrugged. "If you wish, I shall close the door and leave you to your hilarity."

"No!" he screamed and jumped up. "No, please don't g-go! I'll do anything for you if you let me out. Anything."

"You must swear never to steal from me as you did your former employer, Trimmer. Do, and I shall take my time in devising a slow and torturous death for you. Is that clear?"

He lifted his hand. "I swear, ma'am. I'll never s-steal from the w-woman who saved my life."

"And as for the other thing . . . ." She closed her eyes in disgust. Everything in her screamed to slaughter this offence to the human race. But if she was right, he could be the solution to their greatest problem.

"I . . . I . . . ." He looked as if he might be sick.

"I don't care what you do on your own time." She turned her back. "Just don't do it where I have to know about it."

He followed her up to the deck like a whipped dog.

"Are you mad?" the British captain asked. "You have no idea how depraved this man is!"

Trimmer whimpered behind her. "I've heard what he did, Captain," she said. "What does it matter to you that I have decided to take him with me? This way you won't have to bother the magistrate on Saint Vincent."

"My God," the *Albermerle's* master exclaimed. "Only the truly evil would consort with his kind!" He spat at the deck in front of her. "Begone from this ship!"

She smiled sourly as she stepped over the spittle, secretly understanding his revulsion. When she took Trimmer's hand to help him board the *Fury*, she felt filthy and in need of one of her rare baths. She assigned him a place in the deepest hold, well out of her crew's way.

That evening, while she was writing up the accounts on the rickety desk in her sparsely furnished cabin, Petronius came in. "I wanna talk t'you about this Trimmer fellow."

She continued with her work. "You don't like him?"

"Like him? It's all I can do t'keep the crew from throwin' him overboard." He began to pace. "The *Albermerle's* crew told us what the little cockroach did. Makes my flesh crawl!"

"Mine, too," she said, shaking sand over her writing to blot the ink.

He stood over her. "Then why? What's in that skull o' yours?"

"Trimmer was head clerk of a very large bank for ten years." She looked up at him. "What is it that we need most?"

"A tame banker," he admitted.

"And we've had no success with the regular sort, have we?"

"I still think you need t'open your legs for those banker fellows," he said, leaning heavily against the shaky desk.

"That doesn't help." She threw down her quill. "Trimmer's disgusting habit makes him controllable. It's a lever we can use to keep him in line. It's how we'll keep him loyal to us, and keep his fingers out of the till."

Petronius paced again. "I suppose you're right. I don't like it, though. I don't want him on the ship any longer than we have to."

"Agreed. Call the little insect in here."

Petronius returned in a few moments with Trimmer. The banker looked even more nervous than he had on the *Albermerle*.

"Ah, Trimmer. Come. Sit." She indicated the stool beside her. Trimmer sat down, eyes lowered, while Petronius leaned against the door, watching them. She examined him thoughtfully. "We must get you new clothes. Those simply won't do. Did you get enough to eat? You're so thin."

"Y-yes, ma'am," he replied to the floor.

She glanced at Petronius and shrugged. Pouring some wine into a clay mug, Mary handed it to Trimmer. "We need to talk about what you can do for me."

He took the wine and gulped it down. "I told you, I'll do anything. Who do you want me to k-kill?"

Mary and Petronius laughed. "I'm not interested in your killing someone right at the moment. What I want from you is some of your knowledge. In banking."

"B-banking?" His eyebrows flew up into what was left of his thinning hairline.

"Yes, you see, I've long held the idea that pirating should be . . . well, profitable."

"Huh." For the first time, Trimmer looked directly at her. In his muddy-brown eyes there was a little light, a flame of greed that he tried not to show.

Mary noted the change. She knew she had him. "The *Fury* comes across all these items that people have paid dearly for, yet I have almost no way of converting those finds into gold. When I do have gold, I have few places to put it. It seems such a shame to have to bury the money."

"You b-bury it! That's horrible. What good is it in the ground!?"

"Precisely my thinking, Mr. Trimmer. Now do you see what I need from you?" She winked covertly at Petronius. The banker was behaving as she'd planned.

Trimmer stared off into space. "Exactly how much g-gold do you think you've got b-buried?"

Mary shrugged. "Oh, over twenty thousand pieces of eight. Then there's the jewelry." Petronius glared at her. She knew he hated for her to tell anyone precisely how much they had stashed away. But how was she supposed to get this revolting little man's attention, otherwise? Money was all that mattered to him, the bigger the sum, the better. Well, money and that other thing. She shuddered discreetly.

"Have you ever thought of opening your own b-bank?" Trimmer asked.

"Pirates ownin' a bank!" Petronius snapped, "Are you crazed? The government of whatever island we had it on would arrest the lot of us in a heartbeat!"

Trimmer flinched. After Mary coaxed him, he resumed his thought. "It would be a problem, if they knew p-pirates owned it." He held his cup out to Mary to be refilled.

"Go on," she said as she poured.

Over the next few evenings, Trimmer devised a plan to take their booty, or consignments, as he preferred to call it, sell it and bank it. The more he talked, the more possible it seemed to Petronius and Mary. They decided to try Saint John's on Antigua, since it was close to Cache Island, yet far enough away that no one would suspect a connection.

In the first year, they transformed their entire operation into a financial success. Trimmer started the Antigua Security Bank & Trust in an abandoned shack near the docks. He slept behind the counter. Shortly, he knew everyone on the waterfront and developed a circle of people to buy the consignments. In a year, he moved into a nicer storefront on the main street. He slept in the loft upstairs. That was the year he came up with ways to make money off Cache Island. Two years later, they built the brick bank building and gave him a flat upstairs. That was the year he diversified their holdings to many different islands and ventures. Last year, Mary ordered a stunning town-house constructed for him. It looked like the people of Saint John's were going to provide another stream of income for the *Fury* through their legitimate outlets. There seemed no end to this financial good luck.

Trimmer interrupted her reverie as he scuttled back in bearing the ledger. "I've ordered a luncheon sent up from the tavern 'round the corner. Their d-duck is superb. I know you'll appreciate it. Should be here in about an hour."

She yanked the ledger from his hands. "I shall die of hunger before then."

"Well, I have these s-sweets to tide us over," he said as he reached into the liquor cabinet and drew forth a jar of hard candies and held out the crystal jar to her. "Have to hide them from myself or they'd be g-gone in a day."

Mary took out a rum-flavored sweet, then opened the ledger. "I expect you'll want to look at these." She reached into her reticule and pulled out a handful of folded ledger pages.

"Ah." He sank into his chair with a smile. "The consignments." He ran a fat finger over the edges of the many sheets. "You've been very lucky this outing."

"More than you know." She turned a page. "We also acquired a new ship and a doctor for the island."

"A new sh-ship! What happened to the *Fury*?"

"It's in Starfish Cove. We've an additional ship, now. The *Pearl*. It's a sloop."

He frowned. "What do you need with a ship as small as a sloop?"

"We'll be using it as a hospital ship." She told Trimmer about the arrangement with Dr. Coulances.

When she finished, he regarded her suspiciously. "There's something more to this doctor, isn't there? A p-personal concern perhaps?"

"Let it go, Trimmer."

He pulled at his lower lip. "This will c-cost us."

"It will indeed," she agreed. "I want you to scour the Caribbean for hospital supplies. I want the *Pearl* to rival the best European hospitals."

"But the expense!"

"Hang the expense!" She struck the desk with her lace-gloved fist. "What if I'm injured in a boarding? Am I just to expire? There goes your main source of income!"

"So it's for your protection." He sucked on his candy noisily for a moment. His porcine eyes squeezed down to mere slits. "I s-see."

"And yours." Mary aimed an imaginary pistol at him, half wishing it was real. "What if you suffered some accident yourself?" She pulled the imaginary trigger. "The doctor could save your skin."

His eyes widened. The candy made a hard knot in his cheek as he nodded nervously. "What a good idea, adding a doctor to the p-payroll."

"I knew you'd see it my way, Trimmer." She tried not to smile. Trimmer was such a malleable fool. Mary focused on the page before her But these numbers proved his worth. They were making a steady profit from all their ventures, both legal and not.

"F-furniture!" he exclaimed. "Wonderful! I have orders for more furniture."

She looked up and, for the first time since her arrival, smiled genuinely at him. "You know, it's because of you that we can take advantage of finds like that. You have, on the whole, been very valuable to us."

"I live to p-please you, ma'am."

"Here, for example, you have your new clients investing in the *Fury's* businesses. Ordinary, law-abiding citizens are supplying pirates with capital. If they only knew! Trimmer, you're a genius!"

He blushed to the roots of his remaining hair. "You are t-too kind, madam."

She tossed the heavy ledger on the desk. "I had an interesting thought the other day, and now I realize that you could, of course, pull off such a plan."

He straightened. "I hope I can accomplish whatever you set b-before me."

"Good," she nodded, "what I have in mind —"

Dickson interrupted them, bringing their dinner. Soon they set to the delicious-smelling meal. Pulling apart his duck, Trimmer asked, "So, what was it you were going to t-tell me?"

Mary put a piece of the fowl in her mouth and chewed thoughtfully. Petronius' idea was audacious. In some ways, she worried that it was over-reaching their luck. How could they command more ships, more men, if they weren't in direct command? He was right, though. The only way to be truly successful at piracy was to control more of the seas "What if we had one or two more ships?"

"To d-do what?" he queried as he popped a large piece of potato in his mouth.

"It would be a sort of . . . pirate fleet."

His food-moistened fat lips formed a greasy "o" of wonder. "A whole fleet of p-pirates. Why, we'd be incredibly r-rich inside of five years!" Trimmer sat back. She could tell he was imagining the profits from such a venture. "We'd own half the Caribbean!"

"We?" Mary's eyes narrowed. She wished she'd poisoned his drink while he was out. She could just imagine the fat pig gasping for breath, tearing at his cravat for air. With a last squeal, he'd flop face first into his gold-rimmed plate. She'd be rid of him finally. And then what? Who would take care of their finances? As much as his very being revolted her, Trimmer was vital to her plans.

"I-I was speaking institutionally, of course," he hastily amended. She merely glared. "As a representative of the b-b-bank."

Mary pushed her empty plate away. "We'd have to capture some decent ships. How much do you think it will cost to refit something faster, bigger than the *Fury*?"

He paused, the duck leg held in mid-air, eyes focused on his inward calculations. "Over a thousand pieces of g-gold, I should think. Rather a high and r-risky investment."

"But easily affordable with all our assets." She slung her leg up over the arm of the chair. "We need something larger. A frigate, perhaps. You wouldn't believe the livestock I've had to pass up lately. I bet we could've gotten thousands for those Arabian horses I saw the other day."

He stared at her bare calf for a moment. "We just had all that w-work done on the *Fury*, and you were b-beached for three months. Why do you want to g-get rid of it?"

"I don't want to get rid of it, Trimmer. We'd give the *Fury* to the new crew. The new ship would be for me. The flagship, if you will."

"The new crew," he said, pulling on his lip. "They would unload at S-starfish cove just like always?"

"Yes, as would my new ship."

"We'd need to p-put in facilities there. Especially if the plan is to create a fleet." His brow furrowed. "Stone wharves, warehouses, transport, more agents — it'll run up c-costs."

"Yes, but we'll be doubling, tripling, our income! Of course, for the added work required of you, there would be an increase in your pay. Why not change our arrangement from a per visit fee to, say, ten percent off the top?"

Trimmer wiped off a small stream of drool that erupted from the corner of his mouth. "T- Ten percent!"

Mary's eyes narrowed. "How long do you think it would take to refit a ship for us?"

"The p-plans I could have for you next month. The refit," he paused, considering, "would probably take a little over three months, I should think. That would put us well into the new year."

Mary raised her half-empty glass. "Here's to next year then!"

CHAPTER SIX

After the *Fury's* business in St. John's was completed, the ship sailed for the Grenadine Isles at the southern reach of the Windward Island chain, searching for a place to careen. They had to drag the ship onto a beach and scrape all the speed-robbing barnacles and seaweed off first one side of the hull, then tip it over and do the other side. It was a lengthy and exhausting process, but it also gave Karl an opportunity to caulk, replace rotting wood and damaged areas. Usually they did this necessary chore in a little cove at Cache Island, but with the French watching the island for their return, that wasn't possible.

In her cabin, Captain Mary wrote out an accounting of the gains Trimmer had explained to her from the lengthy notes she'd taken at his town-house. He'd spelled out in great detail what they needed to further the grand plan for a pirate fleet. The work was tedious and the flickering lamp made her eyes sting.

Her inkwell and the tin box she kept papers in slid around the desk as the *Fury* sailed through storm-rough seas. With hardly a break in her writing, she stopped them from tipping off. But then the ship dove down a wave and slewed to port. Mary couldn't catch the box in time and it fell to the floor, spewing paper all over the cabin.

As she gathered the loose pages chronicling the *Fury's* business ventures for the past five years, she came upon some older sheets. Mary held up one paper to the light and smiled as she realized what it was. Every crewman aboard all pirate ships signed a document setting out the rules of piracy; the crew of the *Fury* was no exception. This one was signed by Talinn and stated the terms and conditions upon which he would remain a crewman in good standing with the rank of quartermaster. She remembered writing:

If the Shipp fail to capture Plunder, the above named Crewman shall get no pay. Otherwise, He shall receve 2 Shares of each Ships taking.

Talinn shall adhere to the Pyrates Code:

That each Person has a Vote in the Operation of the Shipp, an Equal Share in the Provisions and Likur, and one set of Goode Clothing.

To keep All Wepons in Fit and Ready order at All Times.

No Person shall Game or Dice aboard, as these lead to fites.

That no Person shall keep any Plunder to Himself, nor stele from His Mates. The Punishment if discovered be Keelhauling.

If Crewman deserts the Shipp in Time of Battle, Death by Flaying shall be the Punishment.

Personal Disagreements to be settled by a Duel,
but on Land only.

Then there was the rule which Mary herself had
broken more than once now.

No Lovers shall be kept aboard Who do no Work.

This stricture had caused much debate, since it
was obvious one couldn't forbid women aboard as most
pirates did. Her amended rule was the most sensible
compromise she could come up with.

Finally, there was a section about injury. The
compensations were more generous than most ships,
but she'd felt that it was one more way to bind the crew
to a woman captain.

Knowe ye that Talinn be entitled to the following
should Accident befall Him:
*   If He lose His Right Arme — 500 Pieces of Golde.*
*   If He lose His Left Arme — 350 Pieces of Golde.*
*   If He lose Bothe Armes — 1000 Pieces of Golde*
*   and a Servant.*
*   If He lose One Legg — 400 Pieces of Golde.*
*   If He lose Bothe Leggs — 1000 Pieces of Golde*
*   and a Servant.*
*   If He lose an Arme and a Legg — 850 Peeces of*
*   Golde.*

Without knocking, Petronius opened the door
and walked in. He had a bottle with him. "Finish the
accounts? I brought some whiskey."

"Aye." She stuffed the papers back in the box,
then took the bottle from him and poured them both a

glass. "I'm finished for now, at least."

He sat in the opposite chair. "Marie," he said, calling her a name he used only in private, "I think we've got a problem with Trimmer."

"Why?"

"He gave me trouble."

She nearly choked on her drink. "Trimmer? He's terrified of you."

Petronius drank down his whiskey and poured another. "He told me I can't build Naomi a house like Seashell's. It's my money. I can do what I want."

"Pet, it won't work on Antigua."

He stood and began to pace. "God's Teeth, not you, too!"

"Unless you want to move Naomi to Cache Island, a fancy house for a Negress would raise too many suspicions there. Someone — the English, the French, Captain Dead-Eye — would figure out her connection to us and hold her for ransom to bring us in. You don't want that for Naomi, do you?"

He threw himself back into his chair. "Neither do I want Naomi and Seashell on the same island. They'd kill each other! Or worse, make friends and kill me."

Mary guffawed and poured herself more whiskey. "Trimmer's not against you. He's just protecting our mutual arses. Besides, why is it so important for you to build her a place? She seems fairly content with the current arrangement."

He leaned forward and took her arm. "You've always been free. You've no idea what it's like never to've known your father. My mother was sold when I was only five. I won't allow that t'happen t'my children. They'll live with their mothers. They'll know me when I come t'port."

He got up and paced the cabin. "No, I tell you, my women must have houses that no one can take away from 'em. My children must have a home and a land they can call theirs. And after 'em, their children and on down through time."

"A dynasty? By Hades, but you're an ambitious fool." Mary wondered at his dream. She was busy enough plotting for the present, and here Petronius had grand visions of the future. Should she make plans as great for Melissa? "I'll write Trimmer and have him look into a cove on the Caribbean side of Antigua. Maybe she can have a nice place there."

"I can't stand that little bugger. I'm sure he's stealin' our money somehow."

"I don't think so. I checked the account books. Everything's there. Assets, debits, rents, investments." She shrugged. "It's all there."

"Lemme see the accounts."

She shoved the still-wet pages at him. "I'm telling you, I looked over everything very carefully."

His lips moved, shaping each word silently while he read the documents. Although he was used to Mary's handwriting, he hadn't been reading for very long, and the process took some time. For a while, nothing was said. Only the familiar watery burble of their hull slipping through the sea interrupted the silence. Finally, he looked up. "Somethin's missin'."

"Nothing's missing!" She put the inkwell and paper box back in their niches inside the desk with an unneeded force, trying to suppress her irritation at Petronius's questioning.

"Interest on investments." He threw the pages down. "That's how he's thievin' from us."

"Interest?" She pushed back her chair. "I still don't understand all this high finance stuff. All I know is simple plantation bookkeeping."

"Read the book I showed you."

"I read it. I just don't understand it. Fortunately, one of us does."

He grinned. "The student excels the teacher."

She folded her arms in disgust. "Fine. You do the books from now on."

He wagged his finger at her. "No. Things are fine as they are."

"What are we going to do about Trimmer?"

"We watch him." He poured a little more whiskey into his glass. "In the meantime, I'll teach you about interest so he won't fool you again."

"He did act strangely when I asked to see the books. I should have known. I thought knowing his . . . activities would keep him tame on our leash."

Petronius laughed sourly. "It did for a while. Now he's comfortable. Thinks he can take risks."

Mary yawned. "I'm so tired."

"I'm all in, too. And my foot's killing me."

Mary held out her hand. "Give it here and I'll get your boot off."

"There's a good lass." He put his foot in her lap and groaned with pleasure when she removed his boot.

"Gah!" she gasped as the smell hit her. Hurriedly, she opened the porthole. The roar of the sea filled the cabin. "That toe's getting worse."

"Sorry," he said, grimacing. "Hurts like Hell." Gingerly he wiggled his toes. The middle one didn't move. It was swollen and angry red with pus at the nail.

With a bit of cloth she gently wiped the toe dry. "When we get back to Cache Island, you'd best have the doctor look at it. This time I won't take no for an answer."

He chuckled into his glass. "You were too busy playin' with him for me to get in to see him."

Mary shoved his foot off her lap and gestured for the other foot. She jerked at the boot until it came off.

"Ow!" he complained. "Leave the foot, woman!"

"Since when do you get jealous of my lovers?" She pushed his foot down and picked up her glass.

"Jealous! Are you mad?"

"You acted strange as Hell while he was aboard. You even tried to get me to pay all the *Pearl's* expenses." She stood up and closed the porthole since wind-driven rain was coming in. "So I slept with him — and I like him. He's still an asset to Cache Island and the crew. That makes him an accounting expense, just like every other venture we've invested in."

He sat up. "Keep your voice down, woman. You want the crew to hear?"

Mary put a hand on her chair back and sighed. She hated arguing with him. "I want *you* to hear, Pet. You weren't being fair. Don't ever do that to me again."

He sat back and glowered at her from under his bushy brows. "All right. I'm sorry. But I wasn't — and am not — jealous."

Ignoring his protest, she sat back down. She was glad they were speaking about a subject they'd been avoiding for some time. "There're other things as well. Don't forget we have to pay the crew of the *Pearl* . . . and that damned Ingram. We have to provision the ship — they have to eat. Plus a few luxuries, since he'll be entertaining."

"Bloody Hell, Marie," he groaned. "You're

wipin' out our profits."

"What're you worried about? You've so much gold now you don't know where to put it."

"There's never enough gold for me. I've got all those women t'keep up. And their brats — whether they're mine or not."

"Such a soft touch."

"Don't get nasty, woman. Then there's that mine in New Grenada I'm working."

She shook her finger at him. "I told you that thing would suck you dry."

"Workers, overseers, assayers," he moaned. "Then they need more timber, ore cars, track. And still not one bloody nugget of gold out o' that pit! For once, you were right."

She raised her glass. "Here's to my being right."

"Bitch," he grumbled as he grudgingly raised his glass.

They drank their glasses empty. Then she leaned forward and kissed him. "I love it when you swear at me, you old sea dog."

"Oh, shut up, wench," he said, pulling her to him.

Soon they were in the great mahogany bed making love. They were in familiar waters and took their time becoming reacquainted with the territory. Their moves were languorous as kelp. There was no need of hurry. Gradually, waves of pleasure built up into a typhoon that threatened to capsize them both. Afterwards, the sensual flood tide receded, leaving them both spent in the wreck of the ultramarine quilt. Petronius drifted off to sleep almost immediately.

Mary lay peacefully wakeful afterwards, staring out the porthole at the starless night, split now and then by forks of blue-white lightning. Her mind wandered back to the first time she'd realized Petronius's importance to her, nearly six years ago now.

She'd been pregnant and in prison. In those days, she struggled to find the will to take each breath, though she couldn't have explained why she bothered. Her lover had been executed along with his crew. Instead of fighting the British warship, Captain Edmund "Silver Tooth" Baldric — a pirate who'd stricken terror into mariners for two years — had preferred to stay below decks drinking and gambling with the crew. Only Marie — as she was called then — and the newest member of the crew, a runaway slave named Petronius, fought off the boarding Brits. They killed five men before they were captured. As they were being loaded aboard the British ship, Petronius managed to escape and dive into the water. Mary and her captors thought him drowned.

When she stood before the judge at Spanishtown, Jamaica, she pled her belly. English law forbade the hanging of a pregnant woman — and she was indeed six months gone — though it showed not at all under her loose shirt. It caused an uproar in the court. No one had realized the defendant "A.M. de Tocqueville" was even a female until that moment. The pirate crew testified against her, saying she'd fought and sworn as well as any man. They didn't want her to escape the same fate they faced. There had always been grumbling on the ship against her. It was a mystery to her, because she'd never relied on her relationship with the captain or her membership in the "weaker sex" as a way out of working as hard as any of the crew. But they'd hated her all the same. Captain Silver Tooth didn't testify for or against her. He never looked at her, as if it were all somehow her fault.

After the doctor examined her and confirmed Mary was with child, she was locked in a cell by herself. It had a perfect view of her crewmates and her lover of three years dangling at the ends of their ropes. They were left to rot in the sun as a warning to other pirates in the area. Each day there was less of the men as the carrion birds pecked away more of their flesh. She didn't give her jailors the satisfaction of seeing her cry, but inside she fell apart. She didn't care whether she lived or died.

On the night she'd felt that her huge baby-filled belly would surely burst, she heard a scratchy tapping below her window. Mary struggled up and peered out. There stood Petronius staring back up at her. "What're you doing here?" she whispered. "You're supposed to be dead. Are you a ghost?"

"No, but you will be if I don't get you outta there," he said in such a reasonable tone.

She wondered why he was bothering. "I'm too pregnant to move fast enough to escape, Petronius. Thank you for trying, though."

"Don't you worry about bein' fast. Just tie this rope 'round the bars, will you?" He handed up a thick strand.

After she'd tied the knot, she whispered, "All right, now what?"

"Step back." The rope tightened. Slowly, quietly, the window frame and bars tipped out and into the night.

Mary stared out the opening. There were two other black men with Petronius and a gray horse. "Well, I'm damned."

Petronius reached up to her. "Come on down,

now. Time t'be leavin'."

Mary obeyed immediately, although it was a struggle to squeeze her girth over the window sill. She fell into Petronius's arms. He carried her to a waiting horse, then set her upon it. His confederates refitted the window and bars back into the jail's wall.

"It'll take 'em longer t'come lookin' for you if they can't figure how you got out," he whispered.

The men led her horse down to the harbor. Whenever she tried to ask them a question, they shushed her. Petronius helped her aboard a rowboat, then he and the other two paddled down the coast some way. Finally, they entered a sluggish river. There in the moonlight, Mary saw the chipped bowsprit of a familiar ship. It was the *Sea Witch*, the very ship she'd been taken from. "How — ?" she started to ask, and was silenced again.

They had to winch her up the side of the hull, tied into a bosun's chair with all three men pulling. Afterwards, Mary felt tired and shaky, but jubilant. Petronius and his two friends hoisted the sails and eased out into the Caribbean. They were free, yet no one said a word.

The man who'd saved her stood at the great wheel of the ship, seeming to pay no attention to her. Mary dragged an empty crate over and sat down. "I thank you very much, Petronius. Now you'll kindly tell me why you went to so much trouble."

He barely glanced at her. "You be plenty o' trouble, all right. But maybe you're worth it."

Mary looked down at her bulging belly. "I doubt that."

"You fight meaner'n better'n 'most any man I ever saw." He stared out into the night. "The crew o' this ship hated you 'cause you made 'em look lazy — which they was. They also thought you was bad luck — which's just plain foolishness. You was the best luck this leaky bucket had. If they'd come up and fought with us, we coulda killed those bloody Brits."

She felt the depression of her cell again. "Yes, well, they didn't."

"Then at the trial — God's Teeth, what a stir you caused!" He chuckled.

She stared at him. "You were there?"

"Oh, you whites can't tell one dark skin from another. I stood at the back and pretended I belonged there. No one noticed me." He sounded bitter.

"I still don't understand."

"It got me t'thinkin'. See, me and my two mates decided t'go a piratin' ourselves. But just like on land, dark skin don't win no respect. Know what I'm saying?" His voice was like iron.

"You don't think men would follow the orders of a blackamoor." She considered for a moment. "You're probably right."

"Probably!" he snarled. "There's no probably about it! Even if I could put together a crew o' all Africans and Caribs — and a fleet o' whites didn't destroy us — where could we enjoy our booty? Who'd serve us? What island'd have us? What would we do with our treasure? Bury it? What good'd that do? White people invest money t'make more money. If we could find a white man t'handle our treasure, how could we be sure he wouldn't rob us blind?"

Mary sat for a long while, letting his words sink in. She saw his point, but what he implied was . . . bizarre. "What makes you think men would follow a woman?"

He laughed. "I always knew you was quick. You're quality. Not like the rest o' that trash. Where were you raised? Plantation girl, huh?"

She stared at the deck and told the lie she'd repeated a hundred times. "I'm the daughter of a governess. She told everyone I was her niece, but the owner of the plantation and she . . . ."

"Ahhh," he said with a nod. "Them plantation massers sure got their cocks into any woman they can find. And they say African men're wild!"

"I still don't know why you think pirates would accept a woman as their captain." Her jail-softened muscles felt tired and sore after all the activity. The child inside of her kicked its own protest.

"Oh, it'll be hard at first," he agreed. "We'll have t'take some real wharf rats no one else'd take. Then we build up our reputation. If we don't get caught or killed, we could have a good crew in about a year."

She started to feel nauseous. "I don't know anything about being a captain — pirate or otherwise. Do you?"

Petronius smiled down at her. "Didn't you learn anythin' from that man o' yours?"

Without even thinking about it, she jumped up and slapped him in the face. The baby did somersaults in protest.

Calmly, Petronius continued to steer the ship. The other men drew closer. He shook his head at them, and they went back to their posts. "I could turn us 'round. Drop you off at Spanishtown's wharf. That what you want?"

Mary stood panting. Her heart raced and her stomach was threatening to revolt. She felt stupid for slapping a man who was saving her. "I'm sorry. I shouldn't have done that." She found she was shivering and sat back down. "I'd appreciate it if you would never refer to . . . to that man again."

He braced the wheel with his knee and carefully packed a pipe with tobacco. With tinder and flint, he lit it. It took some time, during which they were both silent. Eventually, he took hold of the wheel and cleared his throat. When he spoke again, it was as if the incident had never happened. "You know how t'pirate. You were on a successful ship for a couple o' years. You could lead raids. Men'd follow you once they realize you know what you're doin'. Gold's a powerful tool for changin' a man's mind. We'll pay our crew more'n anybody."

"And you?" she asked, the nausea subsiding.

He shrugged. "I'm one helluva pilot, lass. That's what my fool masser used t'tell everyone, anyway. I don't mind a little shootin', a little fight now'n then." He puffed for a moment on his pipe. "I also know men. I get people t'work harder'n they really want to." The waves hissed against the hull as he puffed thoughtfully. "We could be rich. Very rich."

"How would a woman conduct business for you?" Mary rubbed her forehead. The whole idea was ludicrous. Yet what choice had she? "You must be aware that women aren't allowed to make contracts, let alone actually own property."

"Well," he said, stealing a glance at her, "you might have t'use, ah . . . womanly wiles on someone."

Her mouth dropped open. She took a deep breath, caught between outrage and hilarity. Finally, she laughed for the first time in months. "You've got balls, asking me to whore for you!"

"Not whoring . . . exactly." He puffed hard on

his pipe. "See, you'd get . . . some o' the money."

"How much?" She leaned forward trying to see his face better.

"I dunno. We'll sort it out later."

"Can you do figures?" she demanded. "Sums? Make letters?"

"Well, no," he admitted grudgingly. Then angrily, "You know what the punishment is for teachin' a slave t'read!"

She nodded. "If I'm gonna have to fight as a pirate, use my body to 'do business' and do all the accounting, I get fifty percent — that's half."

"Half!" he shouted. "There won't be any profit left after we pay the crew. And what about me? Just 'cause I was a slave I'm supposed t'take less? It's my idea."

Mary heard the other two men muttering behind her. "Half after expenses — that's what we pay the crew and provisions for the ship, things like that. You could share your half with your friends." She tipped her head in their direction.

"I'd have t'split my half . . . huh." Petronius stared thoughtfully at his friends. "I think we need a bigger share. Three o' us, one o' you."

"No half share, no me. No me, you get no money." She smiled, pleased to be holding all the cards for once. "Turn the ship around. Take me back to Spanishtown."

He puffed at his pipe and glared into the night. Finally he grumbled, "Did I mention I hate all you whites? I don't have a choice but say yes, do I?"

"No," she said, trying to get comfortable on the box, "you don't."

He sighed. "They won't like this. But we'll

make it work. Somehow."

"Good." She rubbed her uncomfortable belly to settle the baby down. "Where're you taking me?"

"Hispaniola. Place called Les Cayes." His pipe went out and he tapped it against the wheel. "Giscard over there has a woman in the village, Nanette. She's a midwife. She'll take care o' the babe after you have it."

Mary blinked in confusion. She hadn't given any thought to the baby since she'd been jailed. She and Edmund had talked about going to Cuba so she could have it. It hadn't occurred to her until just that moment that there was never any mention of what would happen after the baby was born. One couldn't have an infant on a pirate ship, to be sure. Yet, she couldn't just walk away from it, could she? It wasn't natural. Not that she really wanted the child. Not right now. She was determined never to be as helpless as she had been in the old days. A woman with an infant was the most powerless creature in society — a breeding sow with no rights and dependent on any and all men. To Hell with what was natural or proper! Petronius was offering a way out of that trap. "When do we land?"

She had the baby a week later. The pain of labor was more excruciating than the time she was stabbed in the shoulder with a scimitar. Mary tried to pretend that it didn't bother her to leave the tiny pink baby in Nanette's care to head off to sea with Petronius. But it nearly ripped the heart out of her. How could she have known Melissa — as Mary'd named her — could have such a hold on her from the moment she entered the world? For days she walked around the ship in a kind of stupor. It was such a difficult parting, she'd been reluctant to go back and suffer through that pain again.

Mary'd seen Melissa only once since, almost two

years ago. The toddler was a rosy little thing who spoke the incomprehensible patois of the village and looked like an angel. Certainly she didn't look like her mother. Mary still felt that strong tug on her heart the infant had caused, but it was lessened, since she'd not been near Melissa in so long. As soon as it was possible, she asked Petronius to set sail.

She Anglicized her name to Mary before their first voyage as pirates. Marie had seemed too feminine-sounding. As Captain Mary, she selected the scum of half a dozen Caribbean wharves to serve in the original crew. At first, few of the experienced, worthwhile sailors would ship with a woman. Slowly, she and Petronius built a better crew as word of their successful raids spread throughout the Caribbean.

Petronius's partners died in the first month. Mary felt that their loss was a shame. Since Petronius never talked about himself, they'd been her only source of information — not that they talked all that much, themselves. All she knew about their past was that the three had escaped from a plantation somewhere up North. When they'd landed at Havana, Cuba, the Spaniards had seized the ship and thrown them in jail. They'd escaped and run into the jungle. There they'd joined the Cimaroons — small bands of escaped slaves who fought against the white landowners.

It was only recently that Petronius told her how he'd stolen the ship and its load of grain from his Bahamian master and sailed away with twenty of his friends. Only Giscard and Raul had escaped the Spaniards with him. He refused to talk about his reasons for leaving the Cimaroons.

First Giscard was killed playing cards with some friends in Bridgeport. Mary wasn't sure Petronius hadn't arranged it. Giscard had been the most talkative, and also the greediest. He often argued with Petronius about getting a bigger share of the plunder.

Raul was shot in their second, disastrous, boarding raid. Indeed, half their crew was killed or maimed in that awful action. The *Sea Witch* was so badly damaged they had to steal a new ship. The *Fury* belonged to a lazy band of English privateers. It was a mercy getting such a scurrilous lot off the seas and marooned on that tiny island off Virgin Gorda.

Much to their surprise, Petronius and Mary became best friends and business partners. Even more amazing in light of their initial hostility, they became occasional lovers after the acquisition of the commodious — or so it had seemed then — *Fury*.

Mary sighed at the memory of their first lovemaking, so awkward yet exciting. She wondered if Petronius had enjoyed the thrill of taboo she felt, sleeping with a person of another race. For a month they could hardly leave each other alone. They tried to be discreet, but the crew began to whisper about their behavior. So they stopped making love so often. In the end, their encounters became infrequent, but comfortably intense.

It was hard to believe they had been together nearly six years. Watching his face, so relaxed in slumber, she put her hand in Petronius's and squeezed it. She'd never trusted anyone as much.

He snorted at something in his sleep, then squeezed her hand in return.

CHAPTER SEVEN

Four nights later, the *Fury* lay off the Caribbean Sea shore of Basse Terre, Guadaloupe's largest island. Petronius signaled the coast as before. "He won't come," Mary said. "He's greedy, not stupid."

He continued flashing the lantern. "Oh, he'll come. You wait'n see."

As the North Star started its descent into the sea, there was a bump on the *Fury's* hull. Petronius shook Mary's shoulder, waking her from the fitful slumber she'd found, leaning against the foremast. "He's here," he whispered.

She turned to watch as the little man approached, his slight body obviously trembling. "Henri, I'm surprised you have the balls to show your face to me."

"What have I done, madame? Henri only brings you your letters, as always." Trembling, he handed her three missives.

"You're in the pay of Captain Dead-Eye. You betrayed us."

Vigorously, he shook his head, making his wire-framed glasses glint in the lantern light. "Oh *non, madame!* I would never betray you!"

"I don't know why you bother t'talk t'this poxy little runt," Petronius growled. "I think he'd be good shark bait. Put a nice big hook in his belly and drag him behind the ship till we catch a really big shark."

"Oh, *non! Non!*" Henri moaned.

Mary snorted. "What would I want with a huge shark?"

"You eat it!" Petronius smacked his lips. "Jacoby says he's got a new recipe for shark stew. The whole crew wants t'try it."

"It's tempting."

Henri sank down onto the deck and groveled at her feet. "Please, *belle Capitan,* don't let him make shark dinner of me!"

Mary kicked at Henri's face. He dodged, sprawling to her right. "The Evil Eye knew right where to find us after we sent you back ashore."

"It was that other fellow you sent with me! It was not I!" He wrung his hands. "I am loyal to you. You must believe me!"

"You mean this fellow?" Mary pointed behind Henri.

The little traitor turned. Franz, who had boarded that afternoon, glowered down at him. Henri squeaked in surprise.

Mary yanked his collar to get his attention. "I suppose all that free whoring back on Cache Island's making you so stupid you think you can betray me and get away with it."

"They force me! They come and they beat me! He — Captain Dead-Eye — he read the letters, then whip me. Tell me not to say anything!" He held his arms up in supplication. "What could I do? No one will protect Henri. You are not here when they are!"

"All my letters. He read all of them?"

"*Non*, not all. Maybe half."

She held up the ones he'd just given her. "These?"

Henri shook his head. "He hasn't been here since the battle. I haven't heard from him."

"You disgust me, worm. The moment my back was turned, you went looking for some way to betray me." She turned to Petronius. "Dispose of that."

"*Non! Non!*" he cried. Petronius grabbed him by the arm and hauled him toward the stern.

Mary started to her cabin, taking Franz with her. Over her shoulder she called, "And don't use him for bait!"

Petronius stopped, tightening his grip on the squirming Henri. "Why not?"

"I don't want my stew poisoned!" she snapped, entering her cabin. Mary could hear Henri screaming as Petronius dragged him off. There was a terrific splash followed by the almost immediate thrashing noise accompanying a shark attack. Suddenly, all was quiet. "Sit down, Franz," she said as she took her usual chair. He sat carefully on the edge of the seat, clearly conscious of the unaccustomed luxury. "How went your negotiations?"

He pulled at his scarf and nervously glanced around the room. "Badly, I'm afeared, Cap'n. Them two'r greedy. Took the forty pieces of eight you sent and demanded more. I met with 'em three times and didn't get nowhere."

"I see." Mary was unsurprised. She hadn't imagined this would be easy. "What about the package? Was it in good condition?"

"Ah, the package," he brightened. "Aye, she — that is, it's in good shape. As fine and lively as an item of that sort could be expected."

"You inspected it yourself then?"

He cleared his throat. "Not directly, Cap'n, no. It was kept outside while I talked to that Juan fella — but it seemed right good."

She leaned forward. "How could you be sure it was the package in question?"

Franz eyes flew wide. "You mean they coulda switched . . . . Oh, aye, I never thought! Might not've been her — er, it — at all I suppose."

"Describe it."

"Long brown hair, brown eyes — though in a certain light they were sort of gold-like, tiny li'l mouth, chattered all the time."

Mary could see he was searching for further information, hoping to please her. She knew the child by those gold-touched eyes and small mouth, just like her father's. But she said nothing.

Franz continued, "Spoke that Creole rubbish, like 'em." He shrugged, palms up. "Sorry, Cap'n. Best I can do."

"All right. We'll just have to hope it's her." Mary opened a small cask, took out a bag of coin, and handed it to him. "I want you to take this back to them. Tell them Madam Marie agrees to their terms."

"You're gonna pay 'em their ransom?"

"For the moment." She sat back, considering whether to explain her plan to Franz, then rejected the idea. It wasn't that he was untrustworthy. But she had no idea what kind of friends Juan Carlo had. If someone tortured Franz, he would surely tell all. "I want you to go back immediately and keep an eye on all of them. Learn everything about Juan and Gigi you can and send me the information, all right?"

He stood. "Of course, Cap'n. You can depend on me."

"I hope so." Mary watched him leave, feeling slightly sick. How dare these people hold her daughter! And then to have to bargain for her continued safety . . . . She suddenly realized her jaw was clenched so tightly it felt as if her teeth would surely shatter. With an effort, she unlocked her jaw and took a deep, calming breath. This Juan and Gigi were apparently taking care of Melissa. She had to focus on that, and not the thought that people who would hold a child for ransom were likely to do anything.

Mary tried to put the matter out of her mind and picked up the letters from Cache Island. The first letter was from Alphonse. She opened it and winced.

> *Darling Mary,*   *5 January*
>
> *Your Islande is quite Beautiful, a virtual Paradise. The Harbor is like a piece of Lapis Lazuli in a wonderous Greene Teacup. The Breezes are like Carresses. The Skye is a deep Turquoise the Like of which I have never seen before. But It is as Purgatory with out You.*
>
> *I have been quite welle Receved bye the people Here. The Govenor is quite a jolly olde Fellow. I can scarce Imagine anyone less like the French Authorities than He. And the Stories he telles of You! Then there are the Merchants. A more disreputable*

Lott I've never met! Judging from Their Tales, They
spend as much time trying to steal from Each Other
as they doe in attracting Custom! They too have
Many and Many Stories of You. Is noe One here not
from Your former Crewe?

Frustrated, Mary stopped reading and folded up
the letter. If Henri had shown this to the French,
Spanish or British, Cache Island could be invaded any
moment. No Colonial government was going to stand
for a pirate-run island! She'd sent Alphonse three letters
telling him to use her special code. Had he heeded her?
No, of course not. She threw his letter to the back of the
desk. Later, she might be able to finish it without getting angry.

The next on the pile was from her other lover.
She couldn't get up the courage to open that one. Not
yet. Instead, she tore off the seal from Governor
Donwelyn Briarley's letter. Of course he'd had many
stories to tell Alphonse about her. He'd been one of her
first crewmen, back in the early days. Not a young man
then, Briarley had shipped out with almost every pirate
crew the Caribbean had ever spawned. He'd seen time
with the likes of Calico Jack and Edward Morgan.
Briarley taught Petronius and Mary the finer points of
pirating. When he lost his leg to a Dutch cannonball, she
swore to take care of him the rest of his days. She
installed him in luxury in San Juan, but he wasn't
happy. He didn't like sitting around and watching others. Mary received quite a few angry letters from this
former second mate of hers, demanding that she let him
"doe Some Thingg!"

When Mary's Town was established, she offered
him the position of governor. He was so delighted with

the offer, he threatened to swim to Cache Island if she and the *Fury* didn't hurry and come for him. He ran the island to Mary's satisfaction and profit. In the meantime, he managed to skim just enough from the top to build a public house, amusingly called "The Leviathan's Blowhole." His family was the second richest on the island now.

She struggled to make out his erratic handwriting.

> *Darlin Girle,*   *2 January 1722*
> *Hopin All is Welle with You. Things goe passin Welle Heer. I know Ye don't like fer Mee ta but I'm writin Ye in the clear. I paid Henri 2 Golde Sovrins to keep this on Him At All Times and show it to No One. But Ye gotta heer what I have ta say.*
> *Lasst Monthe, We had Us a Scare. Captain Jubbal of the Ragin Tigerr whatt flys the Three Red Skulls and Crossbonnes reported thet Captain DeadEyye waz thretenin to attakk Our Illand. I made shure Evvery One waz Welle-Armed and sett Lookoutts Day n Nite.*

Damn Dead-Eye! She should have taken a torch and searched those dark waters after the battle till she'd found him and killed him. Now it wasn't enough for the poxy bastard to attack her and the *Fury* — he had to get at her through the island. If she could only stay at Cache Island, she could ensure its safety. Anxiously, she read on.

> *Then lasst Weke Danny 3 Fingers member Him? Use ta saill with Bonney Captain Johnny til the Brits hanged the Poore Olde Salt fer a Pyrate. Any Wayys*

Danny come in from Porto Reeco sez Captain DeadEyye run affole of some Hi Falutin Spanyard. Saw Him rottin on the Gibbet in San Wan Hisself!

Mary felt like jumping up and dancing. Dead-Eye on the gibbet! What a wonderful sight that must've been. Well, that was one enemy she needn't worry about. Wait till Petronius heard. She returned to the letter.

Now heers the tricky part. Right fore They puts Olde DeadEyye on the spike He hollers — Capn Mary owns Cache Illande! If Ye have Cache Illande Ye have Capn Mary! Welle so at first I dint worry cause it was all Spainyards and They speak that gibberish of Theirs. But Danny 3 Fingers sez He saw 2 English Sailors in the crowd. They was looking mighty inner-ested in what DeadEyye had ta say. He followed Them 2 ta a Shipp called Mars Thunderbolt. Have Ye had Any Dealins with that Lott?

Now my girle, I knows Ye can take care of Yerself but I think Ye should steer welle cleare of the Illande fer a wile. There's plenny fer Ye ta do Out Theer, and Thinggs be goin Rite Welle heer. Give it a 6-monthe or more fore Ye chance comin Home. Ye knowe Ill keep watch on the Place fer Ye.

Mary folded the letter slowly. She'd always feared this moment would come. That someone would reveal her secret island. Of course, it would be Dead Eye! Why couldn't he have died during the fight last month. Then he could only have told the fish. And of course there had to be British present! She shook her head at her bad luck: a resourceful enemy and a traitorous messenger.

Petronius came in. "Henri's feedin' the fish now. Waste o' good shark bait, if you ask me."

"Good." She poured whiskey for both of them. "I have good news. Briarley says that Dead-Eye's met his maker." She filled him in on the details. Petronius whooped with delight. They hugged each other, then raised their glasses and drank to the death of their enemy.

She refilled the glasses. "But there's a price to be paid for this good fortune."

He took his whiskey, the smile disappeared from his face. "What?"

Mary took the paper from the inside of her shirt and read him the last of Briarley's letter. "He's right. We've got to stay away from home for now."

Petronius looked down and sighed deeply. "Seashell wrote. It's a girl. Got lots of hair. Says she looks just like me. I'd kinda . . . ."

"You'd like to go home and be with them for a while," she finished for him. He nodded. "I haven't seen my loved ones in a long time as well, my friend. But it's just too dangerous."

"I know. You're right. We'll stay away, maybe go back after next Storm Season is over."

Mary calculated. That would be seven months — making it almost two years between visits. A long, long time.

"Did Franz have good news, too?" he asked.

"No." She sat with a sigh. "We're going to Hispaniola."

"We'll finally kill those swine."

"And then what?"

He flung himself into the chair where Franz had

sat. "What d'you mean?"

"What do I do with Melissa?" she asked.

"Ah." He looked as if someone had taken the wind out of his sails. "Find someone else t'take care of her, I guess."

"Who?" She folded her arms. "Do you have any suggestions?"

"I don't know. Maybe Seashell or Naomi might do."

Mary snorted. "And no one would ask questions about how a Negress came by a white child? Melissa'd be taken by the Brits or the French in a week."

"You have any ideas?" He leaned back and methodically lit his pipe using a piece of straw to get flame from the whale-oil lamp.

She groaned as she scrubbed at her face in frustration. "I don't know." Then her eye fell on her lover's unopened letter. Mary picked it up. "Maybe she . . . ."

"What? Who, maybe?"

"Who are we going to replace Henri with?"

He sat for a moment, blinking at her abrupt change of subject. "I don't know. I suppose Paolo would do. He's wantin' t'settle down somewhere. Set him up in Pointe-á-Pitre. You trust him, yes?"

"Paolo? Yes, he's a good man. See to it, will you?" She took out some paper and dipped her quill in ink.

He peered over her shoulder. "Are you gonna tell me, or am I gonna have t'guess?"

"There's a certain lady on Cache Island, just might fit the bill," Mary hinted.

He chortled. "Elaina Mayhew."

She started writing. "Elaina Mayhew."

He walked to the door. "She'd say . . . what?

That Melissa's hers?"

Mary shrugged. "What's one more brat in that house? If she'll do it."

"If!" He chuckled. "I'll tell Paolo he's goin' t'Cache Island tonight."

"Tell him he has to stay until he receives an answer to this letter."

He opened the door. "When do you wanna set sail?"

"As soon as she agrees." Mary stopped with her pen raised, "Now get, so I can finish this."

He threw her a mock salute and closed the door behind him.

Having come up with the plan, she suddenly realized all might be lost. After what she'd last written, Elaina might never want to speak to her again. Mary unfolded her latest letter and read it slowly.

Dearest Amaritta,   *4 January*

How Terrible it muste have been for You to write that Letter. What an Awfull Moment You surely had as Henri carried It away! Sometimes I can become quite Vexed, that You have soe little Faith in Me.

Are We not Women? Surely God fashioned Us to want Men. There is Nothing quite like the Love of One, is there? It fills a Certain Niche that Nothing Else can. Did I not tell You of My Love for Mosely Summerhazy and the Sharing I had with My Governess? The One Attraction did not interfere with the Other.

As Women, We must fulfill Our Role assigned bye Nature and God. But This does not preclude our having Pleasure with Whom We may. In fact, No One says that a Woman is Unfaithful when She gives

Herself to another Woman. Not Society nor Religion, not as long as One is Properly Affianced.

Perhaps You will Marry him. Even Settle Down. I should Love to see You happily surrounded bye Children. And while They are out at Play, and Your Handsome Doktor is off visiting Patients, We Two will slip up to Your Bedroom and share a Swetty Afternoon!

Feare not that I will Forsake My Darling,
Elaina

Mary found rare tears sliding down her cheeks. How could she ever have doubted Elaina's love? It was so unlike anything else she'd ever experienced, sometimes she could hardly credit it was there. But it was. Far stronger than her feelings for Alphonse. Truth be told, her love for him had somewhat cooled, now that he was nowhere near.

She took up her quill and wrote:

My Darling Elaina,   19 January
To begin, You will have noticed that This was delivered by an Unfamiliar Messenger. His name is Paolo and You may, in Limited Fashion, trust Him. I must inform You that I have discovered a Problem with My Correspondance. Henri, whom You and I have entrusted with All our Letters and Deelings, was, in fact, delivering these Papers to Captain Dedd-Eye. He, in turn, may have been selling Them to the British and French. When I discovered the Problem, I insured that Henri ceesed to suck Air longer. I know how This Sort of Action distresses You. However, as I have told You before, a Certain Behavior is expected from a Pyrate. The Quality of Mercy, in My

Occupation, is somewhat strained.

Now, as to Your last Letter — You are the Beste and Moste Perfekt Person there is. It touched Me to the Pointe of Tears, something unwarranted in a Pyrate. I have noe Understanding how I was Fortunate enough to find such a One as You in a Place so Wilde. Yours is a Generous, Forgiving Nature.

I agree that the Love of a Man fills Certain Niches that Our Special Friendship does not touch and Vice Versa. Many and many a Time when Alphonse and I were talking, I wished, in spite of my New-found Love, that He was You. This could All be very confusing if not for Your Calme and Goode Sense. I will keep Your Letter neare My Heart as I find its soothing Effects moste Wonderous.

You need never meet Him. I have restricted the Doctor to His Ship soe that He can be removed quickly if there is Danger. I worry that Your Last Letter was merely a Collection of Brave Words and that the Proximity of This Man may sever Our Relations.

Now came the ticklish part. Elaina mustn't say no, but she had to be given the opportunity. Of all those whom she controlled, Mary manipulated Elaina the least. That's why she must word the letter as a general question of what to do. Elaina might just refuse. It was rather a lot to ask, that she put up with Alphonse in the harbor and Melissa in her home. But Elaina had surprised Mary before. She seemed such a delicate little flower, yet just when one came to that conclusion, the woman showed that she was made of very stern stuff.

I must tell You of a Matter of some Urgency and

*Importance without feer that Others will get Wind of
it. You will remember My perhaps too Vehement
refusal to allow Converse on the Subject of My
Childe. I thot at the Time that the less said aboute the
Girl the better. Lately, I have been pondering the Fate
of Her, Melissa by Name, thinking that Her Environs
were becoming Unacceptable. The Years press on (too
Fast!) and She is growing Rapidly. You will laff to
know that I worry about Melissa's Education and
Lack of Manners, but It is so.*

*There must needs be a Proper Solution. This con-
cerns Me greatly because of What and Who I am. I
am in a Quandry about Where, Exactly, to place Her.
Those Who would take Money to look after Her could
be bribed to give the Childe up. Or, as in the Current
Situation, Some beleeve They should be paid a Greater
Fee — Do not Trouble Yourself about any Danger to
Melissa right now. I shall rectify the Problem. Those
Who would seem to Act Freely may indeed have Their
Eye on some Future . . . call it Remuneration. I real-
ize in chusing this Life I gave up Certain Rights,
Certain Privileges and Considerations. It is Hard to
see those Constraints transferred to Other Matters.*

*How I wish You were here to discuss This! Your
Keen Insights into Human Nature might show Me
the Way Out of This Trouble. At Night, I cannot
sleep for the Torture of Indecision. I beg You, apply
Your not Inconsiderable Power of Cognition to This
Problem and advise Me as Soon as You are able.
Paolo will whisk Your Answer to Me thru the Night.
I pray You will be swift as Melissa is in a somewhat
Prekarious Situation.*

*I await your Answer,
Amaritta*

Mary recapped the ink and leaned back, satisfied that she had achieved the perfect balance between letting Elaina make a decision on her own and telling her what it was she wanted.

She remembered the first time she'd seen her lady-love. Elaina had been trying to hide behind a trunk in her cabin. That was what? Three years ago, now.

Off St. Eustatius, the *Fury* had taken a Dutch *fluyt* — a long narrow cargo ship with only one deck — called the *Leitsterne*, heading out to the open ocean. The few passengers were quite deliciously wealthy, but the tiny woman trembling behind her voluminous luggage looked the richest of them all. She was dressed all in sky-blue brocade with the finest bleached lace surrounding her neck and wrists. Her blond hair was in long golden ringlets that perfectly framed her heart-shaped face. She wore the most elaborate gold filigree and seed pearl necklace Mary had ever seen. More gold flashed at her ears. On each finger she had rings with diamonds, emeralds and rubies. It wasn't hard to make the decision to hold her for ransom. Where she'd gotten those baubles, there had to be more!

Oh, how the woman had wailed as she was taken aboard the *Fury*! All through the day, as Mary went about the business of dividing the spoils and directing repairs — the damn Dutch put two cannon-balls through the *Fury's* fore-royal sail — the rich woman blubbered away in the captain's cabin.

Finally, as evening purpled the sky, Mary took her captive some dinner. In the humbly-furnished room, the captive looked like a brightly colored exotic bird. Her face was red and puffy from a day spent crying. She cowered on the plain bunk, clearly expecting to be beaten.

Mary bowed and introduced herself. "You're aboard the *Fury*. While you're with us, no harm will befall you. I promise." Still the woman watched her fearfully.

"I brought you some pepperpot stew. It's a spicy chicken and pork dish. My cook, Jacoby, is quite accomplished." Mary put their tin plates down on the rickety table. Despite the delectable smells, the woman shook her head.

"Truly, Madam," Mary said, "it's against my best interest to poison you. No one would ransom a corpse."

Hollow-eyed, the woman stared distrustfully at her.

Mary shrugged and ate a little from both plates. Then she poured two cups of wine into clay mugs and drank from each of those. She was beginning to think she was going to have to consume both dinners when she heard the rustle of cloth.

The woman sat at the end of the bed near her captor. She took a tiny piece of chicken daintily between two fingers and chewed carefully. "You have a fine cook," she said quietly, eyes averted.

Mary smiled. "I discovered him while he was in the midst of creating a dinner for a fat French admiral. It smelled so good, and the admiral was so undeserving, that I offered Jacoby a job at twice what he was being paid."

Bright, intensely blue eyes seemed to bore into Mary's. She felt she was being appraised like one of the woman's jewels. "How is it that a woman is a pirate?"

Mary took a sip of wine. "That's a long tale which interests no one but myself."

"I should like to hear it." The woman tapped delicately at her lips with a fragile-looking handkerchief.

"Perhaps another time," Mary said, as she finished her dinner. "May I inquire your name?"

Holding herself very erectly, the captaive said with some pride, "I am Elaina Pickethall Mayhew Dunnage. My husband is Robert Crofter Dunnage of Bridgetown, Barbados Island."

Mary poured them both more wine. "What does your husband do in fair Bridgetown?"

Mrs. Dunnage looked away. "He's a merchant."

She eyed the necklace. It had to be worth a thousand pounds. "A very successful one, I should judge."

"He has, as they say, a head for business."

"And what does his business include?"

"Mr. Dunnage deals in many things," she hedged.

Mary watched the woman over the rim of her cup. This little woman played things close. "Pray be specific."

She averted her gaze as she spoke. "Mayhew and Dunnage deal principally in the acquisition of laborers for plantations in the various islands of the Caribbean."

Mary put her cup down slowly and almost spat. "He's a slaver."

"Yes."

"I gather that the Mayhew of Mayhew and Dunnage is your father."

"Yes." Mrs. Dunnage stared steadily in front of her, as if undergoing an inquisition. "My family for many generations have been importers. Father deals specifically with sugarcane from the islands, but never, prior to three years ago, did our family deal in slaves. He once told me that to trade in human beings as if they were cattle was a sin against God and nature."

"What changed his mind?"

"My husband." Mrs. Dunnage twisted her handkerchief into a knot. "Robert was the company's manager in Barbados. He convinced Father that he was losing vast amounts of money in shipping and labor costs. He sailed all the way to London to show Father how he could make five times what he'd made the previous year if he took part in the slave market." She sighed. "Father put aside his moral convictions. He told Robert that if they made five times the profit by the same time next year, he'd make Robert a full partner."

"So, when Robert proved successful, your father agreed to your being Mrs. Dunnage as a way of sealing their partnership?"

Mrs. Dunnage's lower lip began to quiver. "Yes," she whispered. "Mother told me marriage wasn't for something as frivolous as love. I had a duty to the family. Just as she had to the Pickethall family."

"Was there someone else you intended to wed?"

She sniffled. "There was a young vicar, Mosely Summerhazy. It's true, Mosely was in reduced circumstances. But he came of good family. If Father had only agreed . . . ."

Mary used the candle to light her pipe. "What was the purpose of your voyage?"

She plucked nervously at her lace gloves. "I was on my way back to London. Father . . . passed away two months ago. Mother died last year. I must oversee the distribution of the estate."

Mary watched the smoke curl around the ceiling.

"Are you the only heir?" Mrs. Dunnage nodded. "Meaning your husband will have control over the entire estate."

A lone tear slid down Mrs. Dunnage's cheek. "Yes."

"Do you and your husband enjoy a pleasant marriage?"

More tears escaped down the fair Mrs. Dunnage's face as she shook her head. "Robert will probably rejoice in my capture."

"Perhaps not." Mary contemplated the fitful ember in her pipe. "Since you haven't completed your trip to London, you've yet to finalize the estate. Without a family member present, the courts could take years to settle the inheritance. And by then, they'll have dissipated it considerably. He could be induced to come up with a rather steep ransom to ensure that the estate is expedited."

Mrs. Dunnage narrowed her eyes. "You are cold and calculating."

"It's the nature of what I do, Madam. One may take an adversarial attitude in our relationship, or one may view the situation at hand as a kind of test for your husband. Certainly others have."

"A test?"

She put the pipe aside. "Even the most strife-ridden of marriages have produced some truly astonishing gestures of largess from worried spouses. Perhaps we can induce Robert to prove his devotion to you in the form of a large sum of money. If nothing else, than to relieve the embarrassment of having one's wife in the hands of pirates."

Mrs. Dunnage crossed her arms. "What if I don't care whether or not he's devoted to me?"

Mary laughed. "That's a problem. But one which you'll have to solve yourself." She gathered up the tin plates and clay mugs, then walked to the door. "These negotiations take some little time, so I advise you to make yourself as comfortable as you can. Goodnight." She closed the door behind her and listened for further crying, but there was none. Jacoby took the dishes from her. She strolled over to Petronius, who stood at the wheel.

"Good. You made her stop cryin'. I hate weepy women on my ship."

"Oh, you'll like this one, soon enough." She patted his shoulder. "Make for Barbados."

He made an adjustment in their heading. "She's very rich, yes?"

"Oh, aye." Mary chuckled. "This'll be our biggest ransom yet!"

"Ten thousand?"

"How about fifty thousand guineas?"

He laughed. "Woman, you think big!"

"That's my job." She smiled as she rigged her hammock.

The trip down the Windward Islands was fairly uneventful. No colonial ships or rival pirates challenged them. Elaina lost her fear of the *Fury's* crew and strolled freely about the decks. Soon she and Mary were on a first-name basis, allowing for more relaxed converse in the evenings after dinner.

"I'm amazed at your collection of books and your fair speech," Elaina began one night. "Won't you tell me how you came by such erudition?"

Mary allowed herself a thin smile. "I wasn't born a pirate, Elaina."

"Where were you born?" she asked.

"On a plantation. And no, you may not ask where." Mary lit her pipe.

"Ah, then you are of gentle birth." Elaina seemed pleased with the news.

"Why does that matter to you?" Mary tilted her head.

Elaina smoothed out her lace cuffs. "One can tell quality, refinement, even in a rough cover. I pride myself on my ability to see it when others do not."

"Ah, and whilst I was kidnaping you, you said to yourself, 'At least she's not common!'"

"Oh, you!" Elaina fluttered her handkerchief. "I could tell by your civility after I was aboard. Also, as I said before, by your speech. That is, by the way, a most singular accent you have."

"What accent?" Mary teased.

"Really, I think I've heard it's like before, but I can't remember." Elaina started to cough delicately. "Do you have to smoke that repugnant thing in here?"

Mary stood and opened the porthole. The room was filled with the sound of the sea rushing by the *Fury's* hull.

Elaina glowered at Mary, then her expression abruptly changed. "Oh! I just remembered where I've heard your accent before. It was at a meeting of Methodist missionaries I attended with Mosely. The speaker was from the American colonies. He said he was from South Carolinda . . . Carolita . . . . Something like that."

"Carolina." Mary had the odd feeling she'd been discovered. It was funny because she hadn't really thought she was hiding.

Elaina's voice betrayed her delight in the revelation. "So you're from the Carolina colony in the

American wilderness."

Mary bowed her head in acknowledgment. "It would seem so."

"You were the daughter of a plantation owner?" Elaina pressed.

Mary directed a stream of smoke out the porthole. "I weary of this game. Shall we read or would you prefer to turn in for the night?"

Elaina sat quietly, giving Mary a most calculating look with her intense blue eyes. "Why won't you tell me of your life? I'm sure it's very interesting, and I promise I shall listen most sympathetically."

Mary tamped down the tobacco in her pipe with her knife. "Madam, I'm a pirate. A person outside the law. Once you're safely returned home — and you will see home again, have no doubt — you'll tell others of your experience. It's best for me if you remain ignorant about my life."

"But Mary," Elaina pleaded, "I would tell no one!"

"No," Mary said firmly, taking down a volume of poems by Sir Walter Raleigh. She started reading over Elaina's protests until she quit trying to interrupt. Although that ended the discussion for the evening, it didn't stop Elaina from taking up the subject of Mary's life on each successive occasion.

"Were you ever married?" Elaina inquired over late tea.

Mary chuckled at the woman's tenacity. "Yes, I've been married. More than once."

"Really? Do you have children?"

"I will not answer, Elaina." Mary lit her pipe. "Would you care to read Christopher Marlowe tonight?"

"You must have children, then," Elaina pressed on. "Were you a pirate when you had the children, or did you live as a normal woman?"

"Elaina —" Mary cautioned.

"I wouldn't tell a soul!" she objected. "I simply want to know about you."

"Why? Of what possible use is the information to you?"

Elaina waved at the smoke that poured over her in Mary's explosion. "Will you please put that out!"

Mary sighed and crushed out the ember.

"Thank you. I want to know about you because . . . well, because you're so in control of what happens to you. No one tells you what to do, where to go. Whom to marry!"

"How little you know."

"But you're the captain of a pirate ship. Men jump to your command!"

Mary wrapped her hands around her knee. "You'd like that, would you?"

"Have you worn breeches so long that you've forgotten the helplessness of our sex?" Elaina demanded.

Mary closed her eyes. "No." It would never be long enough to forget.

Elaina leaned forward. "You see? Perhaps from your experience, I could learn something."

"I assure you," Mary said, pulling a book off the shelf, "nothing in my rather irregular life would be of any use to a lady such as yourself." She opened the book and turned a few pages.

"But Mary —"

"Ah. Here's an appropriate poem by Giles Fletcher the Elder: 'I wish sometimes, although a worthless thing.'" She read while Elaina quietly fumed.

On another night, Elaina tried a different tack. "You know," she began, "I'm surprised at the extent to which you live like a man."

"Oh?" Mary closed the book of Ben Johnson's essays they'd been reading and wondered where this would lead.

Elaina waved at the furnishings. "Look at this room, for instance."

For the first time, Mary saw the room as it looked to her wealthy hostage. The porthole was covered by a ragged dirty-white cloth. There was little furniture save for the original spare naval bunk that had been placed aboard twenty years ago. She'd picked up the scarred carpenter's chest she used to store blankets and clothes in up at Montserrat's Provincetown wharf. It had a warped top that didn't close fully and looked as if it had been through a war. The table she used as both dining area and work desk was forever rocking on its uneven, loosely fixed legs.

Elaina patted the unyielding surface of the bunk, breaking Mary's train of though. "This hard bed is just awful! Granted, you have a pretty coverlet for it, but it's so . . . so masculine."

"I'm sorry you're discomforted by your lodgings." Mary hid her smile.

"And the chairs!" Elaina got up and demonstrated that her straight-back chair was becoming loose-jointed. "They're positively torture racks!"

"Hmm." Mary wished for her banished pipe.

"Surely you were accustomed to better in your youth."

"Ah. That's what this is about."

"Didn't you live well on your plantation?"

Elaina said, giving Mary an innocent look.

Mary laughed. "Bloody Hell, woman! Will you not give up the subject?"

Elaina's ruby lips formed a pretty *moue*, perhaps in offence at Mary's cursing or pretended hurt. "I'm merely making an observation about the environment you've chosen to provide yourself."

"I've experienced better," Mary admitted. "I've also lived in much smaller, more . . . Spartan quarters."

"In jail?" Those piercing blue eyes seemed to drill at Mary's careful armor.

"You are very quick, madam," Mary admitted with a nod. "Yes, I've spent some time in the hospitality of a jailor. Fortunately, I left before my welcome wore out."

"You escaped!"

Mary reshelved the book with resignation. "It was either escape or hang. On the whole, I prefer breathing."

"Were you sentenced for piracy?"

"Yes. But I believe this conversation started with an observation about the furnishings of this cabin. Shall we return to it? You were thinking — what? — blue velvet for the porthole?"

"Oh, Mary! Why won't you tell me of your life? If you've been jailed before, how could my knowing about it possibly endanger you?"

Mary closed her eyes, fighting back irritation. The woman was incredibly persistent. And yet . . . she was the first who had ever taken a sincere interest in who Mary was and why she did what she did. Even Petronious had never pressed her for her history. She felt the need to confide in someone. Should she? She truly liked Elaina. Would it put this clever little woman in danger to know a pirate's secret life as much as Mary pretended? Or was she afraid to let anyone close to her? "I served aboard the *Sea Witch* for two years before we were captured by a British warship," she said quietly.

Elaina leaned forward slightly. A triumphal light danced in her eyes, but she hid her excitement well. In an almost-calm voice, she asked, "Were you the captain of that ship as well?"

Mary got up and poured herself a mug of whiskey. "No. The captain was a man by the name of Silver Tooth." She took a large swallow. "He was my husband."

"Your husband," Elaina exclaimed. "Did you dress as a man then?"

Mary sat back down and smiled thinly despite the sting of memory. "It would be mighty inconvenient to fight a battle in skirts, don't you think?"

"Did the crew know you were a woman?"

"Oh, aye, they knew," Mary stared into her drink, remembering. "They didn't like that I was there. That I could shoot better than most of them. Or use a cutlass like it was attached to my hand. That I slept with their captain. They practically begged the British to capture us . . . because of me."

"Did your husband escape with you?"

Mary twisted the mug around in her hands. "No, I watched from my cell as he and the others were hanged, one by one."

"How horrible." Elaina shivered. "How was it that you weren't hanged with them, though?"

Mary got up and wandered around the cabin. "English law prohibits the taking of an unborn life."

"You were pregnant!" Elaina grasped Mary's arm as she walked close to her. "Oh, how awful for you!"

Mary stared at the wall, forcing herself to steely indifference. It was hard. Elaina's presence, her persistent questioning, somehow brought Mary's emotions to the surface. "The crew testified against me. They wanted me to die with them. My husband . . . said nothing at all."

"He didn't try to defend you?" Elaina asked, withdrawing her hand. "Why?"

Mary shook her head, feeling her control slip further. She whispered, "I don't know. From the moment we were captured, he never spoke another word to me. Perhaps he thought it was my fault." She drank down the whiskey. "Women are supposed to be bad luck on a ship, you know."

After a long silence, Elaina asked, "And the baby?"

"I will never, never, answer your questions on that subject." Mary slammed the cup down on the desk. "It's simply too dangerous for anyone to have that knowledge." She fled out the door and away from the too close questioning.

Mary walked around the deck half the night, reliving over and over that dreadful time. It did no good climbing into her hammock. Rather than sleep, she watched the stars and fought long-held-back tears.

Three days later, off St. Lucia, they raided a Spanish merchant ship. In the captain's cabin was a marriage bed — comfortable for two. Charming, fat *putti* smiled from the crown of the mahogany headboard. It also had a thick, goosedown mattress. Mary ordered it taken aboard the *Fury*. That evening, when she joined Elaina for dinner, she expected words of praise.

"Oh, Mary, how could you!" came Elaina's surprising rebuke.

"I beg your pardon?" Mary asked in confusion. "You complained about the bed. I've provided you with one more comfortable."

She stamped her foot. "You stole it! It's a sin to steal. I'll not be party to the way you constantly endanger your immortal soul!"

Mary sank into her chair, bemused. "Elaina, I'm a pirate. I take things of value. How did you think I would acquire better furniture?"

She crossed her arms and glared down at Mary as if she were a naughty child. "You could buy it, like everyone else in the world. What you do is wrong and a sin."

"I thought you liked what I did, Mistress Elaina." Mary picked up her plate and began to eat.

"I'll admit I'm intrigued by your ability to command men and live as you please. Not the way you break the laws of God and civilization."

Mary said around her food, "But only by becoming a pirate could I do the things that you admire. Without booty, my men wouldn't follow me. If I were to engage in a more respectable occupation, then I would have to dress and act, if you will, like a woman — which would preclude my ability to have an occupation at all. A pretty problem. Now, sit down and eat before your fish grows cold."

Elaina sat in her chair, clearly still nettled. "Your rhetoric is very good. It will take me some while to come up with a refutation."

"Take your time."

Elaina picked at her perfectly cooked snapper. "Were you well-tutored when you lived on your

Carolina plantation?"

Always back to the same subject, Mary thought with a combination of admiration and annoyance. "I lacked for little as a child. Except, perhaps, a mother."

"What was the plantation called? I hear they all have quite fanciful names."

Mary shook her head. "Not ours. It was just 'the de Tocqueville place.'" Even with her new confidant, she wouldn't reveal all the truth. What if Elaina betrayed her? It would be too easy to go to the plantation in South Carolina and arrest Iain Mcnair, her blameless father. With him as hostage, Mary would give anything to ensure his safety.

Elaina nibbled a fritter. "de Tocqueville? Your people are French?"

Mary shrugged. "I suppose." In fact, her mother, Sidoni de Tocqueville, had been a French maid— and sometimes bedmate — of Laird Donaugh's, father's chieftain. The Laird had brought her from Rheims to his castle in Scotland. Iain and Sidoni ran off to the new American colonies to escape the Laird's wrath when he caught the two making love in his own bed. "My father never talked about anything that happened before he started the plantation." At least, not when he was sober. When he'd had a bottle or two of port, well . . . that was a different matter.

"Mary de Tocqueville," Elaina tried out the name.

She took a swallow of wine. "Actually, it's Amaritta Marie."

"Why that's beautiful," Elaina exclaimed. "Amaritta Marie de Tocqueville. I'm surprised you don't go by Amaritta. It's so pretty."

"Well," she said, grinning, "would you respect a

pirate named Amaritta?"

"No," Elaina admitted. "Would you permit me to call you Amaritta?"

Mary took a deep breath. It seemed a hundred years since anyone had called her that. But, she liked hearing it again. Liked the fluid way Elaina pronounced it. "I suppose so. If you promise never to use it unless we're alone."

"I promise . . . Amaritta." Elaina smiled.

Mary finished off her wine, feeling somehow vulnerable. It was at once a frightening and pleasurable sensation.

Elaina appeared to study Mary, then continued, "Your mother, did she die when you were young?"

"When I was five. Papa was quite bitter about her loss. It seemed to compound his outrage that I wasn't born male."

"That must have been difficult for you." Elaina took a dainty sip of her wine.

Mary smiled. It had been a long time since she'd allowed herself to think of home. She remembered the greening fields where the poor slaves moved down the rows in time to their endless, mournful songs. Like sentinels, towering long-needle pines lined the property, scenting the thick, hot air. Underneath a huge live oak was the two-storey brick main house where she'd grown up. It had green shutters and a white portico. Off in the glen, half-hidden by Virginia creeper, was the tiny chapel Papa had built for her mother not long before she'd died. Strangely, it wasn't the place that was as memorable so much as the powerful loneliness she'd felt there. "In some ways it was quite useful. I was taught to shoot accurately, to ride a horse as well as my father, and to make decisions regarding the running of the plantation. Perhaps I was let to run too wild to have ever accepted life as a tame little girl."

Elaina put her empty plate on the plank table. "It sounds as if you were brought up to be a boy."

"Perhaps. However, when I began to show signs that I was indeed a woman, Papa certainly treated me as such."

Elaina leaned her chin on her cupped hand. "Meaning?"

"I, too, had a marriage arranged for me." As soon as the words were out of her mouth, Mary wished them back. What had possessed her to bring that subject up? Her heart beat wildly as she tried not to run out of the cabin.

Elaina leaned forward. "No! Who was he?"

Mary took a sip of wine to moisten her suddenly dry tongue. It had been so long ago. Perhaps she could tell the story now. It might help put the demons to rest. "He was the son of the owner of the plantation down the river from us. I thought at the time that he was older than God — I was only seventeen. I realize now that he must've been in his thirties or thereabouts." Unbidden, Darius's leering face appeared on the bulkhead opposite her.

"Did you marry him?"

"No," Mary said curtly, seeing again the dead body on the newly turned earth. The old priest shouted, *"Thou shalt not kill!"* She shut her eyes.

"Mary?" Elaina interrupted her fearsome memory.

She opened her eyes. Elaina was waiting so patiently, obviously expecting to hear what had happened. But she couldn't tell her about that horrible afternoon. She realized she would never be able to utter the words. "I wanted nothing to do with Darius. When Papa became insistent, I ran away with one of the stable hands, Billy Lorain." That at least, wasn't a total fabrication. As she saddled her big chestnut mare, Billy stopped her. He wouldn't let loose the horse unless she told him where she was going. Too upset to talk, she'd tugged at him till he'd gotten up on the horse. Then they galloped down the oak-lined lane. Billy didn't protest.

"You ran away!" Elaina shook her head. "It never occurred to you to obey your father?"

Mary wished for her pipe. Her head began to throb. "Wed Darius Manchester! Why? He was ugly, stupid and only interested in me so that he could inherit my father's plantation. Besides," she said, trying for a glibness she didn't feel, "Billy was much more fun to roll around in the hay with."

Elaina stared at Mary. "You had relations with this boy . . . . And you weren't married?!"

"Don't be so shocked. We had the captain of the ship we sailed on marry us, first thing out of Charleston." Mary drank her wine, wondering. Why had marrying him seemed so important? She'd hardly known him. Perhaps she wasn't as daring — as against tradition — as she'd thought.

"Where did you sail?" Elaina asked, clearly caught between fascination and horror.

"New Providence in the Bahamas, eventually. Though it took almost a year to work our way there. We had no money."

"You never contacted your father? Let him know what had become of you?"

Mary refilled their cups. "Why? I knew I'd be disinherited the moment I left the plantation." Surely

the priest told Papa what he'd seen. Papa was unstint-
ing when it came to following God's laws.

"He must have been devastated when you left
like that!"

Mary's breath caught in her throat. It'd never
occurred to her that Papa would be hurt. Angry, venge-
ful — wrathful even — but hurt? A picture came into
her mind of Papa at Sunday worship in the family
chapel, his face sorrowful as he prayed for her dead
mother's soul. Did he now pray for her — a sinner — as
well? Could he still care for his murderous daughter?
"You'll have to excuse me from our reading tonight,
Elaina," Mary said, rising. "I find I'm not feeling very
well." The room seemed filled with Papa's mournful
presence and the shadow of Darius's dead body.

Elaina grasped Mary's hand. "Amaritta, dear,
I'm sorry. I've upset you. Please, sit down. We'll read
some of Shakespeare's lovely sonnets together."

Gently, Mary removed Elaina's hand. "No.
Goodnight." She left quickly and made her way up to
the bow, stopping to light her shaking pipe from a
lantern. The *Fury* lay off an island, barely discernible in
the moonless night. She could smell the jungle, hear the
waves crashing on the jagged shore. It did nothing to
ease the pain in her heart.

"Barbados," Petronius said behind her. "I sent
Watu with the ransom letter."

"Good." She didn't turn around, still remembering her father's face.

"Fifty thousand's a lot. You really think he'll
pay?"

She shrugged, indifferent to anything but her
own pain. "Why not?"

They stood in silence, listening to the night noises. "You like this Dunnage woman, yes?"

"I s'pose." She took a deep drag on the clay pipe.

He put his hand gently on her shoulder and whispered, "Marie, whatever she said, it isn't important. You know?"

She threw her pipe angrily into the sea and turned on him. "I'm Captain Mary, dammit!" Mary stormed aft to string up her hammock. "And don't you forget it!"

Behind her, almost lost in the wind, she heard Petronius say, "Aye, Cap'n."

CHAPTER EIGHT

"What is that you're eating?" Mary asked as they dined in the *Fury's* cabin.

"Ackee. Want some?" Petronius asked, around a mouthful.

"Hell no! I don't eat food that'll kill me."

"It's good," he said, offering her a scoop of the scrambled-eggy-looking stuff. "'Sides, I made it myself, just like Seashell taught me. It's only the unopened fruits that're poisonous."

"No." Mary wrinkled her nose up at the concoction that smelled like a mix of sweat and burnt eggs. She was well-familiar with this particular island fruit. On the tree it was a pale yellow fruit the size of a fist. When left to open by itself, the rind split into four wedges revealing four seeds like halves of black olives resting on a kind of custard. It was the custardy stuff Petronius was eating. The seeds were thrown away.

The trouble with ackee occurred when a person forced it open. Then, as if in retribution for being disturbed too early, it would kill. She'd seen a man on New Providence die a horrid, lingering death. The doctor said it was the ackee that did him in. Since then, she had no ambition to eat the killer fruit. "Get that away from me."

"Oh, c'mon." He tried to get a morsel in her mouth. "Live dangerously!"

"No!" She laughed, pushing his hand away.

A knock at the door interrupted their play. A voice called out in a heavy Spanish accent, "It is Paolo, *Capitan!*"

"Come!" Mary replied, rising to meet him.

Paolo entered, striped wool cap in hand. He held out a letter. "I come very fast."

She patted the man on the shoulder. "You did well, Paolo. Was the trip difficult?"

"No," he said, shaking his head. "*Muy facile.*"

"Good." She took the letter to her desk. "Go get some dinner from Jacoby. I want to send a reply back tonight."

"*Sí, gracias.*" He left quickly.

"You're that sure o' her answer?" Petronius lit his pipe.

She slit open the envelope. "I doubt she'll disappoint me." Mary held the letter close to the lamp.

Darling Amaritta,   *6 February*
I am touched that You have written to Me about this Terrible Problem of Yours. Well I remember Your reluctance to allow Converse on this Topic. Now, Your Melissa is endangered and You wonder where She may be kept hid Safely.

Have You ever played Hide the Thimble?

Mary snorted. "What?"

"There a problem?" he asked.

"Nothing." She sipped a little wine to steady herself. Just like Elaina to confuse the issue totally. Mary barely remembered playing Hide the Thimble with Papa when she was a tot — too young to be riding or shooting. Papa had always found the thimble so quickly. When she'd hunted for it, it couldn't be found.

I know It seems an Inanity, but bear with me. What is the Beste Place to hide the Thimble? In the Parlor? In the Drawer? Too obvious! Under the Antimacassar? It would show. No, the Beste Place to hide it is in Plaine View. On the Lamp Fixture, on the Edge of an Ornate Frame, among the Silver Tea Service.

So it must be with the Childe. Why not let her be Here, in amongst the People who revere You? Better still, who should take care of Her but Myself? In the Company I keep, a Childe would be as Unremarkable as a Milke Jug. She will soon be lost Amid the Happy Tumult that is Our Day to Day Life here.

What think You? I am most anxious to take on this Responsibility for You. I do not see you Muche, and long for Your Company. This, at Least, would give me Some Comfort.

I await your Answer with Great Excitement.

Mary refolded the letter.

"Well?" Petronius asked. "Did she say yes?"

"Of course." Mary smiled, eagerly dipping her quill into the ink. "Tell Paolo to come in here when he finishes his dinner," she said, already starting to compose her reply. He pushed himself out of his chair with a grunt. "Foot hurting?" she asked.

"Yeah," he grumbled and went out.

It didn't take long to write the letter. She was so delighted that Elaina was going to take the child. After she taught Melissa to speak properly — that horrid Creole was offensive to the ear — perhaps Elaina would teach her some of the qualities of being a lady. God knew the child could never learn them from her mother. If Melissa grew into a fine woman, perhaps she'd want to live in England or France — even the northern American colonies would be an improvement on the wild island life.

Mary shook her head at herself. She was no better than her father. Plotting and planning without finding out what the child might desire. She wanted Melissa to have a normal life, if that was possible. It was probably too late now, what with her childhood in Les Cayes. If anybody could make a lady out of a pirate's get, though, it was Elaina.

Mary's worst fear was that Melissa would grow up and want to be a pirate. Not that Mary didn't enjoy it. Occasionally it was downright fun. But Melissa should have a home, family, someone to share her life with. Sometimes Mary had thoughts about settling down. One couldn't live the pirate's life forever. She'd heard that the pirate William Kidd had gone north in search of a king's pardon. Why go to all the trouble? Why not give up the sailing life, change one's habits, clothes, old haunts and blend in like the thimble in the game? She'd heard of a new port at the mouth of the Mississippi River. Wouldn't it be wonderful to take her share of the partnership, gather up Elaina and Melissa and go to this new *Orleans*? Start fresh. But then, what would she do?

Petronius opened the door, interrupting her thoughts. "You'd think he hadn't eaten in a week."

Paolo followed Petronius, grinning sheepishly. "Jacoby make eel pie, *mi favorito!*"

Mary chuckled and reached into a drawer. She took out a few coins and dropped them into his hand. "This's a bonus for fast work. Mind you go back and deliver this just as quick." She put the letter into his other hand.

"*Gracias, Capitan!*" He held tightly to the coins and stuffed the letter inside his shirt. "You come back soon, *sí?*"

"We'll probably be back by the third full moon. Watch for the swingin' lantern every night," Petronius reminded him.

"*Sí*, Petronius. I not forget!" He put on his cap and went to the door. "*Vaya con Dios* and good sailing, *Capitan!*" he called.

"Set sail for Les Cayes," Mary told Petronius as he followed the messenger out.

"Aye," he said, dragging his foot.

"Then come back here, and I'll see to that toe."

He peered back in. "Leave it, lass. It's too nasty tonight." Then closed the door.

Mary sighed and sat back down. He was a stubborn old coot. She had to get him to the doctor soon or he'd lose that foot. The last time he let her look at it, the nail of one toe had come off. The flesh was black and peeling. Two toes next to it were starting to look puffy and pus-filled as well. He wouldn't let her take care of him, though. Sleep with him, yes. Fuss over him, not at all.

She picked up the letter and read it through again. As usual, Elaina reserved a few lines to dig into Mary's heart. *"I do not see you Muche, and long for your Company. This, at Least, would give me Some Comfort."* She knew Elaina must be terribly lonely, as she was for her.

Mary was replacing the letter in its cover sheet when she noticed another piece of paper inside it. She pulled it out. It was a newspaper clipping. Elaina had written across the top,

One of the New Girls stopped in New Providence and bought a used Trunk there. Inside was this Article. Isn't it a Strangge and Small World?

With an increasing chill, Mary read the yellowing paper:

New Providence Register, 7 February 1717.
Inquest concerning the Death of William Lorain.
The Honourable Governor Homer Thomas Crowell opened proceedings on the Inquest concerning the Death of William Lorain, a frequent Government Witness, today. Readers will remember that on the Morning of 28 January, a Body, later identified as that of William Lorain, was found stuffed in the Midden behind the Ugly Bastard Tavern. The Carcase had Diverse Cutts about the Chest and Leggs. Also, the Ears, Nose and Nether Parts of the Corpse were removed. These have not been found. The Area directly behind the Aforementioned Establishment, including the Pigg Sty, was awash in Blood, presumably the Corpse's.
Samuel Dingle, the Owner of the Ugly Bastard,

testified that William Lorain left the Premises some-time after Dusk. He had no Idea where Lorain was heading. Under close Questioning, Dingle stated that Lorain had not left with Anyone, nor had Any Person followed him out. Dingle could not recall Any One having Converse with Lorain, not to mention an Altercation. The only Other Customers He had at that Time were Edgar Huff and Hobart Griffith, but Neither had spoken to or left with Lorain.

Next, Edgar Huff was called for Questioning. He admitted being in the Tavern on the Nite in Question. Huff stated that He did not speak to Lorain, but saw Him leave just after St. Bartholomew's Bell rang Vespers. He left Some Time after Lorain and went to Forsyth's Dry Goods Store to play Rummy until welle after Midnite Watch. Several in Attendance stood and corroborated Huff's Presence at this Activity.

Hobart Griffith testified that he left the Tavern sometime after Huff, but went straight Home. He does not recall seeing Lorain at the Tavern. When Questioned about this, his Wife, Mary Elisabett, stood and testified that Griffith returned Home in an extremely Inebriated State at Nine. She remembered the Time exact because She had just heard the Nite Watch Man's Cry. She had got up to lock her Husband out for the Nite, when He fell in the Door.

Governor Crowell called the Assembled back to Order. He then asked those in Attendance to speak up if They had Information about this vishus Crime. None stepped Forward. The Governor promised a Full Investigation followed by Immediate Hanging for the Culprits, when found.

Trembling, Mary put the scrap of paper down. It was strange how a death four years ago could shake a person. Not that she was surprised Billy had gotten himself killed. She remembered Billy as he was before their arrival in New Providence, sweet and funny, but hard-working. Then he'd discovered the world of bribes and secrets and power in the service of the Governor.

Once again, she looked at the witnesses' names. She recalled all of them. She'd worked for Sam Dingle as a barmaid — until he'd asked her to leave. Customers didn't want Billy's wife "spying" on them. Dingle understood Mary had nothing to do with Billy's activities and had been apologetic about firing her. Mary'd thought him very kind, considering that Billy's testimony put Dingle in the stocks for a week for the crime of Blaspheming.

She remembered Ed Huff as an angry, spiteful man. He hadn't been so bad until his two younger brothers were hanged for piracy on the strength of Billy's testimony. Only Mary knew that Billy was out to punish the entire Huff family. On their first day in town, Billy had been carrying their trunk. He'd tripped and fallen right into a big mud hole. The Huffs just happened to be gathered together on their way to a family picnic. Of course they'd all laughed at the sight of Billy completely covered in muck — she had, too. But from then on, Billy used every opportunity to implicate Huff and his family in real or imagined wrongdoing. The year before she left, Billy'd accused Ed of stealing Jobert's prize pig. The charges were thrown out when Governor Crowell admitted he'd been playing Rummy with Huff when the crime was supposed to have happened. Mary had been appalled when Billy brought home that suspicious side of pork — and he'd seemed proud of himself.

She recalled Hobart Griffith as a drunk who spent as much time in taverns as escaping the wrath of his wife. But then, he'd a right to stay inebriated. His only son was hanged as the murderer of a barmaid on Billy's say-so. A year later, a low-life named Venuta admitted to the crime.

It was clear to Mary that they were all in on it: Dingle, Huff, and Griffith. They'd all killed him. Crowell himself might have stood by and watched, smoking his great black-cherry pipe. No one likes a snitch.

Mary held the article with a touch of wonder. Only one person in the world would have realized the importance of this news. Once again, she felt vulnerable and a little in awe of Elaina's hold on her. It had happened so subtly, she hadn't realized what was happening.

She thought back to those first days, while they waited for Elaina's ransom. Dunnage had been slow to answer. Mary worried that the rich man was summoning a fleet of British ships to capture his wife's impertinent captors. She had the *Fury* skulk about the nearby archipelagoes. Each night they drifted into a dark cove on the south side of Barbados after they heard the night watchman's call of "Twelve of the clock, and all's well!" Each night, there was no word. She didn't reveal her concerns to Elaina, who continued to pursue her inquisition at each dinner.

Elaina returned to the subject of Billy. "Was your marriage happy?" she asked, taking a bite of kidney pie.

Mary finished her meal and put the plate on the

table. She wiped her hands slowly. "Happy? In the early days. Deliriously so." She remembered those days as sun-drenched, busy and filled with love.

"How did you live? You said you had to work to get to some place . . . ." Elaina bit her lip, trying to recall. "New . . . something."

"New Providence. Billy did any odd job he could find. On the ship he swabbed decks, scraped barnacles, cleaned holds. I helped with the cooking and assisted the passengers as a general maidservant."

Elaina tittered. "You! A maid?"

Mary smiled thinly and took a sip of her wine. "Oh, it gets better, my dear. When we were on shore, I worked as a lady's maid for a time."

"I can't imagine it!"

She pondered the dregs in her cup. "Neither could that poor woman. I constantly had her hair in knots and her jewelry all tangled up. I was quite a fiasco."

"Oh, dear. You weren't trained for service."

"No, nor, as I've told you, was I trained well in the female arts. I didn't stay in that woman's employ very long."

"I'd suppose not."

"Billy and I moved from town to town, island to island. Mostly we worked in taverns. Billy would work in the stable and I'd work as a scullery or barmaid. Then we got to New Providence."

"Did you work at a tavern there?"

Mary crossed her legs and stared thoughtfully at her worn-down heels. "At first. But then Billy fell in with a new crowd."

"Hooligans?" Elaina looked expectant.

Mary chortled darkly. "Worse! He started to

serve the new governor by spying on people. A snitch is what it's called."

"That's bad?"

"In that society it was. Most of the people on New Providence were pirates or involved with pirating. The British sent a governor to tame their colony. For Billy, being a snitch was a kind of game. He became obsessed with it. He stopped talking to me, unless it was to ask if I'd heard anything interesting at the tavern. Well, of course, no one would speak to me after it became known what Billy was up to. Some even threw things at me in the street. I couldn't stand it. I begged him to stop. But he slapped me and told me to shut up."

Elaina covered her mouth. "He struck you? How could you let him do that?"

Mary shrugged. "I was eighteen or nineteen then. I thought that was how men managed their woman. Certainly that's how the other women I spoke to were treated."

"How horrid for you. What did you do?"

"There was a man who spoke to me." Mary closed her eyes, seeing his chiseled features, his gold-lit brown eyes, hearing that deep, melodious voice again. "Sweet words. Gentle words."

"You fell in love," Elaina whispered.

Mary nodded. "The more Billy beat me, the more I fell in love with Edmund. Finally, I discovered I didn't care what Billy did to me. I wanted Edmund."

Elaina leaned forward, her wine cup clutched tightly. "Did you run away with him?"

Mary smiled ruefully. "Not at first. We tried to convince Billy to let me go."

"Why?"

"He was in the pay of the governor. Billy could

have made it impossible for us — sworn out a warrant saying I'd been kidnapped. That would have guaranteed Edmund could find no work. He captained a small sloop that carried consignments of all kinds."

Elaina remembered her cup and put it on the table. "So what did you do?"

"We went to Billy and asked for his consent to allow me to leave."

"No!"

"It was a stupid idea. I was very romantic then. I believed that love would overcome any objections. I was wrong."

"He had you arrested," Elaina guessed.

"Oh," Mary said with a sigh, "he wasn't content with a mere arrest. He had to humiliate me totally."

"How?"

Mary refilled her cup. "Have you ever heard of Divorce by Sale?"

Elaina sat back, thinking. "I heard something about it when I was little. It's a sort of folk divorce, isn't it? I know it's not legal."

"You know more than I did, then. Billy convinced Edmund and me to go through with it — we had no idea it was illegal. I'm sure he did though. He said it was the only way he would agree to my leaving him."

"What did you have to do?"

Mary rubbed her face, memory prickling her skin. "Billy tied a halter around my neck, as if I was a cow."

"Good Lord!" Elaina moved her chair closer to Mary and put a hand on her shoulder.

"He led me around the market three times." She could hear again the taunts and jeers of people in the market. "Then he stood in the middle of the square and offered me for sale . . . to the highest bidder."

"Oh, my dear Amaritta!" Elaina took her hand and leaned forward, peering into Mary's face.

Mary grasped Elaina's hand tightly as if it was a lifeline. She found it hard to force the words out. "Edmund . . . came up and offered two sea bass he'd caught that morning . . . and Billy accepted. Then Edmund led me away."

Elaina stroked Mary's hand, then her cheek. "I can't believe it! How ever did you stand for it?"

"I believed that it would make everything all right. And for two days, it was. Edmund and I lived as man and wife . . . as we'd dreamed." She bit her fist and tried to stop the tears.

Elaina encircled Mary's shoulders in a comforting embrace. "But Billy didn't let you alone?"

Mary shook her head. "The governor's soldiers came a-and arrested us. We were tried . . . for l-lewdness. Billy and Edmund were put in jail — though Billy was let out by his friend the guard an hour after sentencing."

"And you, dear?" Elaina held Mary's hand to her own cheek.

"I was put . . . in the s-stocks . . . for three days . . . as an a-adulteress." Mary fought back sobs. She felt again the rotting fruit the children had thrown at her. Heard the laughter of the filthy drunks who'd pissed on her dress.

"Oh, you poor dear." Elaina hugged Mary as she gave in to tears. Gently, Elaina kissed Mary's forehead, her cheeks.

It felt so soothing to be consoled by someone who cared that Mary held tightly to Elaina and blindly returned her kisses. At first it was just gentle pecks on the cheek and neck, but then their lips met and it was as if a strong magnet held them together. Mary's eyes flew open in surprise. But instead of pulling away, she let the kiss continue. Elaina's lips were so sweet. The kiss was so delicious as it went on and on. Her eyes closed as she allowed herself to enjoy the moment. Then their tongues touched, ran away and finally intertwined in a slow intricate dance that utterly thrilled Mary. It felt better than with Edmund or Billy or even Petronius. This was somehow . . . better.

Mary felt Elaina's hands gently caress her breasts. Could this be happening? Did women really do this with each other? But Elaina's touch was gentle, not rough like a man's. The more Elaina stroked her, the more Mary craved her touch. Slowly, experimentally, she slid her hand onto Elaina's breast. She fondled it's unfamiliar softness, not firm like her own. Eagerly, she explored her breast's contours. Elaina squeezed Mary's nipples, not pinching them, like men had, but with a firm, teasing grip that made Mary feel as if she were melting. Elaina's kiss went deeper still. Mary felt herself surrendering to Elaina as she'd never given herself to anyone but Edmund.

Elaina unbuttoned Mary's pants. Mary couldn't imagine what two women could do further, but she wanted very much to find out. She unlaced Elaina's bodice. Smiling, Elaina stood, pulling Mary up, and led her to bed. She unlaced the top of Mary's shirt while kissing her deeply. Trembling as they undressed each other, Elaina kissed and sucked each newly exposed area. Mary found herself doing the same and reveling in the texture of Elaina's skin, her delicate perfume. Their passion built and built, finally exploding in a way that Mary had never experienced before. She clung to her new lover as if she were the only thing floating in a vast, harsh sea.

Elaina stroked Mary's back and kissed her ear. Mary was trembling all over from spent passion and amazement. She rolled out of Elaina's arms and laughed. "My God, I never imagined such a thing!" She stroked Elaina's brow, wondering at how such a delicate-looking woman could move her as no man had. "That was astounding."

"Good." Elaina rolled over so that they were facing on their sides and brushed Mary's hair out of her eyes.

"Have . . . have you ever . . . done that before?"

"Um-hm," Elaina said languidly. "My governess and I shared this quite often until I was forced to live in Barbados." She chuckled. "You see? Being a girl does have its advantages."

Mary giggled. "I see that!" Her laughter faded as she traced the outline of Elaina's lips.

Elaina stroked Mary's breast. "You're so lovely."

Mary snorted. "You're kind to say so, but it's not true. I've seen a mirror." Getting up, she refilled their goblets and took them back to bed. Elaina plumped up the two pillows so that they could sit up together. Mary gave her a cup, then climbed back into bed.

"That's another thing you don't have in here is a mirror. How is a woman supposed to make herself presentable without one?"

"I'll obtain one for your ladyship as soon as I'm able." Mary toasted her.

Elaina considered her over the rim of her clay cup as she drank, then said. "I wish that you lived a gentler life. You should be surrounded with fine laces, crystal, beautiful china, exquisite furniture and sumptuous brocades."

"Difficult to have as a pirate."

"Why? You have this cabin. If you continue to live as a pirate, why not allow yourself some luxuries in here. There's no reason to live so austerely."

"Perhaps," Mary said thoughtfully.

Elaina took her hand. "Now finish the story about that horrible island. What did you do when you were released from . . . that situation?"

Mary swallowed down some wine before she said, "We ran away, which was what we should have done in the first place."

"Didn't Billy file charges against Edmund and you?"

She nodded. "Oh, yes. That's why we had to turn to pirating. No port would allow wanted criminals in to do legitimate business. We changed his name, since no one would be afraid of a pirate named Edmund. He had this incisor made of silver, so he called himself —"

"Edmund was Captain Silver Tooth?" Elaina squeezed Mary's hand. "Then you became a pirate not for money, but for love."

"Does that make it all right, then, Mistress Elaina?"

"No, it doesn't make it all right." Elaina made as if to bite Mary's neck.

Mary drew back and laughed, charmed by Elaina's love-play.

"Still, it's terribly romantic all the same."

"Oh, please don't say that. Romance . . . at least with men . . . has never done me any favors."

Elaina seemed to ponder. "But let's see. That

makes you Amaritta Marie de Tocqueville Lorain . . . ."

"Baldric," Mary finished. "Quite a mouthful."

"Are there any more husbands?"

"No, I've sworn off having husbands. The only marriage I have now is to the *Fury*." She winked. "And, of course, all ships are ladies!"

"So you wouldn't be averse to sharing your life with a woman?" Elaina asked shyly.

Mary leaned over and kissed her in their new-found way. "Maybe. But I'm not taking your husband's name!"

Elaina laughed. "No." Then she leaned over and started to tongue Mary's nipple. "Mayhew," she said between licks.

"Whatever you want, Elaina." Mary put her cup on the floor. She took Elaina's cup and put it beside hers before succumbing again to Elaina's mastery.

Two nights later, Watu appeared on deck with an answer from Robert Dunnage. Mary hastily took it to read beneath a lantern.

> *Madam (if One may be so Free with the Term),*
>
> *I have just returned from a Junket and have dis-covered with a Great Deal of Dismay your Missive informing me that you hold my Wife for Ranssom. I find It Incomprehensibile that a Woman would be of so Rough a Character as to become a Pyrate. However, after having consulted with our Sheriff I have learned that you are Well Knowne, Both for your Acts of Pyracy as well as for the Civvil Manner in which you treat your Hostages. I trust my Deare Wife is welle.*
>
> *Then There is the Matter of the Ranssom Itself.*

*Suche an extravagant Demand! Think you that I am
made of Money? I am not, myself, a Wealthy Man,
but a Hard-Working Christian Merchant. I will pay
5,000 Golde Guineas to you at the Place of your chusing. Anything Else is out of the Question — I certainly would never have access to Sums the likes of
which you mentioned! Please be merciful to my Poore
Wife and to my Sorrowing Hearte.*

Awaiting your Reply anxiously,
Robert Crofter Dunnage

"Poxy bastard," Mary whispered.

"What'd he say?" Petronius asked. She showed
him the letter. "God's Teeth! I had a bad feelin' about
askin' that much."

"Now you tell me."

"If you were right, we'd be rich."

"Thanks so much."

"What're you gonna do now?"

"I don't know," she said with a sigh. "Maybe
Elaina has an idea."

"Elaina?" He took her by the shoulder. "What's
goin' on 'tween you two. Huh?"

She glared at his hand until he released her.
"Nothing. She just has good ideas, that's all."

He grunted, then stood back. "You and me, we
gotta have a talk about this lady. Somethin's goin' on
here. Since when d'you listen t'silly rich women?"

"She's as smart as you!"

"Maybe so, but she's the one we're holdin' for
ransom. She's our prisoner. Why would she help us get
a bigger ransom?"

"She doesn't like her husband very much."

He took a piece of straw from its place beside the

lantern and set it aflame to light his pipe. "She likes you, though. A whole lot. Maybe . . . more, yes?" He sat on the hatch behind him.

"Meaning?"

He smiled around his pipe stem. "Don't you look at me that way, lass. I'm your partner, remember? I don't care who you sleep with. I only care when it affects this ship." He tapped the boards of the deck. "This lady may be a fun playmate for you, but her husband's givin' us the run 'round. You gotta decide what t'do and soon."

Mary closed her eyes and leaned her head against the wall. She didn't want to deal with the problem right now. She'd intended to talk to Petronius the last couple of days — but how do you even open a subject like that? In her cabin at night, when she was with Elaina, it was good and sweet and perfect. On the deck, during the day, it had seemed . . . warped and perhaps even a little perverse. No doubt that old priest would call it an abomination. And her father! She winced inwardly. Best not to think of him, now.

She wondered if the crew could guess what was going on between Elaina and her. They'd been so careful to be quiet. Then Petronius had guessed everything — as he always seemed to. She couldn't dwell on how this would affect her relationship with Petronius or even the crew. She had to be Captain Mary the ruthless pirate — not Elaina's lover, Amaritta. "Tell Watu to get something to eat. I'll have a new letter for him to deliver in a little while."

"What'll it say?"

"I'll compromise with him at twenty-five thousand. Not a bloody piece of gold less." She stomped off to her cabin.

"And what if he won't pay?" he called after her.

She threw the door open. "I don't know!" she shouted over her shoulder, then slammed the door behind her.

"Amaritta!" Elaina cried.

Mary's hands were balled up into fists as she paced angrily. "Your bastard husband is quibbling with me over your ransom!" She threw the crumpled letter at her.

Elaina retrieved it and spread the missive out on the bed. Slowly, lips moving, she read it through, stopping to exclaim "Oh!" or "Liar!" occasionally. Finally, she put the letter on the table. "What do you plan to do? You know he's lying about what he can pay." She sat back down on the bed and asked in a too-casual tone, "By the bye, how much ransom did you ask?"

"Fifty thousand guineas." Mary threw herself into the rickety chair and prepared to write a new demand.

Elaina tittered nervously. "Fifty thousand! My goodness! No wonder he wouldn't pay!"

"Why? Isn't he rich?"

"Well, yes." Elaina fidgeted with her necklace and looked distraught at Mary's sharp tone. "But he'd never part with that much unless it was for his business. You'd be surprised at the modest little house we live in. Robert doesn't believe in spending large amounts on oneself."

Mary sat perfectly still, mentally calculating the money spent on Elaina's jewelry. "Then how do you explain your baubles?"

Elaina put her hand to her chest defensively. "These? They're from my parents. Robert doesn't allow me to wear such finery on the streets of the village. In

London, of course, I wore such things all the time."

Mary rubbed her forehead. "Then if I ask your husband for twenty-five thousand, he'll still say no."

"Perhaps fifteen . . . ."

"I've promised Petronius I wouldn't ask less than twenty-five, and that's what I'm going to do." She started to write the letter.

"I don't understand, dear. What has Petronius . . . isn't that the blackamoor? What has he to do with you?" Elaina began rubbing Mary's neck. "My, you're so tense!"

"He's my partner." Mary felt the soothing effects of Elaina's delicate touch loosen her knotted muscles. She finished the letter and sprinkled it with sand. Leaning back into Elaina, she said softly, "He knows about us."

Elaina abruptly stopped rubbing her shoulders. "What do you mean?"

Mary put her hand on Elaina's and said without turning around, "I mean he knows you and I are . . . lovers."

Elaina slowly ran her hands through Mary's loose long hair, bringing it back into one long strand. She leaned forward and whispered into her ear, "Then get rid of him. No one should know. He could be dangerous to you!"

Mary swung around and grabbed Elaina by the neck. She pressed her nose to Elaina's. "Don't dare meddle in what you don't know," she hissed. "I love you, but you'd better understand that what I am and the people who I'm with are all here because of my choosing. I will not change myself — or them — for you!" She tightened her grip briefly, then let go.

Elaina stumbled to the bed and burst into tears.

Mary shook off the sand, folded the letter, and melted wax onto the paper. After applying the seal, she walked to the door. "I'll be back in a little while." She turned, hand on the knob. "I do love you, you know. I didn't mean to hurt you. I guess I *am* little more than a brute." She walked out.

The next day was difficult. The two women were intensely cordial with each other, but distant. After dinner, as had been their practice before they became lovers, they read to each other. After reading two or three poems, Mary read the poem that began:

> Come live with mee, and be my love,
> And we will all the pleasures prove . . . .

When she finished, Elaina's face was wet with tears. "Christopher Marlowe is so wonderful," she whispered.

"That was 'The passionate Sheepheard to his love.'" Mary shut the book, placed it on the table and sat down on the bed. Taking Elaina's hand and pressing it to her cheek, she said, "I hate myself for what I did. Can you ever forgive me?"

"Oh, Amaritta." Elaina hugged her tightly. "I didn't mean to—to intrude into your business. Obviously I don't understand your arrangement with that man. I'm just . . . protective of you. Forgive me for a meddling fool!"

Their caresses of contrition soon turned to passion. Their lovemaking was both fiercer and more heartfelt than it had been before. In the end, they lay exhausted together.

Mary wiped the sweat from Elaina's upper lip. "You really think Robert won't pay?"

Elaina tucked a damp tendril behind Mary's ear. "I would be very much surprised if he parted with that amount, my dear." She sat back thoughtfully. "I don't think he would approve of my spending that much to ransom him."

Mary put her hands behind her head. "Then I can't let you go." She allowed herself a thin smile. "It would be very bad form if a pirate simply returned a hostage. Everyone would refuse to pay — and then where would my business go?"

Elaina drew herself up and looked down at Mary. "And where does that leave me?"

Mary traced Elaina's chin. "*'Come live with mee, and be my love.'* Stay with me, my dear. Become a pirate! We'll sail the High Seas together. You'll love it."

"Be a pirate?" Elaina's blue eyes danced. "Me?"

"Why not?"

Elaina leaned against the headboard. "But I truly believe what I told you before. That you are endangering your immortal soul when you do . . . what you do."

Mary shrugged. "My dear, I lived as a good little girl and a good wife. What did it do for me? Would my immortal soul go to Heaven if I'd married a man I didn't care for, or stayed with another who beat me? Are you happy, married to a man you hate? Do you really think God approves of that kind of arrangement? I'm not so sure the rules you live by are made to favor women. At least living the way I do, I have some say in what happens to me."

Elaina bit her finger. "I don't know. I have to think."

Mary kissed her shoulder. "You don't have to decide this minute."

The next evening, Watu returned with Dunnage's reply.

Madam,

As I stated in my previous Letter, I cannot produce the Sum you ask. I Beg you to accept 7,000 Golde Guineas. It is all I can Manage. I shall place a Bag containing the Money under the Tallest Mangrove near the Port, beneathe a Rock, Tomorrow Evening. Please see fit to release my Poore Wife at that Time.

Petronius read the letter over Mary's shoulder. "God's Teeth. What're we gonna do now?"

Mary balled up the letter. "Do? There's nothing to do, unless you want everyone in the Caribbean knowing the *Fury* can be bargained down to almost nothing!"

"You're gonna keep her on board, aren't you?"

Mary stared calmly into his questioning eyes. "Yes, I am. We'll teach her to be a pirate. Do you have a quarrel with that?"

"If that's what you want." He ran his tongue over his teeth, considering. "And Dunnage? We're just gonna sail away? Let him win?"

"Watu!" Mary called as she continued to hold Petronius's gaze.

Watu appeared at her elbow. "Yah, Cap'n?"

"Any white women die in Bridgetown while you were there?" she asked.

"Womens?" the Carib asked thoughtfully, then, "Yah. Pretty lady in casket, two day ago."

Petronius smiled. "You're up t'somethin'. What?"

"When the moon sets, take a party to the cemetery and dig that woman up. Remove her right hand and put her back. There's a big mangrove tree by the port. Underneath that will be a rock with a sack underneath it. Take it and leave the corpse's hand in its place."

Petronius chortled. "You're cruel, lass. T'do right, though, the hand should have one of Mrs. Dunnage's rings on, yes?"

She smiled. "I think we can accommodate that."

"She's really gonna sign on with us?" he asked.

"It looks like," she said over her shoulder as she headed to the cabin. She explained to Elaina that she needed the ring to fool Robert into believing that he'd caused his wife's death by his penuriousness. Mary thought it prudent not to mention the dead woman's hand.

Elaina cooperated, giving Mary an amethyst ring from her right hand. "He gave it to me for my birthday last year. I hate it."

Mary took the ring. "Have you thought about this? Are you sure you don't want to go back to Bridgeport?"

She nodded. "I'm sure. I will not go back to living with Robert again!"

"Well, we'll be away from here by morning. I'll be back soon."

Mary went out on deck and gave the ring to Petronius. "Middle finger," she said as she handed it to him.

"Nice," he said, admiring it before he slipped it on his pinkie. It stuck after the first knuckle.

Mary put her hand on his shoulder. "I don't want you or any of the crew to mention to Elaina what was done with that, all right?"

He looked to the Heavens for help. "Oh, she's gonna be a fearsome pirate!"

A few days later they were off Martinique when they came upon a French ship. The *Fury's* crew went into action. Mary had Elaina watch from the helm as she led her men onto the frigate and fought with its crew. One was killed, the others surrendered. The *Fury's* crew quickly took the valuables, including two armchairs from the captain's cabin, a barrel of fine china and a crate of beautiful crystal from the hold. Before the sun climbed very high, Mary's men were back aboard and setting their sails to catch the north wind.

That night, as they sat in the new burgundy-colored damask and rosewood armchairs, Mary asked Elaina what she thought. "You killed a man!" Elaina held her handkerchief to her lips. The dinner on the new gold-rimmed china, the fine claret in the newly acquired crystal goblet went untouched in front of her.

"I know. On the whole, I don't approve of killing. But I'm not about to let a man with a cutlass run me through just because I have certain scruples."

"Have you k-killed many people?" Elaina asked.

"More than I like to think about." Mary briefly closed her eyes. On the inside of her lids was every man she had ever slain, starting with Darius. They crowded in on her, forcing her to remember their faces, their existence prior to coming across her. She opened her eyes and tried to pretend she was calm. "Isn't this nice roast pork?"

"How can you kill and then eat as if nothing happened?"

Mary sighed and put her knife down. "Elaina, that's the nature of being a pirate. It's difficult to deal with at first. But when you realize that if you don't kill him, he'll kill you, it makes a little more sense. I try to demonstrate that my superior marksmanship makes it smart to surrender. Most people appreciate the fact that I offer them a chance to see their families again. No one really wants to die. It's been months since I had to kill anyone." The lie tasted sour in her mouth.

Tears slipped down her pretty face. "I-I can't. I c-couldn't."

Mary drank down the rest of her wine. "Perhaps we can think of something else you can do. Maybe we can teach you to be a powder monkey."

Elaina laughed in spite of her tears. "A what?"

"Usually it's a job one gives to a small boy, but I won't have children on my ship." She got up and refilled her glass. "You'd learn to fill the cannons with gunpowder and help bring the cannonballs to each gun. They're rather small spaces, but you're certainly lithe enough for the job."

Elaina dried her tears. "Well, perhaps I can try that."

Mary smiled. "Good. Now eat a little, won't you? Here we have nice china and crystal to eat off instead of that nasty old tin, and you turn your nose up at it."

"But you stole these things!"

Mary threw up her hands. "Not that argument again. You can't have it both ways, Elaina. You can't be a pirate and reject everything we do. I won't ask you to be on the raiding parties, but you must cease to bedevil me over the moral questions. Now eat your supper."

Elaina obediently took a bite of potato.

"I've got a surprise for you." Mary stepped out of the cabin and returned with a bundle. "I got some clothes for you. Your first long pants!" She shook out the shirt and breeches. "Of course, we'll have to sew up some undergarments for you. You can't wear your corset in this."

Elaina laughed and clapped her hands. They spent the evening giggling like girls and sewing up Elaina's new outfit.

Mary later wrote Briarley:

Our Ladye Gueste is trying the life of the Shipp's Crewe. So far the Results are Not Pleasing. The Stint as a Powder Monkay wasn't Successful. She hated being Covered with Dirtt and Gunne Powder, saying It stung Her Skin. I offered Her other Jobbs I thot might suit Her. She only briefly considered the Position of Look-Out. Just Looking Up at the Crowe's Nesst made Her dizzy. The Work of Calker made her delicate Handes bleed from the mere Touch of Tar. As a Sail-Mender She was a Disaster, insisting on making Tiny Little Stiches appropriate for hemming a Shift. The Work was so Fine that in the Time it took My Mann to mend a Whole Sail, She only completed Two Feet. As Cooks Assistant She was a Failyure. My Cooke begged Me to remove Her. He swore She somehow managed to burn Water. In the midst of all this, the Ladye made it Cleare to the entire Crewe She thinks Steeling and Murder are Immoral Akts and hadn't We better Start Thinking aboute another way to Make a Living?

Then there was the Strangge Incident with the Gunne Powder. Just as We were about to attakk a likely-looking French Brigantine, there was a Flash Explosion near the Cannon. No one was Hurtt, tho we were all quite startled. Perhaps the Men got careless. In consequence, We had to abandon our Prey to put out the Fire. Curiously, the Ladye went down there just as the French Shipp was sighted — a Thingg I have never knowne Her to doe. She says She saw nothing and was merely strolling the decks because She was Restless. It does make Me wonder, tho.

I feare She is too High-bourne to fitt in with suche a Group of Wilde Ruffians as Us. But It would be soe Nice to have Another Woman on Board. I doe get tired of always Looking at — and Smelling — Nothing but Men, Men, Men! I'll let You noe how this Little Experiment goes.

After a fortnight of this, Petronius stood on the poop deck with Mary, smoking his pipe. "You know, the men, they can't stand that Elaina."

She turned her back to the sea and leaned against the rail. "Tell me something I don't know."

He stared down at their wake. "She's not gonna work as a pirate."

"This has become evident."

"What're you gonna do about it?"

She studied him. "I want to keep her on board with me."

He took a deep draft from his pipe. "I don't think that's such a good idea."

"You think the crew would mutiny?"

"I think *I* would mutiny!"

"Petronius."

He took his pipe out of his mouth and pointed at her with the long stem. "No, you listen t'me!" As always, he argued — but with fire in his eyes. "Either you put Elaina ashore, or we're finished as partners. She can't pull her own weight, and she nags everybody for doin' their jobs. I won't have it."

"But —"

"No, lass," he said, replacing his pipe. "I know you've feelin's for her, but you've gotta decide what you're gonna do. Be a pirate or keep your ladyfriend — not both." He strode off toward the bow.

Mary stared out at the wake for hours. Elaina had become more important to her than she could have ever dreamed possible. She'd become a pirate for love. Could she give up being a pirate for love as well?

CHAPTER NINE

A fortnight after Elaina's assurances that she would care for "the package," the *Fury* raced through the darkness to rescue Melissa. Mary stood under the velvety black Caribbean sky with Petronius as he consulted his astrolabe. It was a small brass instrument with several movable disks that surrounded a depiction of the heavens. A center pin marked the position of the North Star. Petronius sited along the straight rule, which he'd told her was called an alidade. Then he checked their new charts on the makeshift desk, lit by the light of two lanterns.

The west wind smelled sweet, like a new-mown field after a day of rain. Mary let her body sway to the undulations of the deck as the *Fury* slid over the gentle swells. As if in agreement with her, the timbers of the ship moaned and creaked with pleasure. Rigging tapped lightly together, the same way she'd heard people clapping in time to a slow-tempo dance. There was a feeling to the night, as if wind and waves were a hand pushing them onward. The thought brought Mary back to herself. She turned to watch Petronius.

After many careful measurements, he tossed his protractor and ruling pens on the charts. Shaking his head, he grumbled, "Surely there must be a better way o' navigatin'."

"What d'you mean?" Mary asked, though she had little interest in the answer. She'd come on deck because sleep was impossible.

"More precise than this God-rottin' system we have now," he growled, not noticing her mood.

"We have the latitude. The charts show us the coasts and shoals. Your astrolabe tells you where you are."

"Yes, yes." He traced the arc of the eighteenth latitude on their map with his long index finger. "But where on this line are we exactly? Are we west or east of Saba Island? There's no way t'tell. It's the same for every ship in every ocean. It's why everyone hugs the coasts o' these islands. Few dare cross the Atlantic except at the Bahamas. It's the only way we can navigate. We're like blind men in unfamiliar rooms, feelin' our way along the walls and hopin' not t'bump into furniture or fall down the stairs."

She tried to attend to their conversation. "If they didn't hug the coasts, we wouldn't find them. Then they wouldn't be such easy pickings."

He grinned. "True. It's a help t'us." He turned serious again. "But these charts are a problem themselves. Some of 'em show islands, like Marie Gallant, toward the Atlantic, rather than the Gulf. Lotsa maps show reefs in the wrong place. That can kill you. There must be some way of takin' precise measurements o' where you are."

"Have you given it any thought?" she asked, losing interest before he spoke.

"I heard a Portugee captain speak to that, once. It has t'do with gettin' a clock that'll work at sea."

"A clock?"

"Aye," he said, warming to the subject and describing with his hands. "See, you have a clock, a chronometer, really, on shore. You set your ship's clock t'that one. Then, as you move outward from the clock on land, you can measure in minutes and seconds the difference. The . . . ."

Mary's attention drifted out to the starry sky ahead. Petronius would go on the rest of the night describing his contraption. He was fascinated with all things concerning the sea, but especially any new device that aided navigation. Mary didn't care, so long as they got where they were headed. Even when they got lost, the accidental destinations were interesting. That was how they'd discovered Cache Island. They were trying to find a cove on the southern tip of Grande Terre, Guadaloupe. Instead, they discovered what was now their island.

She'd come on deck hoping to find something to distract herself. During the last two watches she lay abed and fretted about the ship, about Trimmer, Elaina, Alphonse, Briarley — everything except the secret fear that crept away from the light of thought. Those concerns followed her on deck now as she stood pondering the need for better protection of Cache Island.

"Are you listenin' t'me?" Petronius broke into her thoughts.

She patted him on the shoulder. "I'm afraid not. I've a head full of worry tonight."

He rolled up the charts and blew out the lanterns. "I'm finished here. Why don't we get ourselves a tot?"

"A sound idea," she agreed, leading the way.

After she poured them each a brandy and they'd gotten comfortably settled, he asked, "Nervous about the rescue tomorrow?"

She avoided his eyes. "No. No, of course not. I'm sure all will go well. Just remember there's to be no bloodshed. I don't want the child seeing violence."

Petronius puffed on his pipe. "You sound as if you aren't plannin' t'come with us. I'd figgered you were gonna lead the raid."

She played with her knife on the blue leather blotter. "No. I think I'll stay aboard."

"Not anxious t'see your baby, Marie?"

She jammed the knife point squarely in the middle of the blotter. "She's hardly a baby. Melissa's a girl of six — almost seven, now."

"Um-hmm."

"I might lose my head and kill this Juan Carlo person." She took the knife out of the damaged leather and tried to seal up the gash by pushing the edges closed. "I told you, I don't want her to witness violence."

"'Specially by her mama."

Mary tested the sharpness of the blade with her thumb. "She believes Nanette was her mother. Now that mother's dead. What am I to Melissa?"

"Ah." He sighed smoke.

She shook the knife at him. "Don't you ah me!"

He grinned around the pipe stem. "Do you want her t'call you mama, or are you afraid o' just that?"

Mary tossed the knife on the desk and chewed

on a knuckle. "Not on the ship. In fact, I want you to tell the men they're to refer to me as Melissa's aunt — her *Tante*. So far as they know, that's true." She caught his humorous look and pressed on. "We have to hire someone in Jamaica to take her to Cache Island. I don't want the child on board any longer than necessary."

Petronius's pipe went out. "Why, Marie?"

For the first time, Mary looked him in the eye. How could she discuss this with him, when she wasn't really sure what she felt about the child herself? "I . . . don't want the men thinking this is some passenger ship. There's no place for children aboard. Besides, they're a rough bunch. Melissa'll pick up bad habits from them."

"And what would all the other pirates think?" he asked straight-faced.

She took a deep breath, on the verge of exploding. Finally, she let it out and said shakily, "Don't you have something to do?"

"Aye, Cap'n." He winked as he went out.

She threw her knife, just as the door shut. It stuck quivering in the upper panel, about where his shoulder would have been.

Les Cayes was still the sleepy little village Mary remembered. Huts made of palm fronds rimmed the harbor. A stick-built dock jutted out into the calm bay. Blue-white cook smoke crept along the water like a snake of air. Skinny dogs, ratty-looking chickens and naked children wandered aimlessly about. Villagers, not used to a pirate ship in their harbor, dropped whatever they were doing. They ran to the broken-down quay and stood gawking. Presently, Franz pushed his way through the crowd and got in a dinghy. He rowed out to the *Fury*.

"I hadn't expected you so soon, Cap'n," he said, after they exchanged greetings.

She lead him to the bow away from eavesdroppers. "I decided to address this personally after all. Is the package still safe?"

"Aye, and I've asked 'round. It is indeed the right one."

"Good. Tell me of these kidnappers."

He leaned against the gunnel. "They're very unpopular with the villagers here. Juan Carlo is a petty thief when he isn't selling secrets to the colonial military."

"Secrets? What about?"

"Oh, the movements of the Cimaroons. The hideouts of other scofflaws. You know the type."

Mary nodded, knowing the sort of person he was describing too well.

"Gigi's a gossip who makes sure any bad news about a neighbor is spread far and wide."

"They sound like a perfect couple." Gigi would have been a good match for Billy Lorain.

"The villagers say Melissa's been living with Juan Carlo and Gigi since Nanette died. That was a woman everyone liked. Not a few people told me how much she's missed."

"Yes, I'm sure." Mary nodded, once again saddened at the loss. She would never forget the gentleness of the Creole midwife. Nanette had accepted the burden of Melissa's rearing with what seemed like real joy. Certainly Melissa had clearly loved her. But now was not the time for mourning. "Can you lead my men to their house?"

"Aye, Cap'n. It's about a half day's march from

here." He pointed up the river.

"Fine. Why don't you get yourself some supper. We'll start at first light tomorrow." Mary dismissed Franz, then went to help Petronius arrange the rescue party.

Before the gray morning mist was burned away by the puny-looking white sun, Petronius and a small band of pirates left the *Fury* on their mission. Mary watched through her spyglass as the men landed on the beach with the help of excited villagers. Franz led them up the brown river into the wall of dense blue-green foliage where Mary's vision couldn't go. She collapsed her telescope, terribly uneasy about the raid.

Throughout the rest of the day, Mary opened her glass and stared at the blank wall of trees, even though she knew it was too early. She couldn't concentrate and questions coursed through her mind. What if the kidnappers had killed Melissa? What if the child was attached to them — called this Gigi person *Maman* and Juan Carlo *Pére*? Was snatching the child from them the right thing to do? She paced the deck, making her men nervous. *Of course it was the right thing to do! One couldn't leave the child to be brought up by criminals, could one?* Mary stopped, chilled. That thought was a little too close to home.

She started to pace again. Was Elaina that much of an improvement? After all, she was running a whorehouse. But, whose fault was that? Of course Elaina would take good care of Melissa. Teach her gentility and all the things that she herself . . . well, couldn't. Besides, Elaina loved her. She must love her child. Maybe. If she wasn't mad about being stuck on a rock in the middle of the Caribbean running a bordello. Mary's thoughts ran and stumbled over each other as the sun turned hot and yellow. It reached its zenith, then started its journey back down to its home in the sea.

To distract herself, Mary reread Alphonse's latest letter — now almost three months old — even though it hadn't been a pleasant experience the first time.

> *Cheri,*   *5 February*
> *I don't understand whyy Your Missives muste be so Cold. Am I no longer in Your Hearte? There is not the Faintest Hint of Our Passion in them. Then there is the Matter of the Code in which You command me to write. I do not understand what You are Concerned about. Surely no one cares about a Lover's Note? Then there is the problem of translating this Code of Yours. I have spent many Nights studying these Words, but I cannot unlock their Merciless Practicallity to reveal Your True Self. Do You feel Nothingg for Me, now?*
>
> *You muste forgive Me if I begin to Misdoubt Your Love. It has been almoste a Twelvemonth since We were last Together. My Dreems of You seem more real than My Memories. Whyy do You stay away? Even Your Govenor cannot remember the last time You were away for so long. What have I done to Displease You? I beg You, Cheri, find Some Wayy to show Me that You still Care. I cannot go on in this Helle of Not Knowing.*

Mary rubbed her eyes and sighed. She could just imagine him inspecting each word carefully, hoping to find some loving thought embedded in the message. In truth, there were no coded messages concealing her true feelings — she'd written none. And as he pleaded with her, she became less enchanted with him. She couldn't remember the last time she'd dreamed of him, or even thought of him unbidden by another letter. Yet, she couldn't bring herself to cut him off, as she knew she ought. He'd been an amusing lover and might still be again, whenever they got back home. Besides, the island needed a doctor. He might be tempted to leave such a remote village if she had no hold over him at all. She wished she'd put him off at a colonial-held island so he could have gone on with his life.

Mary folded the letter and replaced it in her bodice. Swinging her glass up, she scanned the foliage once more. Suddenly, she espied movement by the river. The group broke out of the trees. Petronius was in the lead, a brown-haired little girl in a plain yellow dress perched on his broad shoulder. She could see the child talking. No, Petronius's mouth also moved. They were singing! Franz, walking a step behind, was laughing at the two of them. No, the others also were singing. "Now I've seen everything," she muttered, putting the glass down, "pirates singing with infants." She swung the telescope back up and watched them walk into the village. Melissa seemed happy and plumply healthy — so the kidnappers hadn't harmed her. Mary leaned on the gunnel in relief.

She watched as the villagers helped the pirates launch the dinghy. Melissa sat on Petronius's lap, prattling excitedly, pointing at the ship, the waves, the sky. He grinned hugely, answering her and stroking her busy brown head. Mary had often teased Petronius about his far-flung brood, and he'd always shrugged it off. Somehow, it had never occurred to her that he loved his children. Yet there he was, taking on the role of parent easily, naturally. Mary felt a knot in her chest.

She had no clear idea what to do with Melissa once she was aboard. What did she know of being a mother? Collapsing the spyglass, she retreated to her cabin.

When she had proposed this rescue to the crew a month ago, she'd told the men about her "sister's girl" and how she had to be rescued. The men were keen to hunt down people who would harm a child and so the vote was unanimous. She'd cautioned them to be careful not to commit any acts of violence in front of the girl — and mind their rough language! — for fear of damaging Melissa's "delicate sensibilities." But still Mary worried that something would go wrong, that Melissa would know she was in the hands of murderous pirates. That her "aunt" was a killer.

Very soon she heard the commotion of the landing party returning. The unfamiliar trill of a child's voice mingled with the sounds of the crew boarding and calls of the men. There was no avoiding it. She had to go out. Straightening her vest, stomach aching with worry, she walked out on deck. All the men were gathered around the new arrival. Mary had to push her way into the crowd to get near the child. Mapana moved out of the way and revealed the child who stood beside her protector, Petronius, eyeing the excited crew uncertainly.

He tapped the child on the shoulder and directed her attention to Mary. He said in French, "Melissa, this is your *Tante* Marie."

"*Tante*?" the child asked.

Mary's smile was uneven. "Your mother's sister."

Before she could say anything else, Melissa broke in with, "You're wearing boy's clothes!" She giggled.

Mary saw several of her men hiding grins. Trying not to show her anger, she explained, "That's because I'm a sailor. All girls who sail wear boy's clothes."

"Can I?" Melissa asked excitedly.

"We'll see what we can find for you," Mary said. This wasn't what she'd planned to happen at all. The first thing she did was corrupt the girl's femininity! She drew in a deep breath. "Wouldn't you like your friend Petronius to show you around the ship?"

Melissa's small head bobbed assent. She asked in her lisping, Creole French, "Do I get to sail away on the big boat?"

"It's a ship, not a boat. It's called the *Fury*, and indeed you shall sail away on her." Mary felt grateful Melissa didn't seem bothered by the separation from the kidnappers. "And tonight you'll sleep in the captain's quarters."

"Oh, goody!" Melissa jumped up and down. "Gonna sail on the big ocean!" The men laughed.

"She's a natural sailor, this one," Petronius said with a grin as he led her away.

Mary bit back a retort. She swung to face her crew. "I charge all of you with watching over her. If any of you let her get hurt or slip overboard . . . ." She paused to glare about her. "There'll be dire consequences." She caught Snowby and Brepa looking at each with amused raised eyebrows. "Cast off! Set sail for Montego Bay."

The crew of the *Fury* rushed off to waiting tasks. Petronius led Melissa over to the wheel and placed her little hands on the lower spindles while he turned the ship into the wind. She gazed up at him in adoration.

A sudden sick feeling gripped Mary. She gestured for Franz to follow her to her cabin.

"Are you all right, Cap'n?" he asked as he shut the door.

"Just a headache." She opened a cask on her desk and withdrew a blue velvet purse. Smiling weakly, she placed the heavy bag in Franz's hand. "Good work. I thank you."

Eyes wide, he hefted the weight in his hand. "Cap'n, this's most generous."

She sat down. "No more than you deserve. Where will you go now?"

He smiled. "Home, eventually. There was this lass whose father wouldn't let me marry her because I was poor." He shook the purse. "This might change his mind."

Privately, Mary very much doubted his ladylove would have waited for him. "That's a fine idea. We shall miss you."

Franz started for the door, then turned back. It seemed to Mary that an avaricious light suddenly gleamed in his eye. "Cap'n, where're you going to take the child — er, package? I thought, if you'd like, I could take her for you."

Subtly, Mary moved her hand toward her knife. Perhaps she was wrong, but it could be that Franz had just hatched a plan to hold Melissa for ransom himself. "Thank you for your most kind offer. I've already made other arrangements."

"Ah, well." He hesitated a moment. She could almost hear him try other angles to his plan in his mind. He shrugged, perhaps unable to think of anything at the moment. "It's been a pleasure serving with you, Cap'n. *Adieu*."

Mary wondered if Franz was indeed gone from

her life or if he would show up again in less friendly circumstances.

Later, Petronius, Melissa and Mary sat down to dinner. Melissa perched on two ledgers stacked on the desk chair so that she could reach the table, telling Mary all that she'd seen and done on the ship. "Then Troni helped me climb up the big mast. But I didn't go very far, 'cause it's so terrible high," she finished.

"Troni?" Mary asked.

He shrugged. "Petronius is difficult for her t'say. 'Sides, Seashell and Naomi call me that." He placed a spoonful of greens in his mouth and stared back at her impassively.

"Huh." She wondered why he'd never said anything.

"Where're we goin'?" Melissa asked. "How long's it gonna take?"

"Montego Bay. That's in Jamaica." Mary planned to put into a nearby cove and take the child into town as the redoubtable Marie de Tocqueville and her niece. She'd book passage for the child and an experienced nanny to St. John's. From there, Trimmer could handle the transportation to Cache Island. "We should be there in two days if the weather holds."

Melissa finished her dinner. "Will *Tante* Gigi and *Oncle* Juan be there?"

Petronius picked up their plates. "Well, I'll leave you two t'talk. G'night." He kissed the child on the cheek.

Melissa flung her arms around his neck, nearly upsetting the plates, and loudly kissed his ear. "*Bonne nuit*, Troni!"

Mary glowered at his exit. He would leave when

it came to the sticky part. Talinn had filled her in on the raid, earlier. Her men had surprised the couple in their ramshackle hovel. It took only the barest flash of their knives and a calm threat to get the pair to release Melissa. Petronius led Melissa outside and slightly down river from the hut while the crew made an end of the kidnappers, quickly and quietly. Petronius told Melissa that Gigi and Juan Carlo had called upon the crew of the *Fury* to give her the greatest adventure of her life, since she was such a very good girl.

"*Tante* Marie?" Melissa called Mary back from her thoughts. "When will I see *Tante* Gigi?"

Mary folded her napkin and placed it on the table, stalling for time. Melissa watched her so trustingly. How would she look at her if she knew what had been done to Gigi and Juan Carlo? "Did your *Tante* and *Oncle* treat you well? I know that it must have been hard for you when Nanette . . . your mother . . . died."

Dark clouds crossed the child's brow. "*Maman* got very sick. I tried to take care of her, but she died. Then *Tante* Gigi and *Oncle* Juan camed and took me to their house." Melissa peered at Mary for a moment, then, coming to a decision, whispered, "*Tante* Gigi, she not very nice."

"No?" Mary leaned forward to hear the child better. "What does she do?"

"She yells a lot and pinches me when I don't do what she say." Melissa pouted. "Yesterday she hit me inna head with her big wooden spoon."

"So that's why you wanted to know if *Tante* Gigi would be meeting you in Jamaica?" Mary asked. Melissa nodded solemnly. Mary took the girl's little hand in hers. "Well, *Tante* Gigi and *Oncle* Juan Carlo aren't going to be taking care of you any more."

"Promise?" Melissa whispered.

"I promise," Mary whispered back.

Melissa leapt into Mary's arms so forcefully she was knocked back in her chair. "*Merci*, oh *merci!*" she cried. "Will you and Troni take care of me now?"

For the briefest of moments, Mary pictured the crew of the *Fury* with their tiny pirate comrade, a long dagger clutched in Melissa's tiny fist, sailing the Windward Isles. "No, my little dear. I'm going to send you to someone who will love and care for you as well as your own mother could. Better, maybe." Better, for sure!

"Will you and Troni come with?"

"No, little one." Mary was touched by Melissa's instant devotion. It would make it that much easier for her to take to Elaina. "Now, it's time for bed. We'll talk more about this tomorrow."

Melissa slid off Mary's lap and struggled out of her dress, with help. Her shift was worn and had rents in it. It was also too small. Mary would have to repair it as best she could before sending the child to Elaina. She tucked the girl into the big marriage bed. Melissa looked trustingly up at her with eyes so like Edmund's, brown with flecks of gold resembling dawn's light on morning waves. Otherwise, Melissa looked like Mary's father, who surely was dead and buried by now. The idea of Melissa as somehow a ghost of people she'd known made Mary shiver.

She kissed the girl on the cheek. "*Bonne nuit*, little dear."

"*Bonne nuit.*" Melissa stifled a yawn. Mary turned down the lamp and started to leave the room. "No!" The child sat up. "Don't go!"

"But Melissa . . . ."

She started to weep. "Please?"

Mary opened her mouth to argue, but what was the point? She'd just snatched the child away from everything she knew. Of course she was afraid. Besides, for these next few days, Melissa would be in her care. For a little while, Mary could pretend she lived that elusive normal life with home, hearth, and child — at least within the confines of this cabin. She slipped off her boots and climbed in beside her daughter. "Better?"

Melissa snuggled in between Mary's arm and side, her head on Mary's shoulder. A perfect fit. Mary fought tears. Almost instantly, the child was asleep. Would Melissa take as well to Elaina? Would Elaina hold her just so? Would it, too, be a perfect fit — some sort of trick of female anatomy that allowed any child to fit any woman? Mary checked herself. Such thoughts would only tempt her to madness in the days to come.

More important to consider how Elaina would take to this new imposition. She told Mary once that she'd always wanted children and was disappointed with Dunnage all the more when any failed to appear. That didn't mean, however, that she wanted Mary's child as a surrogate. As it was, only the love of her had kept Elaina on Cache Island, in charge of that whorehouse. Mary rubbed her eyes. Why hadn't she let Elaina do something more respectable? Why make her run a cathouse? *A test*, whispered her inmost self. *If Elaina would so let herself be debased, then truly she must love me. Do anything for me.* But the "breaking" of Elaina had cost so much. Nothing had been quite the same between them since.

After Mary'd had her talk with Petronius, things seemed somehow different between the two women. Especially at dinner that night, it was as if Elaina could somehow hear Mary's tortured thoughts. By some perversity, she was dressed in her funereal bombazine. Elaina looked incredibly lovely and fragile. She gave Mary furtive, questioning glances, but didn't speak. Mary chewed her squab mechanically, tasting only sand. When they finished, Elaina cleared the plates away and poured more wine for the two of them.

"Elaina . . . ." Mary stared into the depths of her wineglass.

"Yes?" She smoothed out her skirt innocently.

Mary drank down most of the wine. "My dear . . . I think, that is, it seems evident that — well, that you don't make a very good pirate."

Elaina looked down, but didn't really seem all that abashed. "Perhaps not," she whispered.

"I find myself faced with a very important decision," Mary struggled on.

Elaina put her hands to her cheeks. "You're not renouncing your piracy?"

Mary studied her. What would make her jump to such a conclusion? And was the dismay on Elaina's face real or counterfeit? "No, my dear. I'm not."

Elaina looked genuinely confused. "Then whatever is the matter?"

"The time has come for us to part ways." Mary felt as if someone had punched her in the stomach.

"No!" Elaina wailed and threw herself at Mary's feet, her head in her lap.

Mary stroked Elaina's golden hair, fighting tears herself. "I'll pay your passage to England or France . . . or wherever you care to go."

"No," Elaina sobbed. "I want to be near you."

"Perhaps you'd prefer Jamaica or one of the American colonies."

Elaina looked up at Mary, tears streaking her face. "Will you come with me?"

"No," Mary whispered. "My life is that of a pirate captain. I won't give it up." She saw a light go out in Elaina's eyes and felt its loss as if the sun was never to shine again. "Nor can I visit you once you're settled in a nice respectable village." She tried a smile. "What would your new neighbors think?"

Elaina pushed herself up and glared at Mary, hands balled up into fists. "Don't dare to make jokes. You're tearing my heart out!"

Mary took Elaina's fist and pressed it to her cheek. "My love, I'm trying to bear up, just as you are."

"How can you drop me off in a port and never see me again?" Her tears started again. "Do I mean that little to you?"

Mary pulled Elaina down onto her lap and took her face into her hands. "I've never loved anyone the way I do you, my dearest. But you can't stay aboard the *Fury* — we both know that."

"I don't! I don't see why we can't stay together!" She turned her head away.

Mary sighed. "If you stay aboard, my crew will mutiny. They are pirates and expect . . . a certain behavior from everyone. Including their captain."

"So in order not to disappoint a bunch of murderous thieves, you'll put me off?"

"I'm a pirate, Elaina." Mary shut her eyes in exasperation. "I cannot and will not change who I am."

"I'll n-never see you again?" Elaina's tears washed down her cheeks, staining her dress.

Mary wiped them away. "That does seem a harsh sentence for us, doesn't it?" Elaina nodded miserably. An idea occurred to Mary. "Have I ever told you about Cache Island?"

"No," Elaina said shakily.

"Cache Island is a place we found almost three years ago," Mary explained. "The little town there has grown quite a bit. It's now a place that others stop by to do business."

"Hmm," Elaina pretended interest.

Mary smiled. "Bear with me, love. You could live there, in the town. You could have your own business. The *Fury* stops there every few months. We could see each other regularly."

Elaina stared. "I could have my own business?"

Mary squeezed her waist. "Yes, why not? I would finance the venture. We'd be partners."

Elaina slid off Mary's lap. "What's the name of this town?"

"Mary's Town."

Elaina giggled. "How fitting!"

Mary found herself blushing. "I didn't name it."

Elaina got up to pour them both more wine. "What kind of businesses are needed in Mary's Town? A chandlery? A good inn?"

"Well," Mary said, shifting uncomfortably, "first you must know that most of the people who come to the island are pirates."

Elaina inclined her head. "So they have concerns other than regular ships."

Mary nodded. "Indeed. In fact, the business I was thinking you might run was a . . . a bawd house."

"What!?" Elaina put the glasses down on the table with a clatter. Red wine sloshed over her fingers.

Mary raised her hands to forestall Elaina's objections. "I know, I know. It's hardly the sort of thing you were thinking of. But it's something I've been pondering for some time."

Elaina threw herself into her chair. "A house of assignation? I think you're quite mad!"

Mary smiled wanly and reached out to take Elaina's hand. "Perhaps. But hear me out. There's a brothel there — a miserable place. The girls are over-worked, treated roughly, and disease-ridden. Last year one poor girl hanged herself rather than continue on."

"How horrid," Elaina gasped.

"I had in mind a place much more refined." Mary dropped Elaina's hand, got up and began to pace. "You're certainly the most elegant person I've ever met. My thought was that the girls would be well-dressed and clean. The premises would be pleasant — like a respectable home. Gentlemen would be expected to behave themselves, and would be treated like honored guests no matter their color or profession."

"But . . . but what would I . . . ?" Elaina objected.

"You," Mary said, wagging a finger, "would be the Grande Dame of the house. You wouldn't have to take any clients. Your job would be to manage the girls and entertain the gentlemen while they're in the parlor. In many respects, you're already familiar with most of the duties this job would require."

Elaina's eyes seemed ready to start out of her head. "I beg your pardon!"

Mary laughed and drank some of her wine. "It's not as far a stretch for you as you think. You're used to entertaining your husband's friends and business asso-ciates, yes?"

"Y-yes," she replied, quaffing her wine shakily.

Mary pressed on, "You managed the servants, the cook, the upstairs and downstairs maids, the laun-dress. Yes?"

"Well, of course, but — " Elaina started to object.

Mary shrugged. "It's the same thing. The only difference is that you have rather a lot of upstairs maids — whom you and you alone would select. You'd also handle the accounts, the money — most of which you'd get to keep."

"The money would be mine," Elaina said slowly.

Mary watched a familiar light appear in her eyes and smiled. "After expenses — paying the girls, buying liquor, laundry, et cetera — yes, it will all be yours."

Elaina sat blinking at Mary. "You said we'd be partners."

"At some future time, I may ask to be given a share of the vast fortune you acquire, but let's not worry about that right now, shall we?"

"You'd come see me from time to time?"

Mary took Elaina's hand and kissed it. "Every few months, love. I promise."

"I'll miss you terribly." Elaina's tears started again.

"And I you." Mary leaned forward and kissed her. Soon they lost themselves in their passion.

After explaining the plan to Petronius, the preparations went forward to buid Mayhew House — for that was the name Elaina chose, despite Mary's worries that her husband would catch wind of the name.

"How would he ever connect such a place with me?" Elaina asked with a wry chuckle.

Mary wrote Ethan Trimmer to arrange the necessary funds, the bulk of which would go to the building of a grand house. Then there was the hiring of twelve French "ladies" from Martinique to consider. Though Trimmer would chose them, Madam Mayhew would of course, have final say. The furnishing of the house was taken care of by the providential boarding of a Viennese merchant ship. For once Elaina only mildly objected. The tall, gilt pier mirrors and exquisite mahogany salon furniture, she said, were just perfect for the ambience Elaina wished to create. She even wondered openly — though it was phrased as a purely hypothetical question — if Mary ever came across large chandeliers.

Elaina stayed aboard the *Fury*, using Henri — her new and entirely trustworthy messenger — to ferry messages between Cache Island and St. John's. Mary, with Petronius' help, taught Elaina the finer points of bookkeeping. She was so consumed by preparations that she didn't even trouble the *Fury's* crew as they went about their business. Multiple drawings of the house — contributed by Petronius as well as Mary and Elaina — were hung on the wall of the captain's cabin. Trimmer had sent fabric swatches and wallpaper samples from his vast supplies. These Elaina draped over everything, making it look like a millinery shop instead of a pirate captain's cabin.

After almost six months, the *Fury* hove into Cache Island's harbor. People thronged the wharf, waving and cheering as the crew threw mooring lines to willing, helpful hands. Mary dismissed the crew for extended shore leave — possibly a month, she said. The men happily debarked to their waiting families.

Mary and Elaina spent all their time applying the finishing touches to the stunning house. Mary was delighted that Briarley had made sure the plantation-style manor was situated both for the view and to catch the northern breezes to keep the interior cool. There was even a widow's walk with a brass telescope on the roof.

Elaina interviewed each of the "ladies" under

Mary's watchful eye. Two, whom Mary would have hired, after Elaina's careful questioning revealed themselves as thieves. Another one cheerfully admitted having killed her procurer. Although Mary sympathized, she escorted her out of the house. Finally, Elaina settled on twelve pretty, well-behaved girls.

The relationship between Elaina and Mary intensified. Without the constraints of the crew watching her every move, Mary was free to be Elaina's Amaritta. She began to let Elaina make all the decisions. It was restful having someone else take the lead. Soothing to be the follower. They spent delightful hours of lovemaking in the heat of the afternoon. Elaina's sweaty body became Mary's happily conquered land, endlessly to be explored. In turn, Mary felt herself a captured prize of Elaina's, constantly cherished and fondled. It was a delight to be so petted, so thoroughly possessed. There were some days when the thought of her years as Captain Mary seemed an odd sort of dream.

Finally, the preparations were completed. Mayhew House opened its doors to an admiring public. Mary dressed in an elaborate naval uniform sewn up for the occasion — including a new pair of patent leather boots Elaina ordered made for her. Mary longed for her old battle-scarred calfskin boots. The new ones pinched in the heel, making it uncomfortable to walk far.

Mary was also the only one armed, since weapons were against house rules. She toasted the new venture, only half-humorously warning that uncivil behavior would be rectified by a visit from the *Fury*.

The guests danced to an orchestra Elaina brought in from Martinique. Petronius arrived dressed in an elegant, long coat of yellow damask and lavender hose. He danced with his stunning wife, Seashell. She was a woman of sensuous curves and skin the color of dark honey, made all the lovelier in her billowing, lemon silk gown. Seashell's face was like a Roman marble of a classic beauty: a high, intelligent forehead; almond-shaped dark-brown eyes with long black lashes; high cheekbones divided by a perfectly proportioned small nose; and a mouth that looked as if it laughed more often than frowned.

All the *Fury's* crew and two ship-loads of privateers appeared; the *Fury's* crew with their women, the privateers escorting the "ladies" of Mayhew House and other establishments. Both pirates and privateers were dressed as wealthy merchants and tried to behave as landed gentry, but they were clumsy in the role, stepping on each others's feet and bumping into everyone during the dance. Yet, they kept their good humor and forgave transgressions that would have earned the offender a knife in the stomach just a month before. The party wore on until the sun rose out of the Atlantic, golden and promising.

In the afternoon, Mary awoke next to Elaina in their beautiful mahogany canopy bed. The warm Trade Winds billowed out the gauzy white drapes over the open porch doors. Elaina smiled dreamily. Mary kissed her, then got up.

Elaina stretched languidly. "Where are you going?"

Mary went to the wardrobe and brought out her recently laundered pirate gear. Pulling on her breeches, she said, "It's time to set sail, my love. Pirates must go to sea."

"Oh, no!" Elaina tumbled out of bed and hugged Mary tightly. "Please, not yet!"

"I'm afraid I must, dear." Mary kissed her.

"You'll be very busy with the place, now. It shouldn't be too awful for you."

Elaina started to cry. "I was hoping you'd stay."

"You know I can't." Mary stroked her hair, then went to hunt up her old boots, which someone had stuffed far back in a dark corner of the wardrobe.

Elaina sank onto the bed. "I shall miss you terribly."

Mary sat down next to her and pulled on the cracked, stained boots. "I shall miss you too, my love. We'll be back in a couple of months. I bet you'll be too busy to know I'm gone."

Elaina hugged herself. "You must think I don't care for you at all, then."

"Oh, darling," Mary said. She wiped away Elaina's tears and gave her a little squeeze. "Try to be a little happy. Please? If we can't sail together, at least be here for me when I get back."

Elaina dutifully kissed Mary's cheek. "That I can do."

"*Au revoir*, my dear." Mary kissed Elaina long and slowly. Then rose and walked out of the room without looking back.

Aboard the *Fury*, she gave orders for her slightly hung-over crew to cast off. Mayhew House sat on its hill, gleaming white. On the roof stood Elaina, still in her white nightshift with a bright red shawl wrapped around her. She didn't move when Mary waved up at her. Mary knew she was crying. As the *Fury* broke free of Cache Island's protective reef and caught the first winds off the Caribbean in her sails, Mary lost sight of the house. She felt as if her insides were turning to stone. The world seemed to dim.

"You all right?" Petronius asked quietly behind

her.

Mary balled up her hands and straightened. "Set sail for Puerto Rico. I hear there's a big gold shipment coming from Spain, and I bet we can catch her."

Melissa stretched and sighed beside Mary, breaking the spell of remembrance. She stroked her daughter's baby fine hair and prayed she didn't fall too much in love with Melissa before she had to give her up again — just as she had to give up everyone she cared about.

CHAPTER TEN

It was Madam de Toqueville who stepped out of the open ebony carriage in front of the King's Slipper in St. John's, Antigua, but it was Captain Mary's nose that sniffed the air. The wind swept in from the southwest — rather an uncommon direction — and swirls of dust danced in the road. There was a heavy reek of decay from the salt marshes overhanging the town. She felt a prickly sensation between her shoulder blades. Perhaps it was the uncanny wind that made people stop and stare at her all the way from the docks. No one would meet her eye. Something was afoot.

The inn's stiff-backed, overdressed doorman seemed less obsequious than usual. From the corner of her eye, she caught the young black footman making rude gestures at her back. He was new, and she didn't want to cause a scene, but she was going to talk to Mr. Deal about this directly.

She entered the darkened, gold-plush interior.

Mr. Deal glowered at her from behind the massive mahogany reception desk. Odd, very odd indeed. "Good morning," Mary said, pretending calm as she made her way to the banquette.

"Madam de Tocqueville," Mr. Deal said flatly. "What may we do for you today?"

Mary blinked a few times. Something was indeed amiss. "I've come to your fair establishment to stay a few days. I do hope my rooms are available."

Mr. Deal closed the guest register with an echoing slap in the still room. "I'm afraid we won't be able to accommodate you, Madam."

Mary sniffed. "Oh? Can you afford to turn away your wealthiest patron? Business must be very good indeed."

Deal winced at her tone. It was evident he didn't relish losing her custom, but he squared his jaw. "I'm sorry, Madam. This inn will no longer be open to you."

Mary flexed her left thigh, testing the position of the throwing knife there. Would she have to use it on this little man? *Hold,* she cautioned herself. *Don't make a move until you discover what he or anyone else on this wretched island knows.* "Pray tell, Mr. Deal," she said, laughing lightly, "whyever would you insult me so?"

"Surely you've heard of your uncle's disgrace. Barbuda isn't that far away."

"I'm afraid I've been traveling extensively the last few months," Mary explained. "I've come direct from Jamaica. What has occurred?"

Deal's weasel-like face took on the self-satisfied smirk of one about to impart very bad news to the unsuspecting. "Your uncle, Mr. Trimmer, was discovered to be having . . . improper relations with a young boy. A very young boy." He licked his lips excitedly.

"Oh, my heavens," Mary exclaimed, clapping a lace handkerchief over her mouth in mock horror. *Damn the fool! He'll bring us all down!*

"Once he was imprisoned," Deal continued, obviously enjoying his role, "other children — all boys — came forward and told of their trysts with your uncle."

The staff drew near to hear the tale. They watched Mary's face with hungry attention.

Mary whispered, playing to the crowd, "I must sit. I feel so faint!" Gratefully, she sank into a chair someone provided. "What . . . " she paused dramatically, as if overwhelmed, "what's been done about my repulsive uncle?"

"We took care a 'im, we did!" the bellboy broke in.

Deal glared at the lad, who stepped back to his former position. He continued, "As I said, he'd been placed in jail, after the initial discovery. However, the testimony from the other boys rather inflamed the town."

The charwoman snorted. "We took care a 'im proper!"

Deal cleared his throat angrily at her. "As I said, tempers were rather hot. Mr. Trimmer was removed from his cell by angry citizens."

The doorman chortled. "Of which you was a part!"

Deal glared, straightened his cuff and opened his mouth to begin again. Before he could utter a sound, the bellboy broke in:

"Took 'im to the town square, we did!" The young man's face flushed with importance and the excitement of that day. "Then we circled 'im 'round and stoned 'im! Ta death!"

Mary sobbed for the crowd. "Horrible! Horrible!"

"Aw, he deserved it, lady!" the chambermaid snarled.

"Oh, yes," she agreed tearfully. "I meant how horrible it was, what . . . what he did." She clutched the handkerchief to her face. What happened to the bank? If Padgett was still keeping things going, maybe she and Petronius could piece back together the whole scheme by themselves.

"And when we was through," a drudge said, "we went ta his house and we burnt the unholy place!"

"Then we burnt down the bank, fer good measure!" the cook growled. "I hear tell Trimmer had a torture room upstairs where he held those boys!"

"I hear it was a temple ta Satan 'isself!" the charwoman added.

Mary felt icy tingles down her arms and legs. *We're sunk! Our entire fortune wiped out! A hold full of goods, worthless without Trimmer and his connections.* Her stomach churned. "I think I'm going to be sick," she whimpered.

The doorman used his foot to push a reeking brass spittoon over to her chair.

"'Ere now! Don't be makin' a mess on my floor! I just finished cleanin' up!" the charwoman snapped.

Mary asked with a dramatic sniffle, "Mr. Deal, what has become of the excellent Mr. Padgett and his clerks. Surely the town hasn't held them liable for the . . . the sins of my abominable uncle." Perhaps Padgett had escaped and saved the records from the fire. By Hades, if he had, she'd set him up on another island in style.

"Mr. Padgett apparently shot himself in remorse for his choice of employer," Deal said unctuously.

The doorman laughed cruelly. "Or his house-keeper took care o' him!"

"The clerks," Deal said loudly as he glared down the doorman, then continued in a normal tone, "prudently acquired passage aboard the next ship off-island. There are some who suspect they may have helped Mr. Trimmer prey upon the lads of this town."

We are well and truly scuppered. Now what to do? She assessed the staff. They looked like drooling wolves circling in for the kill, but someone was missing. Where was Petronius's Naomi? "I don't know what to say," she said tearfully. "He was always so kind to me."

The chambermaid tittered. "Yes, well, 'e didn't like girls, did 'e now?"

"I'm afraid you're not welcome here any longer, Madam de Tocqueville." Deal seemed delighted with his self-importance.

The doorman grabbed her arm roughly and pulled her to her feet. The chair was snatched away. "I'll see her out."

Outside, Mary shook her arm out of his grasp. She noticed her trunks stacked in the street. Already they had acquired a film of dust from passing traffic. "Call a carriage to take me to the dock."

"Too right I will." He blew his whistle.

As the rig approached, she asked, "What became of the Negress who's been my maid when I've stayed here? I didn't see her in that *rabble* Mr. Deal is pleased to call a staff. Naomi. That was her name. What's become of her?"

The doorman shrugged. "You know nigras. They can't stand to work. Always disappearing." The carriage stopped in front of Mary. Its big bays stamped their feet as if impatient to move on. Throwing her bags haphazardly into the carrier, the footman openly leered at her.

The doorman chuckled darkly as he shoved her inside the carriage. "Though I ain't seen her since we took care o' Trimmer. Maybe she had something to do with him, huh? Nigra girls and little boys — it'd figure!" He yelled up to the driver, "Take 'er to the dock, Zeb. Put 'er on the first ship that comes to port."

When they were a few feet away from the inn, Mary leaned forward and said to the driver, "Take me by the Antigua Security Bank first."

The driver barked a laugh and flicked his whip over the horses's backs. Presently they slowed in front of what was left of the bank. Charred brick walls jutted skyward like burnt, pleading fingers. There was no fancy facade, no oak door with brass filigree fittings. All was as black and empty as Mary felt. *Stupid, stupid bastard!* By Hades, how was she to fix this mess? "When did all this happen, driver?"

He shook the reins and got the horses walking again. "'Bout a month, month an' a half ago, I guess." The driver directed the horse down a side street. Here, again, was a burned building. This time there was nothing above ground. The ornamental iron fence lay on the ground, protection from nothing. Mary hardly looked at the remains of the house where she'd dined so often. Her mind was too busy considering and rejecting plans to salvage her ruined financial empire.

"A evil man, your h'uncle," the driver observed.

"May he rot in Hell," Mary replied wholeheartedly. "I thought you were taking me to the dock, driver?"

The half-day passage back to Barbuda was uneventful. Mary stood at the bow, glaring at the sea the whole time. When they reached port, she spotted Mapana, whom she'd posted in Codrington, posing as a transient dock worker. Mary saw him pale when he spotted her debarking. She'd assigned him the task of waiting for Trimmer's agent. Mary knew that Mapana would think her presence so soon could only mean trouble — and he'd be right. She was pleased to note, however, that he kept his wits about him and didn't approach the elegantly dressed woman who went into the nearby tavern.

She sat in the dark, untidy public house with its uncouth patrons — a far cry from the hushed, genteel interior of Mr. Deal's establishment. The Barbuda tavern habitués ogled her, unsure how to treat an obvious woman of means. Their distance suited Mary well. She nursed her sherry and brooded.

By full dark, the bar's patrons had become quite rowdy and involved with their own concerns. Mary laid a few coins next to her glass and slipped out into the night. She thanked her luck there was no moon. Quickly, she walked to the pier. "Mapana! Mapana?" she hissed.

A glimmer from a covered lantern answered her. She clambered down the ladder, struggling with her skirts, and into the waiting dinghy. As soon as she was seated, he cast off and rowed her to Starfish Cove where the *Fury* lay hidden. As she struggled — damning her skirts again — up the cargo net to the deck of her ship, Talinn saw her. "Captain!"

The cloth of her skirt had tangled in the rope interstice of the net. "Don't just stand there. Haul me up!" she snarled. He tugged at her arm until there was an abrupt ripping sound. She struggled free of the shredded fabric and stood on the deck in her petticoat. "Get rid of that," she ordered and strode to her cabin.

Petronius was sitting at the desk, going over the accounts when Mary came in. "What're you doin' back so soon?" Then, eyeing her disheveled costume, he asked anxiously, "Are we found out?"

"Oh, much, much worse." She poured herself a large glass of whiskey, thought better of it, tilted back her head and upended the bottle. Then she threw herself into a chair.

Petronius drank half of her abandoned whiskey. "How bad is it, Marie?"

"We're ruined, Pet. It's all gone!" She took a swig from the bottle again. "Trimmer got caught playing with one of his boys. The town went crazy. Stoned him to death. Burned down the bank. Probably murdered Padgett as well."

"S' Blood!" he moaned as he sank back into his chair. "The records? The contacts?"

"Gone," she whispered hoarsely.

"I told you not t'trust that worm!" He threw the half empty glass into the corner. It shattered with a loud crash in the small cabin.

Mary stared at the fragments thoughtfully. "It doesn't matter who was right or wrong now. We have to figure out what to do next."

"There wasn't a way you could stay there? See if you could figure out who was workin' for him?" Petronius demanded.

"Madam Marie de Tocqueville has been asked not to return." She waved her bottle emphatically. "They want no more to do with Trimmer or his associates. Hell, they ran his clerks out of town!" She took a deep breath, dreading what the impact of her next statement would be. "It's possible they ran Naomi out as well."

He sat up. "Naomi? What about her?"

"She wasn't at the inn." Mary slugged down more whiskey, enjoying the cleansing fire in her belly and the numbness that replaced fear. "Doorman said he hadn't seen her since they killed Trimmer."

He slammed his fist into the desk. "God's Teeth! If they hurt her, I'll burn the whole damned island down!"

"Pet —"

"Don't get in my way, woman!" Petronius got up and paced around the room. "We have t'go t'Antigua. I have t'find out what happened to her!"

Mary felt weariness beyond measure. "What is it you want me to do? Go in with cannons blazing and take over the town? It's a British colony! We wouldn't last a month in these waters if we did something like that. They'd have every warship in the fleet after us."

He shook his head. "No. We'll anchor in a back cove. I'll take the dinghy into town, ask slaves and freemen about her. They'll know."

She wished he would shut up and leave her alone. What she most wanted was to finish the bottle, then slip into a deep and dreamless sleep. "Pet, we have to deal with a hold full of cargo. We've got to work out a new system for selling our goods."

Petronius snatched the bottle out of her hand, dragged her upright by her pearl necklace and stuck his face into hers. "We'll sort that out after I find out about Naomi. Hear?"

It looked as if he had four angry hazel eyes. "Aye, aye, Cap'n," she whispered. He let loose of her and stomped out of the cabin. Mary took another draft off the bottle. She felt as if she were falling down a deep dark shaft, and there was no end in sight.

Two nights later, the *Fury* lay in the waters north of Antigua. Mary spent the entire day brooding. It didn't help that Paolo had delivered letters to her. Neither of her lovers was happy with her. Alphonse's was more of the same. But Elaina's note seemed distant, remote, cold.

> *My Deare Amaritta,*   *2 August*
> *All is welle here. The Package arrived safeley, save for a Situation that called for the Particular expertise of a Gentleman in the Harbour. The Difficulty soon passed and Life is back to Normal.*
> *There is very little to tell. Each Day is muche the same. We doe welle enuff with out the Founder of Our Isle. The Sun rises and sets. Creatures are born and die. People come and goe.*
> *Write if You find Some Thingg Interesting to Say.*

Mary read the lines six times over, shocked at their tone every time. They must go home. And soon. She had to find out what was wrong.

By the time Petronius walked into the cabin, only one candle was burning, and that was guttering. She sat staring at the wall. "Marie?" he whispered.

For a moment, she didn't move or answer. Finally, she stirred, as if after a long sleep. "That you, Pet?" Her voice was husky. "Find her?"

He sank into the opposite chair. "I found her'n lost her."

Mary lit another candle off the dying one and poured them both a drink. "It looks as if we've come upon some rocky shoals."

"Aye." He sighed and drank down the whiskey.

"So what happened?"

He lit his pipe slowly. "I snuck onto the island yesterday, early. Hunted up all the Africans I could and asked 'em about Naomi. Found out pretty quick she run off with the kids. But I had to hide every time a white showed up. It took forever. Finally, late in the day, a friend o' hers told me she was at her Pa's ol' shack in the swamp, off Johnson's Point. He's an ol' hermit. I didn't even know he was still alive." Petronius paused for a moment, smoking thoughtfully. "Anyway, I spent most o' the evening begging her t'come away with me. Said she won't do it. Won't take the children back to St. John's. Won't come on the *Fury*. Won't go t'Cache Island where I'd build her a house big as Seashell's. Told me she'd seen enough of the so-called civilized white folks in the world. Long as she lives, the sight o' that man bein' stoned t'death gonna always be in her mind."

Mary sighed. "I'll believe that."

He leaned forward and jabbed the air with his pipe. "Then, she said she wants me t'give up piratin' and take up fishin' with her father."

Mary laughed tiredly. "Oh, that must've gone over well."

He drained his drink. "When I said no, she told me t'leave and not come back. Said she didn't want a pirate as her children's father. Can you believe that?" He got up and poured himself another.

"Look, I'm sorry about Naomi, but we have to talk about what we're going to do now."

He sat back down. "I don't know. Maybe she's right. Maybe we should stop piratin'. Settle down."

"What? And take up fishing?"

"No," he grumbled. "Do somethin' else. We have Cache Island."

"And become a respectable lady and gentleman? We'd both go crazy inside a fortnight."

"I didn't plan t'be a pirate all my life, Marie! I wanted t'enjoy that money, sometime. Thousands of pounds disappear — poof!" He threw his hand up.

She rubbed her forehead. "Well, we aren't that rich anymore. We have to put together a new way of selling our goods and investing the money — this time with someone we can absolutely trust."

"Who might that be?" he snorted. "I don't trust anybody, anymore!"

She slowly spun her glass around. "The only thing I can think to do is make Cache Island our new base of operations. I know it's dangerous to put all our interests in one place — but there isn't anyplace else that we can control as thoroughly as that island."

"Who's gonna be our agent?" He shook a finger at her. "And don't give me Elaina Dammit Mayhew!"

"No. Elaina's clever, but I don't want her involved in this. Besides, she'd have the same problems I used to have." Mary felt that Elaina had too much control over her now.

He got up to pace. "Then who? I don't know anybody on the island who's all that smart with business. Half the men you start with stores go outta business in a few months or wander away."

A headache stabbed at her right eye. "I don't know, Pet. I think we need to go to Cache Island and see what we can put together. Maybe you and I can run things as long as we parcel bits out to several different people."

"How do we invest? That's what got us involved with that insect Trimmer in the first place."

She closed her eyes, weary with the same argument she'd been having with herself all day.

Petronius snapped his fingers and sat up. "Wait! Why not use that doctor of yours as a front?"

"I don't think he knows anything about investing."

"No, no! We'd tell him what t'do." Petronius sat back and pinched his lips in thought. "He wouldn't cause suspicions. He's just your average French rich man, lookin' t'increase his family fortune. God's Teeth, we could even use that big planter's bank in Jamaica with Coulances as our front."

Mary shifted uncomfortably. "I don't want him to live clear up in Jamaica. I like where he is now."

"So we take him up t'Jamaica occasionally and he stays in the damn harbor!" Petronius sat on the edge of his chair. "And isn't that gettin' old? How long're you gonna keep that poor man on the *Pearl*? He's been there over a year. And it's almost a sixmonth since the French stopped showin' up at the island."

"I don't know." Mary rubbed her eyes in frustration. She still didn't want to let go of Alphonse.

"'Sides, we can't afford the *Pearl* right now. Not with all our money burned up. He'll have t'live on the island, Marie."

"Fine," Mary retorted. "We'll do it your way. Everything I set up goes to Hell, anyway!" She stood with her back turned to him, fists bunched on the desk.

Petronius put his hands on her shoulders. "Don't take on like that, lass," he said into her ear.

"That's all past now. We gotta look t'the future. Let's go t'Cache Island and start fresh, huh?"

She nodded and put her hand on his. "All right, Pet."

CHAPTER ELEVEN

The *Fury* sailed into Cache Island's protected harbor as the gusty wind shifted to the south. Even though there were no clouds on the horizon, the abrupt change in wind direction worried Mary. Anxiously, she surveyed the village that had sprung up to support her ship. Mary's Town seemed tranquil enough. It had doubled in size since she'd last been there. Houses and shops crowded one another at the wharf's edge. More crept up the gentle slope of the extinct volcano with its tree-filled gaping crater. It was nearly a legitimate city now, almost as large as St. John's.

Standing proudly on the western side of town was the white confection of Mayhew House. Over on the northern end was the smaller — but not by much — more formal-looking plantation house belonging to Seashell. The *Pearl* sat at anchor near the mouth of the harbor, ready for a quick escape, should the need arise. It was neatly painted and looked shipshape. At the dock were two foreign sloops, a four-masted barque and a fishing smack. The bigger ships probably belonged to traders or pirates — it didn't matter — they were custom for her town. It brought her a great deal of satisfaction to know that these people were here because of the *Fury*.

All of the people Mary most loved were here. It frightened her for a moment, to think how vulnerable she was. The incident with Trimmer made her realize how easy it was to lose a great deal very suddenly. How could she protect Elaina, Melissa, Alphonse, or even Mary's Town itself? She'd have to install a garrison on the island if they were going to concentrate all their trade here. That meant hiring a mercenary force from somewhere. Very expensive. How many men at arms were enough to protect her island from her fellow pirates, privateers and busybody foreign navies? Bloody Hell! She was beginning to think like a governor.

Work at the new stone quay ceased as the laborers stopped to wave and cheer. People came running out of their homes and shops to greet the *Fury*. *This is home.* The realization brought her close to tears. There were many familiar faces in the crowd, but even more people she'd never seen before. She wanted to stay and come to know them all.

"Look! There's Seashell!" Petronius pointed to his lovely lady, dressed in blue calico. She held a child who looked to be over a year old and stood next to a gangly, handsome-looking lad. "God's Teeth! Is that my Virgil beside her? He's gonna be an oak!" He elbowed Jacoby next to him. "There's my baby girl! She's beautiful!"

All around her, Mary heard her men pointing

out friends and loved ones to each other. It'd been too long since they'd been home. Now they'd come to stay. She scanned the crowd. Elaina wasn't there, nor was Melissa. Would the child recognize her? They were probably busy at Mayhew House, taking care of the men from the foreign ships.

"Petronius," she called.

He was leaning over the gunnel, waving to his son. With a smile, he returned to her side. "Aye, Cap'n?"

"Set two on watch. Declare shore leave for the rest of the crew. But I want everyone on board tomorrow, first light. We've unloading and repairs to deal with."

"Aye, Cap'n." He turned and started directing the crew.

As Mary walked down the gangplank into her town, people stopped and shook her hand or doffed their hats to her. Most she hadn't met before, but they knew her and acknowledged they owed their livelihoods to her. It was a heady feeling, this respect from strangers. She'd grown so used to the fear, coerced obedience or scorn she experienced as a pirate, it seemed odd to have this quiet acceptance. Perhaps she was wrong. Maybe she wouldn't go crazy if she gave up the sea to settle down here. She could run the place to her satisfaction, provided Briarley would step down as governor. He was always saying he'd hand over the reins to her the minute she decided to come home and run things — but was that the truth? Mary couldn't imagine resigning from running a whole island to manage nothing more important than a public house.

She went into the Leviathan's Blowhole Publick House for a drink. "Cap'n!" the attractive young barman shouted in greeting.

A white-haired man playing cards in the rear looked up. "Well, look what the wind blew in."

"Donwelyn Briarley, you old buzzard! How the Hell are you?" Mary went over and gave him a sloppy kiss.

"Ah, if you'd only marry me, lass!"

She smiled. "I'm sure your goodwife would object to that. I'm glad to see you. Drinks for everybody!"

The patrons cheered and shouted their orders to the barman, Briarley's son Kevin.

"That's why it's good to have ye back, lass. Yer allays good fer business!" His daughter — or was it his granddaughter? — Umalora, delivered their drinks, then rushed to fill the orders of the other patrons. The other card players excused themselves. She and Briarley were left alone. "So, ye got some nice things fer me this time?"

Mary nodded. "Oh, aye, you won't need to buy wine for a long time. Nor whiskey."

Briarley stared hard at her. "Something happen this time out, lass? Yer all over worried."

She sighed. "Nothing gets by you, old man. We've, ah . . . had some setbacks. Looks like we'll be staying here for a long while."

He chewed on his pipestem. "That bad, eh?"

She wished for a smoke. "Yeah. Petronius is talking about settling down. Maybe he's right. I'll want to discuss some thoughts with you." She pointed with her eyes to the people listening in. "But it'll keep till a quieter moment."

He nodded his understanding and said cheerily, "Well, you can have the job of gov'nor anytime ye likes, lass. I got plenty ta keep me busy as 'tis."

She scanned the full bar. "Seems like you've got so much custom, not a lot could bother you."

"True. Business be right good. Hey, Loxie baked up an eel pie. Ye want some?"

"I've been looking forward to having some of Loxianna's fine cooking." Presently she was tucking into a hot meal and more ale. While she ate, Briarley filled her in on all the happenings in Mary's Town since she was last there. Mostly it was a roster of who'd shot whom for what — insults, cheating, sleeping with a woman who was already spoken for and the like — newcomers to the island and their quirks, and ships that visited the port. On the whole, it seemed mind-numbingly dull to Mary. But it amused Briarley and the people who were eavesdropping and muttering editorial comments from time to time.

When the news seemed to peter out, she asked, "So what do you think of the doctor I sent you?"

"Oh, he's a fine one, he is!" Briarley pushed himself out of the chair. "Cured Loxie of rheumatism and stopped little Nyla's cough like that." He snapped his fingers.

Mary watched him closely. Suddenly he seemed restless. He rambled behind the bar, peg leg thumping, as if he'd rather be running away. "But?"

"Oh, no arguments a'tall, lass. We're all mighty grateful ta have him at the island." He directed Kevin to pour drinks for a pair of newcomers.

Something wasn't quite right, but she couldn't put her finger on it. "I'm thinking of moving him ashore."

"Oh, aye! Now there'd be a help. It's absolute Hell for the likes a' me ta get out ta that bloody ship, now."

"What is it, Briarley?" she asked quietly.

He threw up his hands. "Nothing, lass! Am I actin' queer like?"

"Aye."

"Must be the storm headin' in. Makes me ghost leg twinge somethin' fierce." He rubbed the stump. "Ya see the weather glass?" He pointed at the glass container of red-tinged liquid mounted on the wall. From its long, upwardly-angled spout a continual drip spattered onto the brass splash plate below. "That's a Devil Storm movin' in, by all indications."

"You have any preparations going on? Battening down the town?"

His eyes twinkled merrily. "Aye, lass. Everyone's on the alert. No fear."

Mary finished her drink, realizing he knew his job quite well without her interference. "Think I'll go and see things are tied down tight on my own ship. G'night old man."

"Night, lass," he called as she walked out.

It was just dark out and gusty. Palm trees lashed the air. There was a dense, tropical smell to the wind. Mary went to the dock, hopped in the nearest dinghy, and rowed out to the bobbing *Pearl*. Another dinghy was there. The watch challenged her, then gave her stammering permission to come aboard when she announced herself.

She clambered up the rope and accepted the crewman's assistance getting over the rail. Captain Ingram came running out of his tent, which had taken on the dimensions of a fabric palace. Straightening his coat, he saluted her. "Cap'n Mary, what an honor!"

She brushed herself off and shook his hand.

He'd become absolutely huge in the last year. The buttons of his coat just barely held the two halves together. "Captain Ingram," she said, looking around, "is all well with your command?"

"Oh, aye, Cap'n!" He gestured to decks gleaming in the lantern light. "We keep the *Pearl* ready at all times, just as you ordered."

"Good," she said, eyeing the neatly kept rigging. Everything seemed in order. "If this storm comes for us, you may have to take her to the lee of the island."

"Aye," he agreed. "I think it'll be a helluva blow. We'll be ready."

"Is the doctor seeing a patient?" she asked pretending indifference.

"Aye, Cap'n. A crewman from one o' yon ships, what gots an earache."

Just then, two men came up from below decks. First, a swarthy sailor with a bandaged ear emerged. Dr. Coulances followed him out, giving instructions in Portuguese and shaking a medicine bottle. He didn't notice Mary until the man started for the railing. Then he gasped, "Mary!"

"Hello, Alphonse." She strolled over to him, feigning a casual air. He looked even more handsome than she remembered. "I didn't know you spoke Portugee."

He kissed her on both cheeks. "I'm delighted to see you. You've been gone so long."

She smiled and took his arm. "Why don't we go into your cabin and talk."

"Please." In the few steps down the gangway and into the cabin, Alphonse was quiet. He darted small glances at her, as if unsure she was really there. When they stepped inside, she peered around his cabin. It was nicely furnished with goods she'd found on her travels, including the Jamaican botanical survey lying on the table next to the overstuffed wing-back chair. Yet it was uniquely his. His medical texts and equipment stood in one corner. The room smelled of wood, sea, some sharp antiseptic . . . and Alphonse. As soon as the door closed, she took his face in her hands and gave him a long, lingering kiss. He responded slowly, but finally returned her passion.

When they paused, he went to his desk and took up a decanter of wine. He poured Madeira into a delicate crystal glass, then handed it to her. "Are you going to be in port long?"

Mary admired the gracefully shaped goblet. She remembered taking it and the matching set from a Venetian merchant ship not long ago. "Perhaps. Things have changed for us recently and we must . . . ." she groped for the proper description, "restructure our operations."

"Is all well?"

"Well enough. But there'll be certain changes to come. One of which will affect you."

"Oh?"

She wondered at his obvious discomfiture. Had he given up on her? Would it serve anything to try and rekindle what they'd had? Now that she was back in his presence, her body reminded her how much she'd enjoyed him. "How would you like to live on the island instead of this little ship?"

"Very much." He seemed worried, though. "I've always wanted to be on land. Some of the more ill have not able to come out to the *Pearl*."

"I know. We argued about that some time ago. Well, now's your chance. I need the *Pearl* for other duties and I think the French have stopped hunting you."

He toyed with his glass. "When will this happen?"

"As soon as we get your house built. Is there a particular style you fancy? Or shall I surprise you?" She pictured a charming bungalow for him on the eastern plateau of the volcano. It would be just perfect for a lovenest.

"Mary, we must talk."

When she tried to look into his eyes, he averted them. Was he angry with her, that she'd been away so long? Had he forgotten their feelings for each other? Perhaps she could remind him — remind both of them — of what they'd had. She leaned over and kissed him. "Later, my dear. I've missed you so!" They kissed again. At first, Alphonse didn't respond much. But as the kiss lengthened and Mary's hands wandered, his passion grew. He caressed her the way she remembered. Slowly, she pulled him up from the chair. They made their way into bed.

If Alphonse had seemed reluctant before, now he was the more aggressive lover, taking initiatives where he never had. Mary delighted in his newfound technique. He seemed to have an appetite for her that was unquenchable. Late that night they fell asleep, exhausted, in each other's arms.

In the morning, Mary arose. Alphonse still slept. The ship rocked heavily and wind wailed eerily through the rigging. Briarley's Devil Storm was coming for them. She and the *Fury's* crew would have to hurry if they were to survive the big blow. She opened the door to leave.

Alphonse called from the ruins of the bed,

"Mary, we must talk."

"After the storm, my dear. I promise." She held the door against a wind swirling down the gangway that wanted to slam the door shut. "Then we'll have dinner and talk about all the things we've been reading and thinking these past months."

"Tonight, then," he said, seeming resigned.

She threw him a kiss and left the cabin. On deck, the sight of the sky stopped her. She'd never seen clouds this strange pewter color. There was an eldritch yellow-green to the daylight that made all the hairs on the back of her neck stand up in alarm. Mary ordered Ingram to make ready to sail out of the harbor by afternoon, then shinnied down to the dinghy and rowed to the wharf.

Aboard the *Fury*, Petronius had the crew working to unload the holds and ready for the storm. "I think we should weather the blow outside the harbor, Cap'n. Have you seen the weather glass?" He pointed to the instrument, much like the one at the Leviathan. The red liquid of the weather glass was coming out in a thin, steady stream. "Never seen the like," he said quietly to her. "It's a fierce storm comin'."

"Aye. This evening we'll stand off the western end of the island. That should be safe enough. Where are you storing our goods?"

"Over at Omanshay's store." He pointed down the street. "It's empty and has plenty o' room. I think we outta keep some of the heavier goods in the hold as ballast, though."

She eyed a flock of seabirds nervously wheeling overhead. "Yes, you're right. After the blow, we'll start work on selling the stuff. If we can get a house built for the doctor quickly enough, we can employ the *Pearl* to sail to the nearby islands."

Petronius leaned into the windshadow of the mainmast and lit his pipe with a spill from the lantern. "Using the *Pearl*'s a good idea."

She glared at him for a moment. "Besides, Ingram is getting fat as a house. He needs something to do besides sit in the harbor and eat."

"I don't trust him much." He watched the men hoist a walnut highboy out of the hold and into the air. "Careful there!" he barked. "Don't let it get twisted up in the rope!" The crew jumped to obey.

She wished she hadn't given up her pipe. "Who is it you do want captaining the *Pearl*?"

"Mapana's a good seaman. Been with us a lot o' years." Petronius nodded toward the man.

Mary watched him work. She knew Mapana well and thought highly of him also. "Perhaps. I still think it's risky to put a black man as captain. It invites notice, which we don't want."

"I know, I know," he said, sighing. "I swear, one day Africans will get the same treatment as whites. Not in my lifetime, maybe not even in Virgil's, but someday."

Mary said nothing, considering it unlikely even in a hundred years.

When she didn't reply, Petronius returned to the subject at hand. "How about Talinn?"

"Fine. What're we going to do with Ingram?"

He shrugged. "Maybe he can be your precious doctor's valet."

She shut her eyes. "Don't start with me, today. Try and think of something useful, hmm?" She turned and started down the gangplank.

"Where're you goin', Cap'n?"

"Into town. I'll be back later." There was nothing further for her to do aboard the *Fury*. Petronius had things well in hand. At least that was what she told herself. What she really wanted was to see Elaina and Melissa. If the *Fury* was to spend the night at sea weathering a storm, she wanted to steal a little time with her lover. Elaina's letters had become so strange lately. Mary knew she shouldn't have left Elaina all alone here for a year. She wondered how Melissa had changed.

As she made her way to the house, Mary studied the people she passed. Women and men of all color and class passed her. She noted just as many female names on shop signs as men's: "Lilita's Fine Clothing," "J'mbaray's Chandlery," "Telinka's Tavern." All these people worked to make Mary's Town profitable to themselves. It was the only place she'd ever come across without all the taboos of European society. Look how well things worked when people were simply let to find their own way in life. But she knew that didn't mean the rest of the Caribbean was ready for the freedoms allowed on Cache Island. Instead, it made the islanders vulnerable. Mary was aware that the colonial governments found this society deviant. She wondered how long it would be before the Europeans would try to stamp it out. After the storm, she'd have a serious discussion with Briarley about the defense of the island. What Cache Island had and was becoming must be saved.

Mary was still turning over the island's possibilities in her mind when she stepped onto the broad front porch of Mayhew House. She stopped to admire the thick orange trumpet vine shrouding the supporting posts. Then she went to the door. Her ring was answered by a doorman in blue and green livery who bowed deeply to her. He was a new addition, but he obviously knew Mary. He led her directly up to the private quarters. Tapping gently on the door, he opened it, announced her, and gestured her in. Then closed the door behind her.

"Amaritta!" Elaina called. Her voice was rich with delight. "Come in, dear!"

Mary stopped at the threshold. This was the new parlor Elaina had written about. It was a large, airy room with light-rose damask wall coverings stretching up fourteen feet to the snow-white ceiling with exquisite plaster moldings. Huge English landscape paintings gave the impression that the views in the elaborate gold frames were more real than the views of the Caribbean harbor out the three north-facing glass-paned doors. There were loveseats with French embroidered scenes and delicate gilt chairs. Beautiful vases and figurines adorned each intricately carved walnut table. Turkish carpets of amazing colors covered the brightly polished wood floors. Elaina was almost lost in the lovely clutter of the room.

"*Tante* Marie!" Melissa shouted. She ran to Mary and hugged her tightly.

"Melissa!" Mary picked the girl up. She had grown so! Her features decidedly favored her father. Yet, there was an openness, a special quality of joy to her that was unlike Edmund — and certainly not like Mary. "Look at you. You're such a great girl now! Have you been good?"

Melissa nodded. "Oh, yes. I've been very good. Did you bring me something from your long trip?"

"Yes, of course," Mary lied. She'd forgotten to look for toys and the like. Hopefully, there'd be something in the holds a beautiful little girl would like.

Perhaps that walnut highboy they'd just unloaded would do.

"Melissa, what did I tell you about pestering people for gifts," Elaina scolded.

"Sorry, Mama." Melissa slipped out of Mary's arms and bounced back to Elaina.

Suppressing the twinge of hearing her daughter call yet another woman Mama, Mary stepped around a marquetry commode. She paused to admire the cosmos plant that sat on its gray marble top. It had wine-red blooms and the strong odor of chocolate. She was pleased to see that it had survived the long trip from its jungle home where she'd found it.

Continuing across the room, Elaina, in a sort of tableau, was revealed to her. She sat on an ornately carved rosewood loveseat with rose upholstery. Illuminated in the lemony glow of the cut-glass whale oil lamp beside her, she held a suckling infant to her breast. Melissa was seated to the right of the couch on a leather hassock, a poorly executed embroidery sample forgotten in her lap.

"Well, you've been busy!" Mary chuckled in confusion as she stood before the three. Why hadn't Elaina written of this development?

"See Mama's pretty baby?" Melissa prattled. "That's my new brudder! His name is Etienne."

"Brother," Elaina corrected. "Use your "th" sound."

"Broth-er," she struggled.

Mary sank into the delicate gilt chair behind her. She didn't know what to make of Melissa's "brudder." He looked to be at least three months old. "He's a love-ly child."

"Melissa," Elaina said, shifting the baby to a

more comfortable position. "Why don't you go down-stairs and ask Zula to make us some tea and scones?"

"Why don't you ring for it, Mama?"

"Because I'd like for you to do it. A lady must sometimes supervise things herself instead of relying on others."

"All right." Melissa skipped out of the room.

Neither woman spoke until Melissa closed the door. They stared into each other's eyes. Elaina's were the same intense blue, but they held something else. A challenge? "Are you here for long?"

Mary detected a hint of falseness in her manner, but pretended all was well. She leaned forward, elbows on knees. "It, ah, could be, Elaina, that I'm here for good. We could finally be together, just as you've always wanted."

Elaina's eyes narrowed to catlike slits. "Well, isn't that nice."

The sarcasm wasn't lost on Mary. "This," she said, pointing to the infant, "is a surprise."

"Yes, well." Elaina finished nursing and adjusted her clothes. The baby turned to peer at the stranger in the room. He had soft black curly hair and a nose that already looked strong. But those green eyes! "It wasn't planned."

Mary held her breath, staring at the child. She denied to herself what she instantly recognized to be true — because it couldn't be! They wouldn't. Not to her. "Who might be the father of this little angel? Are you taking clients of your own these days?"

Elaina's eyes sparked blue fire. "Don't dare insult me! You stuck me on this barbarous island in this demeaning occupation. Then you hardly trouble your-self to come and see me. I'm alone. All alone, because of you. Now, after over a year without so much as an appearance, you show up and announce we're going to live together. What if it's too late?"

"Too late?" Anger and confusion warred in Mary's mind. "Is there a time limit on love? You would throw me out? Spurn me because I've been at sea for a year? After all we've meant to each other?"

"*I* mean something to *you*? No one and nothing means as much to you as that disgusting ship and that filthy crew of yours. You live to be a pirate! Stay here on the island? Ha!" She threw the laugh in Mary's face. "You're too in love with murder and thievery to stay here and understand what real love is all about."

Something in Mary hardened. "You know all about real love, do you now?"

Elaina patted the fussing baby angrily. "Despite you and your evil ways, I've built a life for myself. I have a family. Respect in the community here, even if they're only pirates and miscreants."

"I note that some of your little family isn't yours."

"Fine," Elaina said with a snigger, "tell Melissa you're her mother. She'll tell you it's a lie. She knows who takes care of her when she suffers the ague. Who quiets her nightmares. Who's with her night and day!"

Elaina's words came to Mary from a distant frozen place. It seemed as if all the light was stealing out of the room, and with it her reason. The windows rattled. She couldn't tell if it was the wind or her own anger. "There's more family not currently present, am I right?" Mary realized the hard flat words had come from her mouth. She didn't remember shaping them. There was no air in the room. In its place was the cloying scent of the exotic flower. The smell of love, she'd once thought. Her sight narrowed until all she could see clearly was the eerily familiar face of the baby. "Who is your new lover, Elaina?" she asked, her voice empty of emotion.

The baby began to squall.

Elaina smirked at her. "It's of interest only to me."

Mary found herself standing menacingly over Elaina. "Tell me who fathered this child!" she heard herself shout.

"Look at his face! No one could miss who the father is."

Mary could barely force the word through her clenched teeth. "Alphonse."

"Yes!" Elaina laughed. "We didn't plan for this to happen, but now I'm glad — glad, do you hear!" The baby started to shriek. She bounced the child automatically as she continued. "At last I have someone of my own to love. Someone who isn't another's lover. Or someone else's child."

Mary felt as if something was strangling her. Her head throbbed. She picked up the potted plant and threw it into a tall pier mirror. Glass smashed with a satisfying sound. She reached for the howling infant, intent on doing the same with it. Elaina screamed and covered the baby, huddling in the corner of the loveseat. Their combined shrieks echoed inside Mary's head until she had to make it stop! She picked up Melissa's hassock and hurled it through the nearest glass door. Expensive panes shattered explosively. Elaina's sobs were drowned out by the raging of the storm's winds as they swirled into the room. The gusts seemed to combine with Mary's fury as she demolished vases, figurines, dainty chairs and anything else she could lay her hands on.

The door flew open. "Mama!" Melissa cried.

Mary ran to Melissa and snatched her up, intending to hurl her at the wall. After a brief squeak of fear, the girl fainted.

No, not this one! warned what was left of her reason. *She must live.* She held Melissa's limp little body over her head. Her breath came in ragged gasps as she fought her internal battle. *Elaina will corrupt her. She'll grow up to be as scheming and vicious a bitch as her so-called mother. Better to kill her now before she grows to betray someone else's love!* Turning in painful torment, Mary shakily brought the child down to her chest. Melissa's charming face was relaxed in repose. The echoes of Edmund and Papa were stamped so clearly on her face. *You can't hurt her. Melissa's yours.*

She looked up and saw Elaina watching, still clutching the infant to her breast. A strange smile bent the lips that had once driven Mary mad with passion. *She wants you to hurt Melissa. That would be her ultimate revenge.*

Slowly, Mary placed Melissa on the floor. Little lashes fluttered open. The girl looked up and began to wail. Mary stepped over Melissa and strode out of the house.

Mary could hardly see where she was going for the red fog of anger that clouded the world. She heard people speak to her, but brushed by them. They all wanted something from her. Wanted to take and take — but never give! It was all lies. No one — nothing! — was really as it seemed.

The *Fury's* gangplank appeared, seemingly out of nowhere. She stormed aboard her ship.

"Cap'n!" Petronius called. "My boy Virgil,

here," he said, clapping the tall lad on the shoulder, "has a letter for you."

Mary snatched the missive from the boy's hand. Then, suddenly noticing something, she grabbed Virgil's chin and peered into his face. He didn't look a thing like Petronius. Had Seashell done to Petronius what Alphonse and Elaina had done to her? "Stay here. I want you to take some letters to shore."

"Aye, Cap'n," Virgil said in imitation of his father.

"Cap'n?" Petronius said with concern in his voice, "Anything I can do for you?"

"Make ready to cast off!"

"But Cap'n — "

"Now!" Mary shouted as she slammed into her cabin. She shook and panted like a whipped dog. Struggling to regain some control of herself, she poured a brandy, spilling much of it on the desk, and downed it quickly. Pouring another, she sat down. Mary ran her hands through her unruly hair, tearing plaits out of the eelskin sheath. Strands arced out around her head.

She felt as if she'd taken a direct hit from a mortar. How could Elaina — *Elaina* of all the people in the world — how could she do this? Hadn't Mary bared her soul to the woman? Didn't Elaina know all Mary's secrets? Hadn't she tried to keep Elaina with her? Was it her fault Elaina didn't take to the pirate's life? Ah, God! Was this how love was returned?

She took out a quill and wrote out all her angry thoughts.

> *I am completely undone! I cannot believe how*
> *You have Betrayed My Truste and My Hearte! Did*
> *We mean so little to Each Other, then? You — and*

You alone — I beleeved I could Depend upon not to cause Me Pain. But You have struck a Dagger Directley into My Hearte!

All those Nights We spent Together in Each Other's Arms. How welle I remember Our Lovemaking, Our Letters filled with Fantasies. Did That mean Nothing to You? Are You like all the Men I have encountered — interested only in the Game of acquiring Lovers but not in the Love Itself? Oh, You are Cruel! Cruel! Say I!

And then, the hardest Blow of all. When I bared My Soule to You, entrusted You with My Feelings about Alphonse — You Lied! You said It was perfektly understandable to You that I should have a Man to Love, that it would Change Nothing between Us! Liar! You always planned This, didn't You? The Momente I told You that I would keep Him at Cache Island, You rubbed Your Greedy little Hands with Glee! You could not Wait to Revenge Yourself upon Me could You?

Looking at that Babe in Your Arms — ah God, how I wanted to Smash It! It looks just like Him! I hope and pray this Ettienne will be as Faithful to You as You and He have been to Me! I Curse Your Childe! May Nothing Goode ever come to Him or His Heirs! Then, to add Insult to Injury, My Daughter — Who calls You Mama — asks how I like Her New Brother!

You will Not see Me againe in This Life. You can have Your Precious Childe and Your Duplicitous Doctor and Be Damned! To Hell with You! To Hell with Alphonse! To Hell with the Whole Stinking Island! I call upon God, the Devil, Neptune, or Whoever answers such Prayers to Demolish the

Place! Wipe It Clean from the Vermin Who infest it.
There are Many More Islands in the Sea. There are
Others Who would be Loved by Me — and Keep My
Truste!

    Goode Bye Forever,
    Captain Mary

By the time she was finished, the tip of her quill pen was badly bent. No amount of shaving would salvage it. She threw it on the floor. The letter didn't make much sense, but it would have to do. She never wanted to hear from that harpy again. She folded the letter and slipped on a cover sheet. Let the treacherous wench rot!

How many of the town knew about this? It was too small a place for everyone not to know everyone else's business. For how long had people — her friends! — hidden the truth from her? Surely Briarley, that old goat, knew when he saw her yesterday. That explained his sudden nervousness. Damn him! They'd been friends for years and now he took that vicious wench's side. Then there was Ingram. Ooh, he must have known! How humiliating to have that poxy fool know about her shame. Not one of those who owed their whole miserable existence to her had stopped the affair or tried to warn her. She realized she could never stay in Mary's Town. She drank down another glass of brandy, but it failed to dim the unspeakable pain.

Mechanically, she turned her attention to the letter Virgil had given her, still wadded up in her hand. She noticed Alphonse's handwriting. Well, he'd tried to tell her, hadn't he? Too bad he hadn't tried harder. But what would she have done, then? Killed him? Burned down Mayhew House? Nothing made sense anymore.

Opening the letter, she read:

Dearest Mary,

I have tried to muster the Courage to say this to You in person, but I find I am a Coward. I have been Unfaithful to You — my Lover, my Benefactress, my Friend. I have repaid your thousand Kindnesses by betraying you. I am Unworthy of being called a Dog.

The moste despicable thing is that I would never have mentioned this to you, nor would She, if not for the Childe.

At least he realized how much he owed her. Rather more consideration than Elaina gave! But how it cut like a knife to know that those she loved would've continued to deceive her had not the baby come along. Had Elaina hidden the pregnancy from Alphonse until she was well along? She was just clever enough.

I knowe You must be angry with Me and with Her. Please do not fault Elaina. She is your beste and moste True Friend. It is I, a Weake, Immoral Man Who is to blame. I led Her astray. I corrupted Her Faithfulness. I was lonely. She is lovely and almoste as welle read as You. There are No Excuses.

I submit Myself to Your Justice. Do with Me what You think beste. I accept All Punishment. But do not harme Elaina or the Childe, I beg you. They are blameless. Pawns in a badly played Game.

I await Your Decision.

Mary threw the letter down on the table. The paper soaked up the spilled brandy. The words blurred to illegibility. Poor fool! It was almost laughable how thoroughly Elaina had twisted him around her finger. He didn't even realize how thoroughly he'd been used.

How had Elaina convinced him to take the blame?

Mary shook her head. They could have each other. She didn't need them or the whole stinking island. She and Petronius could set up somewhere else. She'd heard rumors that her home colony of Carolina was the perfect spot for pirating. Perhaps that's where they should go.

Mary was willing to wager that Alphonse wouldn't interest Elaina at all once it was clear the *Fury* wasn't coming back. Oh, the look that would creep across Alphonse's face when Elaina spurned him! Elaina had Mary's child, his baby and her revenge — what did she need him for? One could almost feel sorry for him.

She wrote a note to Alphonse of considerably less heat than the one to Elaina.

> *Doctor,*   *9 September 1722*
>
> *I answer Your Poisonous Note via Your Messenger Virgil, my own Petronius's Son. How shabbily You use Him. He is a Goode Ladde and deserves to do more than carry such Scaberous Missives.*
>
> *I am Wounded beyond the Scope of Your Healing Artes. How have I wronged Either of You that You should serve Me thusly? Have I not taken the Very Beste Care of You? Protected You from All Harme, including a King's Wrathe? Have You ever Wanted for Any Thingg that was in My Power to give? I am Devastated, but Not Surprised. It seems always thus with You Men. As for Her, alas, the Damage there is so Deep You cannot imagine. You have Bothe betrayed Me utterly!*
>
> *I have decided Not to Return to Cache Island ever*

*againe. How could I show My Face? It is a Small Ile,
and surely Every One knows what has Occurred.
They will hold Me in Contempt and soon My whole
Crewe would as well. Cuckolds are always amusing
to Every One but the Cuckold herself. It is Harde to
be a Woman and a Captain. It is All Balanced on
Feare and Respekt. Without One or the Other, It All
falls down like Your pretty little Card Houses.*

Farewelle

Alphonse would be so surprised when Elaina
dropped him. Would his heart be broken? Or would he
shrug in his Gallic way and look for new conquests?
No, he's not that way. He fancies Elaina genuinely loves
him. Soon enough he'll discover his error. There was
some satisfaction in knowing what Elaina would do
with him. That was almost punishment enough. Mary
sprinkled sand on the page and blotted it carefully
before folding it and adding the cover sheet.

She picked up the letter to Elaina again. Mary
got up and paced nervously around the cabin. She
could picture that cat's smile on Elaina's face as she read
Mary's pain. Elaina would gloat at having won the
game: she had the doctor's love — instead of Mary — she
had the devotion of Melissa — instead of Mary — she
had a beautiful baby — which should have been Mary's.
And with this letter, she had proof that she had the ultimate prize — the power to break Mary's heart. Well,
Mary wouldn't let her have the satisfaction. Slowly, she
tore the letter into thirds, then smaller pieces. *You'll
never know how you've hurt me, you sneaking bitch!* She let
the pieces flutter to the floor.

Picking up the letter to Coulances, she went back
outside. Gusts that shrieked and whistled in the rigging

pummeled her as soon as she set foot on deck. The palm trees that ringed the harbor lashed the air. Somewhere in town, the raging wind rang a bell, again and again. Black clouds scudded across the dark-gray sky. Rain would come soon, the air was pregnant with it.

The ship was ready to sail; the crew tense in anticipation of the storm and her mood. "Here," she said, stuffing the letter into Virgil's hand, "mind you take it to the *Pearl* swiftly, now, before they cast off!" She handed the lad a guinea. He stood staring at the coin. Likely it was the most money he'd ever seen.

Petronius tapped him on the shoulder. "You best go do as the Cap'n tells you." Virgil started toward the gangplank.

Mary called him back. "Come say goodbye to your father." She turned and watched Petronius. Confusion showed in his eyes. She brushed past him on her way to the helm. By the wheel, she watched as he hugged his son, stroked his head and sent him on his way. Later, she would tell him that it was probably the last time they would see each other. How would he respond? Although she'd known him through thick and thicker, that was as a pirate. She was coming to realize that, regarding those he loved, Petronius was a man she didn't know at all.

"Cast off!" she ordered, as Virgil's foot hit the dock. Her crew rushed to obey. She glanced up at the rigging. Already the sails strained with the violent gusts of the coming storm. It would be difficult getting around the harbor reef.

Petronius took the wheel and barked orders to the crew. Soon the *Fury* was making its way out of the harbor. Mary tried not to look as they passed the *Pearl*, but she could hear the crew making ready to escape the harbor. She kept her eyes riveted on the protective reef where angry waves dashed themselves in white ferment, trying to reach what she had once thought her place. It didn't matter now. None of it mattered.

The *Fury* breasted the breakers and headed out into the Caribbean. Mary felt the doors of her heart slam shut with a metallic clang. Petronius turned the ship northward. The sailcloth filled with the roar of the storm wind. Huge swells tossed the *Fury* around the white-capped seas with no more regard than a child's toy. Mary went to the bow, letting the stinging spray blast hit her. It was an exhilarating feeling, having the wind in her face and her troubles at her back. Quickly, they made for the tip of the island.

Just as they were rounding the jutting cliffs, Jorge up in the crow's nest shouted. It was impossible to tell what he was saying through the thunder of the wind. Mary lifted her glass and scanned the storm-darkened horizon. What did he see?

All at once, as they passed the rocks of the cliff, a frigate was revealed to them. "Hard about!" Mary ordered, racing back to the quarterdeck so her commands could be better heard. She scanned the rigging of the on-rushing ship for a signal of their country. The British flag! The profile of the ship was familiar. She strained to read the writing on the prow. Her spyglass nearly dropped to the deck when she pieced together *Mars Thunderbolt*. There was a bright flash from their hull. Moments later, an ominous boom thundered through the cacophony of the stormy sea. Then again. And again! Cannonballs began pelting the waves off their starboard side.

"It's Effington!" she shouted to Petronius. Just then, a howling mortar slammed into their bow. The deck exploded with shattered wood and flame. The *Fury* shuddered as if she'd taken a blow to the chin. "All hands! To the bow!" Mary commanded. But her well-trained men were already running to the area.

Petronius was trying to outrace the larger ship by cutting East. The *Mars Thunderbolt* had already turned in that direction and was soon gaining on them. Their forward cannons fired. One cannonball narrowly missed the *Fury's* stern. It arced near the hull with a sizzling noise before falling into the sea.

"Fire's out, Cap'n," Talinn reported. "Damage ain't much, but Karl got hurt bad. Nearly took off his arm."

"Give him a bottle of whiskey. Make him as comfortable as you can." Talinn went to obey. She turned to Petronius. "Take her to the edge of the storm!"

He gaped at her in surprise, then studied the cloud bank on their left. It was black as Death, pierced by brilliant pitchforks of lightning. In places, the inky sky was shot through with an unearthly turquoise. Waves boiled out of the darkness, as tall as mountains. Through it all came the evil keening of the wind. "Are you crazed?" he shouted over the storm. "We'll be killed!"

She hauled out her pistol, cocked it, and placed its muzzle squarely in the middle of his forehead. "Devil take you if you question me again. Take her into the storm!" Their eyes locked. He wasn't afraid of the gun at his head, she saw. Had he ever feared her, as others had? Did Mary only command respect because of Petronius and the crew? Who was she then? She blinked hard against the stinging drops of rain that began to fall. He must obey her or there was no Captain

Mary — never had been! She realized she was peering over an abyss of madness more terrifying than the storm.

Petronius eyed his captain. All the feeling leaked out of Mary onto the drenched boards at her feet. He didn't blink. She saw her pistol hand twitching spastically with the mad beats of her heart. Nearby crewmen stood still, watching the silent struggle. All the while, the *Mars Thunderbolt* drew closer. Finally he said quietly, "Aye, Cap'n. Headin' her into the storm."

Shakily, Mary removed the pistol from his forehead and put it back in her belt. There was no way she could ever make it up with her oldest friend. What she'd done exceeded all bounds. He would either find it in his heart to forgive her, or kill her at his earliest convenience. She wondered dimly which it would be.

With a terrible shudder, the *Fury* turned into the fierce wind. Sails flapped and roared. Men clambered up the wet masts and along the slippery yardarms to reef the sails before they ripped. Petronius began tacking into the heart of the storm. With the *Fury* heeling almost to the gunnels, water poured in the scuppers and sluiced the decks. Mary held tightly to the rail so that she could still stand at the stern. She watched the *Mars Thunderbolt*, whose sails luffed while Effington made up his mind. The distance between the two ships increased. Mary beat her free fist on the railing. "C'mon, you poxy bastard! Give it up!" As if in answer to her, the British ship's sails tightened. Her bow slowly turned toward the *Fury*. "Damn you!" Mary yelled.

She spun around and confronted the storm. It looked like the gaping mouth of Hell. Her crew, thinlipped, tried to perform their duties. It was almost impossible with the wind and waves working against them. Uncanny light made them glow like voodoo wraiths. Timbers shuddered as huge waves crashed over the bow. The impact threw Mary to the deck. "Tie yourselves down!" she screamed over the shrieking wind. Her men struggled with their tasks. It was unclear whether any heard her.

As they entered the storm, the whole world was swallowed up by an ominous blackness. Purple and yellow Saint Elmo's fire danced along the rigging and yardarms. Jorge scrambled down from the lookout's post, his mouth soundlessly open in the gale. His arms and legs were shrouded in eery flames. Suddenly, he lost his grip. His body plummeted to the deck. The *Fury* pitched to port and Jorge's corpse slid across the wet boards, over the gunnels and into the angry sea.

Most of the crew hung onto lines rigged amidships struggling to stay upright. A sudden gigantic wave caromed over the rails amidship. It threw Mary into the wheel. Petronius caught her before she could fall farther. When the water subsided, none of her crew was to be seen.

"Talinn!" Mary screamed. "Mapana! Watu!" But they were gone, swallowed in the storm. *Dead, because of my foolishness.* She had failed them — her crew, her men, her friends. Everyone.

Like an angry child frustrated by a toy, the howling wind snapped the sails right off their spars. Mary stared behind them. She could just make out the *Mars Thunderbolt* as it tried to turn away from the wind. "They've given up!" She pounded Petronius on the back. "We've won!"

He grabbed her arm and lashed it to his own on the wheel. "We've lost, Marie!"

She stared up at him, slowly comprehending. As

she heard the snap of their mainmast, she knew she'd doomed them. "Oh, God, Pet. I'm sorry!"

He lashed her other arm to the wheel and wrapped his arm around it. "If we're goin' to Hell, we're goin' together!" he shouted into her ear.

She could hardly see their bow as rain, sea and wind combined into one, bearing down on their small broken ship. While the storm around them intensified, so did the one inside her. Images danced in her mind's eye. There was Billy looking startled as she'd dragged him on her horse, as she fled her father, Darius and the judgement of the priest. Then she saw Billy dancing around her with a mop as he swabbed the deck and sang a silly love song to her. The moment was quickly replaced with his snarl, just before he backhanded her for not giving him enough information on the Huff family.

Suddenly, Billy's snarl was replaced by Edmund's young, handsome face. It was the moment he'd leaned forward to kiss her behind the protection of Billy's newly washed linsey-woolsey shirt. The delight of that moment dissolved to confused pain as she saw again the sullen glare he'd worn at the trial. It changed into the terrible rictus of pain caused by the noose. She felt again the lancing pain in her heart that she'd tried to hide from her captors.

Then Mary saw the small, red wrinkled face of tiny Melissa just after she was born. She experienced again the joy and terror of having brought a new life into her tumult-filled world. The face shifted to the laughing little imp Melissa became. Mary's heart had been stolen in the few days of the voyage from Hispaniola to Jamaica. Laughter changed to the contortion of terror as Mary struggled not to destroy Melissa in her furor over

Elaina's betrayal.

Melissa's face blurred and became Elaina's delicate features peering timorously at her from behind a trunk. Avaricious thoughts swept Mary, swiftly replaced by the wonder and passion of their lovemaking. She saw again Elaina's lovely, sweaty face, her normally coiffed hair a disheveled wreck. The face melted into the evil delight on her cat face at the brothel. Mary felt her anger boil over again.

Quickly, Elaina's face disappeared and she saw Alphonse when they first met, bruised and battered by his captors. His compassionate skill intrigued her. Later his knowledge and insights had delighted her so that she'd been unaware when, exactly, she'd fallen in love with him. She pictured him last night, as he'd fallen asleep in her arms, so apparently loving, so utterly corrupted by Elaina.

Through it all had been Petronius. She remembered him as he'd looked when she'd peered out of her jail cell. Aloof, competent, yet somehow caring. She recalled the frequently scratched and cut face he'd had their first year together, as they'd tried to discover how to pirate and then how to make it pay. She'd had no closer friend. Once again, she saw his gentle face as they made love with no expectations or claims upon each other, other than their body's needs — or that's what she'd thought. Yet, when the other lovers were gone, it was to him she always returned. She knew his face in anger, joy, laughter and pain — every wrinkle and graying hair. She was swept up by the realization, only possible now. "I love you, Pet! I love you!" she yelled.

But a roaring wall of water coming over their bow prevented her from hearing any answer.

EPILOGUE

High up in the mountains of South America, in a dry riverbed near the entrance to a narrow mineshaft, a dark-haired woman in a simple blue and white dress was talking to two miners. Suddenly, a fat old *niñera* came waddling and hollering down the dusty path toward them. "*Doña* Marie! *Doña* Marie!" She waved her arm, as if Marie couldn't see her. "*Doña!*"

"What is it, Esperanza?" Marie called, irritated at being interrupted.

The run to the mine had made Esperanza breathless. She leaned against a tree, signaling her mistress that she'd speak in a moment.

It wasn't an emergency, then. Marie turned back to the miners. "Tell the *Don* I think we need to work the upper reach of the vein until we've exhausted it. If he disagrees, send him to me."

"*Sí,*" Ramón said with a grin.

Marie stayed expressionless, knowing why he

smiled. Ramón, the foreman, had delivered many such messages in the last few months. They invariably infuriated the *Don*. Her workers thought it funny that a woman should tell her man what to do.

"Well, go on, then," she ordered when they seemed inclined to stay and find out what the old woman wanted. Then, she turned to Esperanza. "What is it this time?"

"Oh, *Doña* Marie," she panted. "The *bebé*, she cry and cry. She wants her *comida, sí?*"

Marie bit back a retort. Yelling did no good with this one. Besides, the old fool was right. Her breasts had been aching and leaking for some time. But there was work to do and the child would just have to wait. "I know, Esperanza. Just another few moments and I'll go up and see to her."

"No, no, *Doña* Marie." Esperanza started pulling her up the hill. "*Bebé* first. *Oro* later. Even men know this!"

"All right, fine." Marie sighed, letting the old woman lead her back to the house. As they reached the top — actually a saddle created by the confluence of three mountains — she was again taken with the magnificence of the view. The jungle formed a dense, lush green wall sloping sharply down to a raging turquoise river. The gorge was narrow here, but some miles further it broadened and led to the Pacific. Late in the evening, when the breeze came from offshore, she could smell the tang of the ocean. Although she missed the sea, she had come to love this life all the more.

She studied the new house as they approached it. Just a rough thatch shack when they'd arrived nearly two years ago, it was now a beautiful home, like the grand Spanish mansions in *Santa Fé de Bogotá*. Sandy brown plaster walls reached two stories into the air. The walls were a foot thick, making it cool in the day, warm at night, and incredibly secure. She was especially proud of the red tile roof, since she'd helped shape and dry many of the tiles. With its commanding view of three valleys, the house seemed a stout ship on a vast green sea whose waves were frozen. It was the first place Marie had ever felt completely at peace with herself.

A slender girl, whose Indian face looked more like the mask of some goddess then a cook's, stood out on the path before the house. "I'm coming, Lohía," Marie said, laughing at the woman's obvious impatience. None of the women servants liked to hear the baby cry and were alarmed at her apparent disinterest.

She followed the women into the nursery, where she could hear the baby wailing. It was her hunger cry, and she was very angry with her mother, besides. *This one is going to be a handful when she grows up,* Marie thought as she went in the room. "All right, little one. Mama's here. Quit your yammering."

Almost immediately, the cries halted. A tear-stained face peeked over the crib wall. Her hair was a wild curly-black tangle from her tantrum. The red ribbon, so carefully tied on this morning, was knotted on one strand nearly straight up from her brow. Her beautiful skin was the color of coffee with cream, although her father argued that it was more like brown sugar. There was no doubt about the color of those incredible hazel eyes. The child sniffled.

Despite herself, Marie was moved by the pathetic little face. "Come to Mama, Evie sweetie." Evie reached out and Marie gathered her in her arms. She loved the silky feel of Evie's skin, the smell of her hair, even the weight in her arms. She'd never had this with Melissa. She'd been in too much of a hurry to go out and pirate. The maidservants cooed at them as she sat to feed the girl.

In the evening, Marie watched the path. She'd never behaved this way before, but ever since they'd come to live in New Grenada, she'd wanted to catch sight of her man the minute he came over the rise. Two men were coming up now. One, tall and sandy-haired, one gray-headed and supporting himself on a crutch, his missing right leg all too apparent.. She went outside and called out, "Troni!" The man with the crutch waved back.

The storm had taken his right leg below the knee. Troni pretended to be philosophic about it, saying, "Better t'lose the foreleg all at once, than endure that slow rot that was eatin' away my toes and foot." But she knew it was merely bravura. If they hadn't been rescued when they had, he'd have surely died. The pain of the recuperation, or perhaps the anguish at losing the *Fury* and her crew, had turned his hair grey overnight. In disgust, he'd made her cut it short so that he wouldn't have to look at it.

She welcomed him home with a kiss, then patted the other man on the arm. "It's good to have you back, Elbert."

"Thank you, Madam Marie," he said, shyly not meeting her eyes.

"Let's have somethin' t'drink, lass, and I'll have von Loos tell you o' his trip." Troni went into the parlor and put his stump up on the big leather hassock with a sigh. Esperanza brought Evie to him and placed the child in his lap. He cooed at her and played peek-a-boo to her giggling delight.

"It went well then?" Marie motioned for Lohía to bring them glasses and wine.

"Oh, yes." Elbert leaned against the large marble mantle. "The assayer was quite impressed with the quality of the ore. Of course, I checked around to make sure of finding the most honest one in town. After he weighed it, he handed me this." He withdrew a paper from inside his striped vest and handed it to Marie. "They also have a bank, you see. So it's on deposit."

Marie read the figure twice, not believing it. "My God! Ten million pesos?"

"We're rich," Troni said quietly. "We could close the mine, never move another muscle and we'd be wealthy for the rest o' our lives. Evie and her children can live three hundred years on that sum alone."

"Unbelievable." Who could have known that their great loss would turn into riches beyond imagining? It wasn't just the money from the gold — though that was sufficient unto itself — but the baby, being with Troni, and having good friends like Elbert, had made Marie feel richer than any queen who walked the Earth.

Lohía reappeared at the door. "Dinner?" Marie asked. The cook nodded. "Gentlemen, shall we?" Esperanza took Evie back from her father and headed upstairs. Marie, Troni and Elbert went into the dining room and started on one of Lohía's spicy creations.

Later, when the fine rich coffee was served and all felt that they had eaten slightly more than they should have, Troni said, "Elbert, we thank you for your excellent work in settin' up our account." The younger man smiled at the compliment. "Marie and I have another favor to ask o' you."

"Anything," he said, staring into Marie's eyes.

She knew how much in love with her he was. Troni tolerated it because he was grateful to Elbert's father for rescuing them.

She thought back to those awful times. For two days after the hurricane, she and Troni had clung to a piece of the *Fury's* hull. Troni's life was ebbing away and Marie's interest in living was fading as well. Then a fisherman spotted them and pulled them out of the sea. Heinrich von Loos was a Dutchman out of Dominica. He took them to his home where he and Elbert nursed them back to health. They stayed with the von Looses three months while Troni relearned to walk and Marie tried to figure out what to do next.

Marie couldn't go back to Cache Island and face her lovers, who were by now, probably living together with their child. She hadn't the heart to try and restart a pirating career. Almost daily she was haunted by the faces of the men she'd lost because of her madness. It didn't help to remember that Effington would have hanged them all if he'd caught them. She couldn't go back to the sea. For the first time in her life, Marie realized she wanted to settle down, and she hadn't the faintest idea how to go about it.

Dominica was one of the places that Trimmer had invested their money. Marie remembered the bank from her examination of the secret bank books some months before. More importantly, she recalled the names their money had been invested under. The manager of the Island Fiduciary Trust pleaded with the strange woman not to remove all her assets, but she was insistent. She went on a buying spree, ordering simple dresses (fewer petticoats and leggings than current fashion demanded), handsome suits for Troni, and new fishing gear for their hosts.

It was Troni who decided they should go to the New Grenadian mine. Especially once it was apparent that she was pregnant. He was delighted with her revelation, even though she couldn't guarantee him that it was his. Using friends of the von Looses, they took ship with anyone who let them on board, appearing to all eyes as a lady of quality with her faithful, if broken-down, manservant. They both chafed with the fiction and looked forward to when they could be together as themselves. Because at last, they had discovered their love for each other.

They laughed when they thought back and recalled how each had pretended total disinterest in the other. Marie had been trying so hard to be a tough pirate, she'd lost sight of the love she felt for her companion and partner. Troni admitted that at first he'd thought of her as nothing but a business partner. Later he'd ignored his rising feelings, thinking them nothing more than lust.

Their love wasn't apparent until Troni started to walk again. Marie stayed up long nights, nursing him back to health. She knew how sick he was by the way he allowed her to fuss over him. She prayed — something she hadn't done in an age — that he would mend. Slowly, he healed. As he sat in the sun, trying to gain strength from the very rays that poured down on him, he held fast to her hand, not wanting her to be very far away. Only after he stumped around the von Loos shack on his crutch twice by himself, did he feel confident to tell Marie that he'd heard her last words on the *Fury*, and he loved her as well. Marie wept in surprise. She'd been so sure that her love would never be returned. He proved to be an even more tender and devoted mate than she could have hoped.

They found freedom in the Andean mountains. The Indios and the poor Spanish at first thought them a strange couple, the *dama blanca* — white lady, and the *caballero negro* — black gentleman. But they worked just as hard as their laborers and were fair, so they commanded respect. When the big house was finished, the fiesta lasted a week and drew a crowd to the isolated mountain top.

Troni interrupted her reverie as he instructed Elbert: "In a fortnight or so, once you're well rested, we'd like you t'take another little trip for us. I'm gonna give you a draft for fifteen thousand."

Elbert raised his eyebrow. "Where am I to go?"

Marie and Troni looked at each other. Then she said, "We want you to go to a certain place. It's called Cache Island. There are some letters we need you to deliver. Perhaps bank accounts to set up. If all goes well, you'll be living there for a while." She and Troni had argued about this for almost the entire month that Elbert had been away. Troni told her that he must send a percentage of the profits back to his families, even if he never intended to go back. They had to be cared for. Furthermore, he said, Marie had to set up an account for Melissa. It wasn't her fault that the child had gotten caught up in the machinations of that conniving Elaina Mayhew. Marie fought it, but to no avail. Troni believed strongly in taking full responsibility for one's family and he demanded that she take care of Melissa.

Secretly, Marie had to admit that she never thought about the child. It was as if Melissa had only existed in a dream. The last time she'd seen her, Melissa had acted so much like Elaina. Elaina had proved to be the most implacable foe Marie had ever faced — the only battle she'd lost utterly. Anything having to do with Elaina Mayhew, Marie wanted to forget. To make Troni leave her alone, she had written to her daughter.

Dearest Melissa,   17 December 1723
*   I imagine You have no further Wish to Hear from Me, given My Behavure the Last Time We saw One Another. I was Upset at Some Thingg that had Nothing to doe with You. I utterly regret My Actions towards You on that Terrible Day. I hope that if You will not Forgive, at least be Tolerant of Me for I have Some Thingg moste Important to tell You.*
*   The Woman whom You call Mama is Not, indeede, any Relation to You at All. She was, for Many Years, My Dearest Friend in the World. I asked Her to Take Care of You, because I Could Not. You see, Melissa, I am a Pyrate — as Your Would-Be-Mother would say, a Thiefe, a Murderess, and a Rogue — or at least I was. Some Day, if You wish, We Two will get Together, and I will explain to You how It was that I became an Out Law. Recent Events have proved to Me that I can No Longer live that Way, and so I have come to Live in a Far-Away Land called New Grenada where People speak a Strange Tongue and No One has ever heard of the Pyrate Captain Mary.*
*   Thinggs are Goode for Us here. We have had Some Fortune with a Golde Mine, and that is why the Mann who is reading You this Letter will shortly Deliver to You Five Thousand Golde Coins. As the Mine continues to do Welle, I will be sending You More Money. This is Not to Buy Your Love. You have had enuff of My Meddling in Your Life. I have No intentions of Ever returning to Cache Island. The Woman whom You call Mother and Your New Father*

knowe All too Welle why It is Not Possible for Me to Return. I am content that You stay There with Them, If that is Your Choice. If ever You should need Some Thingg or wish to contact Me, but speak of It to the Man Who brought You the Letter and It will be taken care of.

   I hope You are Welle and the Storm did You no Harm.

   I will always be Your moste Loving
Mother

Actually, the only person on Cache Island she really wanted to contact was Briarley. And it wasn't he that interested her so much as Mary's Town. She couldn't stop wondering if it had survived the hurricane and what shape it was in. Marie wrote a longer letter to Briarley, full of instructions and inquiries, as well as directions to the hidden cache of two hundred thousand gold coins to be used as the new island state's treasury. His reply she looked forward to. She was afraid to think about Melissa's response. Or the possibility that Elaina would intercept it and cast it away. She'd asked Troni what would happen if they all — Seashell, Melissa, and Naomi — refused the money, or anything to do with her and Troni. "Then we'll've done our duties toward 'em and that'll be the end of it. We'll go on as if they never existed." Secretly, Marie hoped that would be the case.

Elbert smiled at Marie, bringing her back to the moment at hand. "I would be delighted to see your home. Perhaps on my way back, I shall stop and visit with my father."

"An excellent idea," Troni said. Marie knew that he wished Elbert would take some money from them and strike out on his own. Though he said he wasn't worried about Elbert's crush on Marie, it was clear he preferred not to have younger, healthier competition around.

"I shall plan to leave in a few days." He yawned hugely. "But first, I beg your pardon, I must go to bed." They said their goodnights and watched the young man leave.

Troni poured their glasses to the top. "I told you I'd get my gold from this mine. It only needed the two of us t'come down here and run it ourselves."

She laughed. "You were right. You were so right!"

He raised his glass to her. "Here's to me bein' right."

Then she kissed her partner and lover, feeling like a storm tossed ship returning to it's safe harbor once more.

From *The Bridgetown Clarion*, Barbados Island, 28 February 1724:

Traveler Found Murdered

Constable Hertige reported that the Boddy of a Young Man was found in the Swamp just Weste of Towne Saturday Eve. Apparently this Person was stabbed to Death during a Robbery as his Personal Effekts were strewn all about and his Wallett is missing. The Constable had hoped that some letters found on the Boddy would help identify the Man, but has had No Lukk locating a "Melissa," "Naomi," or "Seashell." One Other Letter was too smeared to read the Recipient's Name. If you knowe Who these Peeple are, Pleese contact the Constable.